# The Defrosting of
# Charlotte Small

# The Defrosting of Charlotte Small

## Annabel Giles

W F HOWES LTD

This large print edition published in 2006 by
W F Howes Ltd
Unit 4, Rearsby Business Park, Gaddesby Lane,
Rearsby, Leicester LE7 4YH

1  3  5  7  9  10  8  6  4  2

First published in the United Kingdom in 2006
by Penguin Books Ltd

A CIP catalogue record for this book is available
from the British Library

ISBN 1 84632 603 6

Typeset by Palimpsest Book Production Limited,
Grangemouth, Stirlingshire
Printed and bound in Great Britain
by Antony Rowe Ltd, Chippenham, Wilts.

For all those who loved me
until I learned to love myself.

You wouldn't know it, but I'm only about three years old. I may look like a big grown-up woman on the outside, but inside I'm just a little girl.

I'm going to start at the end, which came before the beginning. You wouldn't have liked me then, I know I didn't; and I certainly wouldn't have liked you. I'd have found something wrong with you, even if I'd had to look really hard. I'd have told Mary Magdalene that blue didn't suit her.

But today I'm a different person. I love my life, I look better than I ever did, and I feel fantastic. In fact, I'd even go so far as to say that I'm happy. Most of the time.

What happened? I'll tell you.

This is my story.

*Charlotte Small*
*London, 2006*

# CHAPTER 1

'My heart was like a secret garden, and the walls were very high.'

William Goldman, *The Princess Bride*

'The trouble viz it,' yelled the latest au pair to walk out on us, I can't remember her name, 'is here is no love, you heff not love!'

'Yes, thanks for that,' I said, holding the dog by the collar to stop him running out into the road yet again. 'Now could you just get out of my house? Please?' (Apart from anything else, it was freezing outside and having the front door open for too long was letting out all that expensive heat.)

Vic, her boyfriend, grabbed another handful of bagged-up possessions from the hallway and, dislodging a tile from my crumbling but authentic Victorian path as he went, grumpily threw the baggage through the open back doors of his white van, which was parked, flashers a go-go, right in the middle of our narrow residential street.

'Hey!' I said. 'That's my smart Joseph cardboard bag, isn't it? I'd been saving that, how dare you?!'

'Voteffer,' replied Helga, or was it Anya, employing the only new English word she'd learned since she'd been here.

'That everythin'?' asked Vic, smiling, impertinent little shit.

Miss Eastern Europe put on her coat.

'And what,' I asked, as she wound the very nice scarf I'd given her for her birthday around her pretty little young neck, 'shall I say to your parents when they ring on Sunday evening?'

'Tell zem,' she said, with a smile as she stepped over the threshold, 'zat you are a monster!'

Behind her, Vic sniggered.

'Could I have my keys back, please?' I demanded, as imperiously as I could, in the face of a laughing plasterer. 'You're not going to steal them as well, are you?'

Bipbip! Outside in the street, one of those awful 4x4 oversize jeep things (they've all got them round here, so useful for London's rocky terrain) wanted that van to leave, and so did I.

She didn't hand me the keys, she sort of threw them at me and ran down the path, giggling.

'Oh, how childish!' I shrieked, as I scrabbled about on all fours in the flowerbed. 'Thief!' I yelled over the hedge, pathetically, as Vic started up the engine.

There was a terrible squeal as they drove off, but not of tyres, of dog. I stood up, just in time

2

to see the Chelsea Tractor finish him off. The driver didn't stop – a little Jack Russell probably doesn't make much impact underneath such huge wheels.

With the impeccable timing of an eight-year-old girl prone to hysteria, Amber appeared at the open front door. 'Mu-u-u-u-m!' she wailed. 'What's happened to McQueen?'

'Er, well' – I looked at what was left of him on the road, and stood between that and Amber – 'he's finally made his Great Escape. Let's face it, it was only a question of time till he started tunnelling his way out. I saw him eyeing up next door's motorbike the other day . . .' Not amused. Too young to get the cinematic reference, probably. 'Look, he's free now, he'll be happy at last.' I walked into the street and looked down at his blooded corpse. 'Yes, see, he's smiling!'

Covering her face with her hands, Amber screamed just long and loud enough to wake up the nosy nurse on nights opposite, and ran back into the house, slamming the front door behind her. Bang!

Could I find those keys? Could I fuck. The neighbours had a spare set, but I'd fallen out with them. Amber was apparently too upset to let me in, all I could hear through the letterbox were the racking sobs of a supposedly heart-broken child. (I wouldn't mind, but it wasn't even our dog – we'd been looking after it for my friend Arthur while he was on holiday.)

In the end I had to walk, coatless, in November, to the newsagent's shop on the corner. I had to beg the owner to give me a packet of sweets to bribe Amber with. It took a while, as we still owed him £72.30, a hangover from those halcyon days of getting a newspaper delivered daily to the door. Sandip finally cracked when I offered to leave him my watch as a deposit, although I could tell he was seriously thinking about it.

Finally, finally, Little Miss Drama Queen deigned to let me in. Freezing and furious, I slammed the door very hard behind me. So very hard that the original-feature Victorian etched-glass in one of the panels shattered on to the doormat, in hundreds and thousands of sparkly-sharp pieces. Thanking god the dog wasn't around to cut his paw open and bleed all over the carpet, I fetched two bin bags from the kitchen – one to stick over the missing door panel, and the other to contain the remains of Arthur's pet, once I'd scraped it off the road. (I thought it best to keep the bag outside the back door until he came back, he'd probably want to hold some bizarre little gay funeral ceremony for it.)

Having plugged Amber into a video of *Harry Potter and the Temple of Doom* or something, I did what any self-respecting single parent in my situation would do; I poured myself a pint glass of red wine, and took me and my fags off to sit on the downstairs loo with the door locked behind me, reading that old copy of *Elle Decor* yet again, hating all those people who had nicer houses than me whilst at the same time wanting to be one of them.

It wasn't until I had to lean forward to flick my ash into the little basin that I spotted my grandmother's diamond ring, just sitting there, glinting at me from the plug hole. So the au pair hadn't stolen it after all. Oh. Well, good riddance anyway, she ate far too much.

Leaning back against the cistern, I blew smoke rings and allowed myself to indulge in my latest obsession, planning my suicide. Currently, my favoured method was slashing my wrists in the bath, as that would be the least messy. But would a disposable razor be OK? Or would I have to buy a man's razor blade, and would the woman in the chemist's guess what it was for and call the police, or the Samaritans? Perhaps I could confess, and she could tell me which was the best one to buy . . . hmm, there was lots to think about. As yet, I hadn't had the courage to do it as I just couldn't bear the thought of Amber finding me face down in a pool of blood or vomit or vodka. I'd have to wait until she was away, on a school trip or something.

I spent the rest of the afternoon staring up at that ominous crack between the wall and the ceiling, designing my funeral, my poor lifeless body having been mercifully run over by a double-decker bus, or felled like a tree thanks to a handy brain tumour. It would be a classy affair; my highly polished black-lacquered coffin would be carried in a black horse-drawn carriage, the horses resplendent with black plumes on their heads and black ribbons through their tails, there would be much wailing from the crowds in the streets, the service would be broadcast around the world, there would be huge screens outside Westminster Abbey . . .

. . . Amber was banging on the door. 'Mum! I'm hungry! What's for lunch?' She hadn't had breakfast either, unless you count that elderly jam tart, and it was only a couple of hours until bathtime. There was no food in the fridge, and little in the cupboard, but I was too tired to leave the house, so Amber had some pasta with tomato ketchup and a packet of jelly cubes for pudding. I ate a whole packet of rice cakes with Marmite, which were not delicious.

To you, this probably sounds like the day from hell. To me, at the time, it was completely normal.

There's just so much to tell you, I don't know where to start. Yes, I know Julie Andrews would say start at the very beginning, but what does she know? This is the woman who thought it was a good idea to flash her breasts at us to further her career, which then went, somewhat gratifyingly, totally tits up.

But do you really need to know where and when and how I was born? Or even

6

what I look like? No. Suffice it to say that on the outside I look completely normal. It's the inside that was the problem.

I think it all started at boarding school, when I was just eight years old. I was duly despatched from Paddington Station, along with lots of other little girls just like me, in green scratchy tweed coats and green felt hats secured under the chin by too-tight elastic.

Funnily enough, the car journey into central London was more harrowing than anything else that followed. It was the first time I had seen my father cry. (This was a man who'd passed all his exams at Stiff-Upper-Lip School with honours.) In fact, he was so upset about my departure that my mother wouldn't let him out of the car, he was told to keep driving round the block until he had pulled himself together. (She had been Head Girl at Don't-Make-A-Scene Ladies College.) Unsurprisingly, there was no trace of emotion on her face as she left her only child with a bunch of complete strangers for the next four months. In fact, she couldn't even wait for the train to leave the platform; she just left me there, muttering something about having lots to get on with. Not for the first time, I felt inconvenient.

With the benefit of fifty/fifty hindsight, I

can see that my parents thought they were doing their best for me. My father worked abroad a lot (he was a troubleshooter for ailing businesses) and besides, in those days, boarding school was considered the only way to give your child the best start in life. Not, sadly, for the education, but for the social status. To their sort of people, there was no question of whether you could afford the enormously high fees, you just did. And, oh, how we heard about those fees: 'Now, come on, girls, your parents are paying a lot of money for you to be here, you should be grateful, you're very lucky. Lucy Gubbins, will you please get a move on!'

But we didn't feel lucky. No, we felt rejected and abandoned, but we didn't know those words back then, just the feelings. Our childish logic said that we must have done something terribly wrong; we had been so bad that our parents had to give the school lots of money to keep us away from them. We were naughty, wicked children who needed to be locked up, for our own good. Maybe that was what we were supposed to be grateful for. It didn't make sense then, and it still doesn't now. Why have children if you don't want them?

Some of the more weedy little girls cried at night because they missed their mummies and daddies so much; we thought they were just wet. (It was a tough world; any show of emotion was seen as weakness, offenders were laughed at/branded a freak/sent to Coventry.) Of course, the reality is that those girls are probably out in the world having happy, well-balanced, grown-up lives, because they managed to deal with the pain of such rejection in a reasonably healthy way. Those of us who laughed at their home-sickness and didn't allow ourselves to feel a thing – we're the totally fucked-up, neurotic crazy-makers. You know who I mean.

Anyway, I adjusted to my new life quite quickly. Even though I had been allocated a 'shadow', an older girl who was supposed to make sure I was OK, she quickly tired of all my questions and I was left to find things out for myself. There was quite a lot to take in: for example, 'top-to-bottom-bottom-off' was the only way to remember how to change your sheets, which all had to have hospital corners, of course, and which were inspected at random, during spontaneous Bed-Checking.

Then there was Egg-Checking, which was a ceremony performed at the beginning of every term. This involved having your hair examined for nits with a mean-toothed steel comb doused in a stinging disinfectant. Needless to say, this was carried out by a tough old matron, who'd forgotten long ago that having your hair pulled really hurts, even hair on the spoilt-brat heads of posh little boarding school girls. (In fact their heads hurt even more, they don't have mummies to comfort them afterwards.) If, horrors, you were unfortunate enough to have a head crawling alive with lice, then not only did you have to have it saturated with the foulest-smelling toxic insecticide which could have easily taken out a horse; but you had to wear your rubber swimming hat all day and all night for a week, thus ensuring that the whole school knew that you were a dirty girl.

(Years later I discovered from a leaflet Amber's school sent home with her that the humble nit actually prefers clean hair, as it can get a better grip. Ah, the shame of shame.)

After I'd been at this baffling institution for a couple of days, a squashy rosy-cheeked girl of about ten approached me in the Recreation Room. (If I'd known then that her name was Victoria Plum – yes, really – things might have gone slightly differently. Anyway.) I was trying not to feel lonely by quietly playing clock patience by myself on the floor. She was clutching a little note-book, a pencil had been attached to it with salmon-pink bloomer elastic, the kind usually only seen in the Haberdashery department of Peter Jones. 'Have you been excused properly today?' she asked.

'I beg your pardon?' I stood up, on best behaviour. (Scared, actually, but not prepared to show it.)

She sighed, clearly bored of having to explain this to all the New Girls. 'Have you been excused properly today?' she asked again, eyes bulging. 'You know, have you been to the lavatory?'

'Well, yes, of course,' I replied. 'It's six o'clock in the evening!'

'No,' she sighed again. She was very good at sighing, actually. 'Properly.'

'Well, I wiped – um, myself with that tracing paper stuff, if that's what you mean.' (We had Izal Medicated at our school, it was shiny instead of absorbent.) I was completely confused. 'And I washed my hands.' Was that the right answer?

'Look,' she took a step closer, I took one back, 'have you done a Number Two today?'

'Oh!' I got it now. 'A poo? A Big Job, you mean?'

She was really, really fed up with me. 'Yes!' she hissed.

'Well actually,' I thought, 'now I come to think of it, um, no – I don't think I have.'

'Really?' She seemed surprised. 'You sure?'

'Er, yes, I think so.'

She bulged her eyes again. 'Really sure?' She was trying to tell me something, but I didn't know what. I was only eight, and as yet unskilled at the art of Hinting. 'Certain?'

'Um, yes. I really haven't done a poo today.'

She took another step towards me and hissed under her breath, 'Last chance!' She stepped back again and spoke in her official voice. 'Have you, or have you not, been excused properly today?'

'No,' I said, sure of my answer now, 'I have not.'

She shook her head, despairing of me. 'What's your name?' she asked, as she consulted the little book with her pencil.

'Charlotte.'

She tutted. 'Charlotte what? There's loads of Charlottes here.'

'Oh, sorry, Charlotte Small.'

She put a big 'X' beside my name in her book. 'Right, report to Nurse, just before bedtime.'

That night, I was given a large dose of Syrup of Figs and told to get my bowels in order. Although this was the beginning of a long childhood blighted by severe constipation, I never told the truth to the girl with the Excused Book again.

Arthur was really upset about his wretched dog. Luckily he dyes his eyelashes now, this had been my suggestion of course. He'd already tested the waterproof mascaras (in brown, more discreet) to their limits. Arthur's big on crying.

'But I thought you knew this would happen one day,' I protested. 'From the minute you dropped him off, that dog was hell-bent on getting out of this house. Isn't that why you called him McQueen, after Steve McQueen in *The Great Escape*?'

'No, Charlotte, it is not.'

Oh.

'Then why is – sorry, was – he called McQueen, then?'

'It was Jimmy's idea.' He buried his tanned face in his man-manicured hands. His bald spot was getting bigger, I'd have to tell him. Maybe not now.

'Oh, Jimmy's idea, right.'

(Jimmy was The Ex, a nasty little spotty youth from Glasgow, who'd looked and behaved like an impoverished rent boy, whilst purporting to be a fashion student. Arthur was not and had never been a great beauty, although he was a very sweet man. But personality's not enough in the cruel world of gay, and if you haven't got a proper long-term live-in boyfriend by a certain age, and you're not famous or rich or fabulous, you're buggered. Or rather you're not, and won't be ever again. So his whole future had been pinned on this wretch

Jimmy, who had yet to see Arthur as anything more than a passing fancy with a wallet. It was so pathetic. I'd been trying to get him over it, but Arthur was still tiresomely devastated about the break-up, nearly a year later. Jimmy had run off with some girl from college, who – as Arthur repeated over and over again through his tears, drunk or sober – was a punk. Literally. She had a purple mohican and wore a mini-kilt. In this day and age.)

'Oh, I get it – it's a Scottish pouff thing. "Me" and "Queen" – very amusing.'

He took time out from his grief to explain. 'We christened him after Alexander McQueen, The Greatest Designer Of Our Time.'

'Yes, thank you, I knew that, I do work in fashion myself, you know.' I took a swig of Arthur's scotch. 'How very stereotypical of you both. Gay, gay, gay.'

'You're unbelievable!'

'Thanks.' I drained his glass. 'Fancy another?'

'You really don't care, do you?' He was looking at me as if he'd only just seen me for the first time. Must be jet-lagged.

'Oh, Arthur, do shut up. Look, I'm sorry, but I've already told you, twice, it was an accident. Just let it go.' I got up from the kitchen table. 'So. Tell me about your holiday, how was it? Don't tell me, a bloody nightmare. Was it like I said, all shell-suits and nylon wedding dresses? Still,' I took another glug, 'if you will go somewhere as common as the Caribbean, you're bound to encounter the great unwashed ... what is it?'

'He was part of my family.' He actually had a tear in his eye and a lump in his throat.

'He was a pet!' I retorted. 'He was a dog, who is dead now. I'm sorry if that's upsetting, but, hey, that's life!' I laughed. 'Or rather, that's death!'

I could sort of tell I was perhaps being a bit insensitive at that point, and so I put a soothing hand on Arthur's arm. 'I'm sorry, really I am. Look, why don't we go and buy another one this weekend? Does Harrods still have a pet department? I remember my grandmother coming home with a mongoose from there once –'

'No!' He stood up, distraught. 'Nothing will replace McQueen. He was my friend, my best friend in the whole world, I loved him and he loved me.'

'But how can he be your best friend?' I remonstrated. Actually, I was quite pissed off as I'd thought I was Arthur's closest friend. I'd never liked that dog. 'He can't talk, he can't laugh at your jokes, he can't tape *Will and Grace* for you, can he? Tell me, Arthur, when did McQueen last buy you a drink?'

'Oh, don't be so literal, you know what I mean.'

I frowned. Humans with deep attachments to animals had always mystified me. I'd quite gone off Amber's rather fierce headmistress when she revealed to me that she cried at *Animal Hospital*.

'Don't you know how this feels?' He looked at

15

me and shook his head. 'No, you probably don't.' He sighed as he took his coat from the back of the chair. 'I suppose I'm really upset because he was the last remaining piece of Us. I've done everything to get over that boy – I've slept with everybody else, I go to different bars, I've moved house, I've replaced all the furniture, the bed linen, even the kitchen utensils, anything to try and get rid of the memories.'

'Well then, isn't it a good thing that McQueen's dead, like the relationship? Maybe it's symbolic . . .'

'No, it's not!' he looked really distraught now. 'I suppose I thought perhaps Jimmy might come back one day, just to see McQueen, he loved that dog. We both did.' His voice cracked, he was about to cry again, and all over a dog! 'Now there's no reason for him to get in touch with me ever, ever again . . .'

Good, I thought, Jimmy was a little shit. 'Honestly, Arthur, I do think you're getting your knickers all in a twist about this – it's really not that big a deal. In fact, you've always been a bit over the top about Jimmy. I mean, I know exactly how you feel, but I think you should –'

'Do you?' His stricken face reddened. 'I don't think so, Charlotte. I mean, have you ever really loved someone?'

'Oh, don't be so silly, of course I have!'

'Really?' He looked like someone who was angry. I'd never seen him like this before. 'Who?'

'You know, lots of people. Look, Arthur –'

'I don't think you have, actually.' His eyes narrowed, unattractively. 'You certainly didn't love Joe, that's for sure –'

I was a bit taken aback. 'And how would you know? You never even knew him!'

'Neither,' he pulled his coat on and brushed imaginary specks off the shoulders, 'did you, as it turned out.'

'Arthur!' I was shocked. 'That is completely below the belt! What a bitchy thing to say, you know it wasn't like that . . .' We'd never been like this before, what on earth was the matter with him? 'And, anyway, I love Amber.'

'Really? Is that why you palm her off on your parents every weekend?'

'I do not "palm her off"! She likes going there.'

'Yes,' he said, buttoning up his coat, 'to get away from you. I'm sorry, I know that must be hard to hear, but it's quite obvious.'

Wow, the worm really was turning. How rude was that? And completely untrue. 'Right, that's it, Arthur, I think you'd better leave, now!'

'Don't worry, I'm going!' He flounced through to the hallway and grabbed the handle of his trolley suitcase on whizzy wheels. 'Goodbye!' he announced, and slammed the front door behind him. He must have been upset, he didn't even stop to kiss the framed photo of my brother on the hall table before he left.

'Drama queen!' I shouted, through the black plastic panel.

'Hard-nosed bitch!' he shouted back, as he closed the gate behind him. (He knew the rules.)

Ridiculous fuss about nothing, I thought, as I put the dog's rotting remains out for the binmen and went to finish off the scotch. I did feel a little uneasy, though. We'd had our little tiffs in the past, but we'd never fallen out like this.

I'd known Arthur for about six years. We met at the end of the London to Brighton Veteran Car Run, you know, as featured in the film *Genevieve*. Dad's pride and joy is a 1902 Panhard, which lives in their garage the rest of the year, although it is polished every Sunday, without fail.

Mum had stopped accompanying him years ago, as she reckons the first Sunday in November is not the right time to be sitting in an ancient open-top car with uncomfortable seats, which is allowed to go no faster than 20 mph, even if it could, waving at people with nothing better to do than cheer at you. She didn't find the prospect of it breaking down at any minute dangerous and exciting either; mind you, nor did I, but it was an Important Event to Dad and one of our traditions now.

Arthur was a steward at the Brighton end, and as Dad was being congratulated by the other old codgers for coming fourth again for the fifth year in a row (oh, the excitement of it all) he offered me a swig from his hipflask. I don't know how or why, but things just took off from there. What had begun as a tedious dutiful-daughter day for me,

18

ended up in a fabulous gay night club with Arthur and I declaring true love to each other and promising that if neither of us had found the right person by the time we were forty, then we would definitely get married, but have no sex. (Forty had recently been raised to forty-five, various birthdays having come and gone since the pact was made . . .)

To be honest, I didn't think I'd see him again after that. But about six months later, he'd quite literally turned up on my doorstep, absolutely frantic at discovering that his Big Love of NEARLY ELEVEN YEARS, Ben, had not only been having an affair with, but also bought a flat in Pimlico with, a young American banker called Clay.

So he'd left Brighton once and for all and had come to seek his fortune in London. I'd let him stay on my sofa for weeks on end, and we'd had a great time crying and laughing and cooking (him) and drinking (me) and smoking ourselves silly. We'd just clicked. Then he'd got an apprenticeship with one of London's leading interior designers, and the obligatory 'living space' in an 'interesting' part of east London to go with it. He was a loyal person, Arthur, and had never forgotten what he called my 'kindness' at putting him up and putting up with him – I don't think I ever actually told him I'd loved his company and was sad to see him go, but I think he sort of knew. We still spoke most days, just to keep in touch. Unless he was 'on' with Jimmy again, and then

19

he disappeared for weeks on end, until their next row. In the words of the great philosopher, Robert Palmer, Arthur was addicted to love.

Silly old queen, I thought, as I hid the bottle in the dustbin. (I was pretty sure the nosy nurse opposite had been counting how many there were in the recycling bin each week.) He'd get over it, he'd be back tomorrow, tail between his legs – oops.

He'd ring.

He didn't.

So by the time I left that school at thirteen, I was quite tough.

I'd become almost completely institutionalized. I got used to living as a large number, I got used to never having a choice in what I ate, what I wore, what I did. I became one of many. Our life was run by The Bell. The Bell told us when to get up, The Bell told us when it was time to eat, to study, to stand up, to sit down, The Bell even told us when to go to sleep.

And I didn't miss having a couple of parents all to myself either. We had a big old fat matron of our own, called Nurse, who wore a white nylon overall which swished when she prowled the corridors to see if anyone was talking after lights out. She was there to 'mother' us, that was her job; but we never asked her to, in case she told anyone.

I think it was her idea to give us a calming drink the night before exams – you could choose between hot Ribena or cocoa made with water. It is probably a testament to her that even now, when I've got a big day tomorrow, I make myself a hot Ribena.

After I'd been at the school for about two years, she died. They gave us time to grieve – we had an hour to walk round the hockey pitch in silence – and then it was back to work. I don't remember wanting any more than that.

I'd got used to not seeing my parents. In fact they'd become a bit of a bore. We had to correspond with them every Sunday, which was very difficult as nothing much ever happened to us, certainly nothing to write home about. On a good week there might have been a netball match which I wasn't in, or someone may have had a birthday; but generally most of our efforts went into doing our biggest writing possible in order to fill the compulsory two sides of notelet. We weren't allowed to seal the envelope until the letter had been checked for spelling and grammar – and, thinking about it now, any get-me-out-of-here-now-it's-horrid-and-I-want-to-come-home passages.

My parents would take it in turns to write back, which highlighted their different styles perfectly. My mother wrote on a Sunday also, which meant that our letters crossed. Her letters were short, almost in note form. They were full of things she'd meant to do, but hadn't because she was too busy; what cake she'd made for what fête, and news of members of the Women's Institute I'd never met, with accompanying operations.

My father's, on the other hand, were much longer, elaborate descriptions of seasons passing, opinionated accounts of world events and updates on the progress of his anti-dogshit campaign. And he always waited until my letter had arrived, responding to my schoolgirl tedia with great passion and interest. Oh, and he never forgot to include a typewritten page of Ten Interesting Facts, by way of an extra educational top-up for me. It was boring, and I never read it, but I missed him.

Of course we had school holidays, and because we knew we were supposed to look forward to going home, we drew up charts with boxes to cross off, which we stuck inside the lids of our desks, headed 'Days Until The End of Term'. We'd allow ourselves to get very excited once the count-down was in single figures, then the people being picked up by car were allowed to go home the day before us, and then hurrah!

We were back on that train, 'behaving very badly' by talking too loudly and being too excited, much to the exasperation of the school secretary who had to accompany us. The sight of Mummy waiting at the end of the platform was almost too much to bear. We ran towards her like they did in films, quite often forgetting our hats, carelessly abandoned on the train seats. Mrs Cox and her limp had to chase after us with them, but at least she had the decency to save the lecture until the journey back to school.

Once home, I'd say hello to the dog and the cat, and rush up to my bedroom to check it was still there. Then I'd do a quick tour of the house, to see if there was anything new. Then I'd hang round my mother, because I wasn't sure what to do next. She hated that, because she wasn't sure what to do next either. We'd both become so used to being apart, it felt strange to be together.

Some budding little statistician in my year (now married to a vicar, oddly) once worked out that we spent many more days of the year at boarding school than we did with our families. Maybe that's why I secretly preferred being at school – it felt more like home.

My mother's Sunday lunch is disgusting. I don't know what she does to the chicken, but it's always slimy. And have you ever been browsing in the supermarket and idly wondered who on earth uses instant mashed potato? And tinned carrots? And that marvel of E-engineering, gravy browning?

'Mmm, this is delicious,' said my father, who was scowled at for talking with his mouth full.

'Mum,' said Amber, wrestling with a roast potato – or was it a piece of coal? – 'what are we doing for Christmas?'

'What d'you mean?'

I saw her glance at my mother, who nodded her permission to continue.

'Well, are we going away?'

'Yes, dahling, I thought Bahbados this year, what d'you reckon?' I popped in a Brussels sprout, which turned out to be still frozen in the middle. 'Don't be silly, Amber.'

'Oh.'

Silence. My father busied himself with his so-called food, and my mother nodded at Amber again. I put my knife and fork together and waited.

'Well, you know Matt?'

'Uncle Matt to you.' I took a gulp of my parents' favourite wine-box Soave, to buy me time for what I suspected was coming next. 'Yes, I do know him, Amber, he's my brother.'

'Well, you know he lives in America now?'

'Yes, I am aware of that.' Oh god.

'Well, um . . .' She took a mouthful.

'Come on, Amber, spit it out!' As she shot the Brussels sprout back out, I looked at my parents, the conspirators. My father was chasing peas around his plate, and my mother was picking tiny bits off the scrawny chicken wings she'd insisted on having so that someone else could have the legs, which were still on the chicken. (She would have to be persuaded to eat them for a second helping, once we'd all refused and there was a danger of them going to waste. It was a ridiculous dance she made us all go through, especially as none of us even liked the legs, which she knew perfectly well.)

'Look,' I said, 'I can't possibly take two weeks off to go to LA for Christmas, I've got a lot on at the moment, what with –'

'– yes, we know that, Mum,' said Amber. It was the 'we' that irritated me. 'Which is why we –' she smiled at my mother –

'– thought we'd take Amber out there, visit her uncle,' interjected Dad, now that Amber had done the difficult part for him, 'poor girl hardly knows him. Y'mother could do with a bit of sun, still trying to shake off that ruddy cold. Thought we'd try Christmas on the beach. Make a change from the usual.'

('The usual' involved the four of us in their chilly, damp dining room with the best silver, slimy turkey and droopy paper hats. The Queen's speech was followed by we three doing the washing-up to give my mother a rest, and then a brisk walk during which we nodded and smiled at complete strangers just because it was Christmas Day. Dad would then drive us back up the motorway to

25

London at about six, just as my mother was reaching for the *Radio Times* to see what they'd circled in red pen for tonight's viewing. I'd always had to be on parent duty for the actual day, as Matt was usually busy elsewhere. He'd breeze in and out a couple of days later, during the boring bit between Christmas and New Year.)

'And they said I could come too!' trilled Amber, cutting to the chase. 'To America!'

'But I can't pay for that! I can't possibly afford to go away for Christmas. Come to think of it, I can't really afford to stay at home either.' How dare they ask her without consulting me first?

'All on us,' smiled my father. 'Found a very good website the other day, perfect for this sort of thing.' He'd recently become a silver surfer, Matt having given him his old laptop during the last prodigal visit. 'Took the precaution of reserving a seat for her. Be our Christmas present to you both, eh?' He looked at his wife for approval. He carried on. 'Y'mother and I thought the break'd do you good, chance to recharge the old batteries. No need to worry about Amber, we'll look after her, won't we?'

Mother said nothing, just dabbed either side of her mouth with her napkin.

'Please, Mum, please? Please can I go?' Amber's little face was at its most beseeching. 'They've got Disneyland out there, and a film studios thing with a shark and ET on his bicycle, and it'll be sunny, and –'

'All right!' I sounded as snappy as I felt. I just

caught my mother's frown as she put her knife and fork together.

'Yay!' Amber got off her seat and hugged me tight. 'I love you, Mum!'

Do you, I thought, do you really? Why do you want to spend Christmas with my family, but not me? Why didn't my family want to spend Christmas with me either?

Looking back, it's not surprising that my parents didn't invite me to go with them. I'd never made any secret of the fact that I hated Christmas, I hated LA and I really, really hated my brother.

'Charlotte Small?' The school secretary stuck her head round the classroom door. It was Geography; we were learning how to tap rubber from a tree. Useful.

'Yes?' I stood up.

'Your mother's had a baby.'

This surprised me, I hadn't known she was 'expecting', as we called it back then. (Heaven forfend that the true description be used, when there was a codeword available.) But it was the end of the summer term, and I'd gone to a friend's for the half-term weekend, so I hadn't seen her for a while.

'Gosh,' I said.

'Don't you want to know whether it's a boy or a girl?' asked Mrs Cox.

'Oh, er, yes. Is it a boy or a girl?'

'A boy. A brother for you. Called Matthew. Marvellous news, isn't it?'

'Yes, Mrs Cox, it is.'

'Three cheers for baby Matthew!' shouted someone in the back row. 'Hip hip –'

'– hooray!' shouted the rest of the class. This was the only way we knew to celebrate, we did this at every Good Thing, although it was usually confined to winning a sporting fixture of some kind.

They sent me a photo of him in my mother's arms. He looked like a baby. But it was her expression that was odd. Her face said that she was really happy, really alive. I'd never seen her look like that before. And he was all wrapped up in fluffy blankets, all snug and smug. And they were sitting in my bedroom, on my bed. Hmm.

Sure enough, when I went home for the hols a couple of weeks later, I discovered that he'd been moved into my room, and I'd been moved out. (If I'd allowed myself any feelings, I'd have probably indulged in a bit of jealousy right then.) I was in the spare room now. 'More space for you,' said my father, by way of explanation. They'd redecorated it, in Laura Ashley, tiny little pink flowers all over the place. Pink used to be my favourite colour, but actually it wasn't any more, I preferred maroon now.

We didn't even go on holiday that

summer, because Matthew was too small. And I know it's not a competition, but he got loads more Christmas presents than I did, loads. That boy could do no wrong, my parents absolutely adored him. If he hiccupped everyone would laugh – if I hiccupped I'd be told to get a glass of water. If he farted everyone would laugh – if I farted I'd be sent out of the room. If he poo'd his pants, it would be called an accident – I'd given up by then.

And he was clever, too. Really, really clever. Clever enough to win a scholarship to the local private boys' school, so he didn't even board. He was nice to have around and cheap to educate.

Each time I came home for the holidays, there was evidence of people having enjoyed themselves without me. Pens from souvenir shops, maps from theme parks, photos of a table for three. They were quite the happy little trio.

Do I need to tell you he was handsome too, or had you guessed that? And good at sports, and really popular, and covered in beautiful, witty, intelligent women. He'd started his career as a humble runner for the somewhat sporadic British film industry, but now he was something in 'development' for one of the big studios in Hollywood – I forget which one – which as far as I could see meant sitting behind his desk waiting for the Next Big Thing to walk through the door. He'd already had a few successes, so he was unbearably wealthy and best friends with film stars. And he was always in those Top Ten Eligible Bachelor lists, but so far no woman had managed to nail him down.

But worst of all, he was very keen on me. I found that really hard to take. He worshipped at my altar, he thought I was fantastic. He'd follow me round the house when I came home from school, smiling at me like a little lapdog, wanting to be my slave. He'd do anything for me; he was pathetically selfless where I was concerned. You could say he loved me.

Yuk.

# CHAPTER 2

'Remember that the whole point of house-
work is to keep the place functioning effi-
ciently as a cheerful background for living –
so live! Decide on something positive, or
simply pleasurable, to do for yourself with
the time you save. Otherwise life . . . just . . .
slithers . . . a-w-a-y . . .'

Shirley Conran, *Superwoman*, 1975

Monday was my day off. I didn't think it
was good for Amber to have a mother
who worked five days a week, and
besides, I was usually exhausted from the weekend.
Monday was the day I was supposed to be
attending a local college to do a free computer
course, but as we didn't have a computer, I didn't
see the point in going yet. I hated computers
anyway; they looked horrible and they went wrong
a lot. Unlike a pen and paper, they were always
'crashing'. The cashpoint was about my limit, and
I'd gone way over that. I hated technology – I didn't

even have a mobile phone. I was a troglodyte, and proud of it.

On Tuesdays and Wednesdays I worked in a local boutique, Shades, as the girl who owned it was having an affair with a married man and this was their 'weekend'. It wasn't enormously well-paid, but it was cash-in-hand, which was useful. I'd only been working there a few weeks – previously I'd thought it must have been a front for laundering drug money or something, I'd hardly ever seen anyone going in or coming out. But then I realized that she only needed one or two customers a week. Just a simple pale pink T-shirt with a tiny diamanté heart on it cost £60!

But for as long as there were people stupid enough to pay these prices, Sadie charged them. The clientele consisted mainly of two types of women: the properly-rich, and the property-rich.

The properly-rich were those blonde women married to wealthy bankers and barristers, who came in to finger the goods, probably because they were bored. They must have wanted five minutes off from Looking Busy. The nanny was looking after the kids, the housekeeper was looking after the house, the husband was working like a maniac in order to pay for people to look after. She just had to look nice, book the holidays, and drive the Range Rover up and down the motorway every weekend, ferrying a sausage and an occasional rasher of bacon from one fridge to the other. These women bought the casual stuff – 'Be good for Padstow/Portugal/The

32

Hamptons, actually' – and they were all called names beginning with 'c': Carina, Camilla, Candida (which had been shortened to Candy ever since it had become known as the proper name for thrush).

The property-rich were usually blonde single women of a certain age who were sitting on a goldmine. They'd bought in Fulham years ago, and had watched the house prices going, almost literally, through the roof. But they had no cash flow. And no kids. But they were desperate for both, so they were kept busy doing their best to hook one of those rich bankers. This involved going to a lot of 'do's, and one had to have the wardrobe to match so that one didn't look desperate, didn't one? These women bought the formal stuff. They'd head straight for the sale rail, which never changed from one week to the next and was full of fashion casualties such as very transparent fluorescent tops or bargain designer items in a size 6 or 16, Sadie was no fool; and then they'd ask me if we had anything suitable for a chic dinner in the city/charity auction/polo party.

The more disorganized ones would dash in from the hairdresser's next door at about five o'clock (where they got their highlights done on the cheap by Docker Dawn) in a mad panic, because they still didn't have anything to wear tonight. Either He had seen everything already, or Aziz had shut the dry cleaner's early again. 'Have you got anything suitable for a man I've done lunch and two dinners with and tonight's probably the night? Anything really sexy?' they'd ask, unaware that they had 'desperate' tattooed on their foreheads, that it would take more than the right clothes to get the right result.

Like I knew. I wasn't exactly an expert. Being a bit of a jeans and a jumper girl, it was all I could do to find something good enough for me to wear while I was working in the shop. (Black everything, obviously. Oxfam, but you couldn't tell.) But I did my best to advise them, and prided myself on not being one of those simpering saleswomen who told everyone they looked lovely in everything. I told my customers the truth.

On this particular Tuesday morning, I was perhaps a little grumpier than usual because I'd left two messages on Arthur's machine, and he hadn't called me back. He was clearly still in the throes of a queenie fit about the dog thing, which was bloody annoying of him, and rather selfish too. I needed a good whinge about my parents kidnapping Amber for Christmas.

It had been too cold to walk and I could only find one glove, so I'd waited for the bus which had taken ages to come and then when it had finally arrived it had been too full to take any more passengers and so I'd had to walk anyway. So I was a bit late to open up the shop, I didn't get there until about eleven. There was an arsey-looking girl waiting outside, shivering in the cold.

'Yes?' I'd said, as I fumbled for the keys with one hand and wiped my streaming nose with the glove.

'Aren't you supposed to open up at half past nine?' she'd said. She had dark hair and a Thames-estuary accent, she wasn't one of the usuals.

'And?' They must be in the other pocket.

'Well, it's quarter past eleven.'

'What's your point?' I peered into the teeming abyss that was my handbag.

'I've been waiting.'

'Really?' Couldn't see them. 'Why?'

'What d'you mean, why?'

'Well why –' I spilled my handbag out on to the pavement, 'didn't you go and do something else until I got here? Are you insane?! It's freezing!'

'I wanted to do some shopping,' she said, through gritted teeth, which I mistook for cold teeth, 'and you're an hour late.'

'So? Have you got an emergency clothing crisis on, or something? I mean I've heard of not having a thing to wear, but this is ridiculous!' Where the fuck were those bloody keys? 'Why the urgency? Aha!' I'd found them in the inner zipped pocket, where I was supposed to keep my lip balm and pocket tissues, only it never worked out like that.

'Come on!' she chattered, 'hurry up!'

'Bloody hell, calm down, will you!' I'd retorted, 'and don't come in, I've got to turn the burglar alarm off first. And put the mail in the drawer.

And spray some air freshener so that the customers can't smell the damp coming up from the basement. Tell you what,' I pushed the door open to an ear-splitting electronic scream, 'why don't you go and get us both a coffee, come back in ten minutes? Mine's a latte with two sugars.' She looked a bit shocked, but I shut the door on her anyway, safe in the knowledge that I'd never see her again.

She came back with them on a mini cardboard tray five minutes later. Cunningly, I'd 'forgotten' to give her the money for mine. (You get like that, when you're really poor. You pretend to be absent-minded about money, whereas in reality you're thinking of very little else.) To compensate, I decided to be Really Helpful.

'Looking for anything special?' I asked, as I lit a fag. I wasn't really supposed to smoke in there, but if you have a whole case of air freshener from the Cash & Carry on demand, well, it's just too tempting.

'Not really,' she said, as she looked round.

The phone rang. It was my new-best-friend Sabrina, wanting a gossip.

'Are you going to be long?' I asked. 'Only this is my doctor ringing to tell me the results of some tests.' She didn't look up. 'For cancer.' Bit of a fib, I know, but it was clear to me that she wasn't a serious shopper, she was just a browser with a lot of time on her hands. And anyway, what kind of freak buys clothes first thing in the morning?

36

'This is nice,' she said, holding a strappy vest top up to her skinny chest as she looked in the mirror.

'Hang on, Sabrina,' I sighed into the receiver, and put it down on the table beside the till. 'Listen,' I said as I walked round to her and put the top back on the circular rail, 'you can get these really cheap in Shepherd's Bush market. That's where the woman who owns this shop gets them – all she does is stick on a few studs and sparkles and triples the price!'

'Really?' said the girl.

'Yes!' I announced. 'It's a complete con, isn't it? I'd get down there sharpish, if I were you, while there's still some left.'

Thanking me for my advice, the girl left the shop, leaving me to while away the morning listening to Sabrina waffle on about some boring man she'd met the night before.

When I arrived at the shop the next day, Sadie was already waiting for me, already furious. She sacked me on the spot. I thought it was completely unfair, and told her so. But she'd had complaints from some of her regulars; apparently they'd taken offence at me telling them they looked fat in that. So she'd sent her sister along yesterday, to spy on me. Shockingly, it turns out that honesty doesn't always pay after all.

At thirteen I went to public school. I don't know why it was called that, it was where we were 'privately educated', it wasn't open to the public at all. Neither was it open to Catholics, or Jews, or anyone else who wasn't Church of England. There were two black girls allowed to be there (their father was king of some tiny African country) and an Indian who must have been at least a Gandhi grand-daughter; they stood out, but they were largely ignored by the six hundred other boarders, who were mainly the daughters of diplomats, military men and gentlemen farmers. Some were from a business background, like mine, and there was the odd politician's daughter there too.

The education itself wasn't great, but we learned lots about detail, tedium and pettiness. For example: we were only allowed to have five items on the chest of drawers beside our beds, one of which had to be the Bible, and two of which had to be your brush and comb, so really we were only allowed to have two items of our choice. If you didn't have a picture of your family on display then you were deemed by your peers to be a weirdo, so the show-offs had a whole photo cube of all back home including the horses, with no less than six photos counting as one. Which left you free to choose precisely one item for your bedside table. Mine was my glasses, because I had nowhere else to put them.

Our dormitories were divided into cubicles; singles and doubles, separated by wooden partitions just a little bit taller than us and a curtain that served as a door. Only it didn't, because if you pulled it across everyone thought you were either in a bait (a bad mood) or hiding something. I never once had a single 'cue' (words were always shortened, natch) but it didn't really matter, as we all lived on each other's beds anyway.

But not in them. I've had many men listen patiently to me talking about boarding school, hoping for tales of lesbianism in a shared soapy-foamy bath way. Or at least a spot of furtive midnight fiddling with each other. Not at my school. The closest we got to each other's vaginas was shoving Tampax up the younger girls, to show them how to do it, but in a medical way, not a sexual one. And we did share bathrooms, but only to wind up the matron, who'd knock on the door saying, 'Who's in there?'

'Charlotte.' That was me.

'Who else?'

'Claire.' My best friend.

'Who else?'

'Judy.' Another best friend, but not my best best one.

'Who else?'

'Sarah.' Judy's best friend, and so a best friend of ours too.

'Anyone else?'

'Just Jessamy.' The fifth one, who was forever trying to get in with us four.

'Open this door, right now!'

So we would, and she'd see that there was only one of us in the bath, and the others would be sitting on the floor, chatting. I have no idea what picture that woman had conjured up in her mind's eye, but she always looked slightly disappointed . . .

We did everything together, you see. Everything. We were never alone. We had communal living down to a fine art. If you ran out of shampoo, you just used somebody else's. If you wanted to borrow a top, you just took it out of someone's drawer. If you complained about any of this, you were declared – the highest insult of all – boring.

God, we were bored. It said in the school prospectus that pupils could spend our free time in the Art Room or the Music Wing if they wanted, creating. What it didn't say was that this depended on a teacher being prepared to give up part of her weekend to unlock it and supervise you.

We were allowed to go shopping in town on Saturdays, but certain stores were out of bounds, due to one or two selfish girls who had stolen lots of nail polish and body glitter from them, therefore spoiling it for us all. (The fact that they'd distributed their booty amongst us when they'd got back to school was neither here nor there.)

On a Saturday night there'd occasionally be a film showing in the Great Hall. We were allowed to wear mufti (non-uniform clothing) to this, but no trousers – apparently they encouraged bad behaviour. Neither were we allowed to wear backless shoes (known to the rest of the world as clogs, all the rage at the time) on Saturday nights, in case we broke our ankles. We'd get to see films like *The Incredible Journey*, the allegedly inspiring tale of a plucky cat and its two dog friends who found their way home, against all odds. Or *Born Free*, the fascinating tale of a lion living in Kenya. And its enthralling sequel, *Living Free, Tarka the Otter*, anyone?

It was the 1970s, we were teenage girls, for god's sake – some of us were eighteen years old! By way of rebellion, we began to boycott these evenings, preferring instead to sit on our beds and have a competition to see who could cry real tears first. So they let us write our suggestions for films we would like to see on a list on the notice-board, along with a catalogue of available titles. Needless to say, we put down anything that even looked slightly rude, like *Virgin Soldiers*. They ignored this, but showed one ancient James Bond movie – which we all missed – and took to not telling us in advance what film it was going to be, we had to take a risk. I've seen *The Incredible Journey* three times.

On Monday nights we would be subjected to lectures from visiting dullards on subjects like 'The Song of British Birds', 'The Lesser Cháteaux of Versailles' and 'Samuel Johnson – The Women in His Life'. There was one on 'The Guitar' which was completely over-subscribed, as we thought it might include the collected works of someone like Pete Townshend – but it was a History Of, from the Lute to the Spanish, and stopped just short of the Electric. We boycotted these too – so they made it compulsory to attend at least three a term.

We had little contact with the outside world, except for the *Illustrated London News*, which was later replaced by the *Daily Telegraph*. So it would be more truthful to say that we had little contact with the real world. Strangely, however, we were allowed to watch *Top of the Pops*. But it was on the same night as Choir Practice, which started at the same time *TOTP* finished. So we had a choice – you either missed finding out what was No. 1 (surely the whole point of the programme) and got there on time; or you stayed to find out but got extra prep as a punishment for being late. We tried to tell the Choir Mistress that it was just another kind of music, and that it was in fact beneficial for us to study this modern art form; so would she please consider starting the practice ten minutes later? Certainly not. So we rang the local under-takers and asked them to come quickly to pick up her body, which they did, much to her fury, their irritation and our hysterics.

Anyway. There we were, six hundred teenage girls, stuck together in one big hormonal lump with Victorian values indoors and a post-60s sexually liberated world outside just passing us by. It's no wonder that as soon as we left the school, some of us went completely mad.

On Thursdays I worked in television. Not for the BBC, or indeed any channel you might have heard of, but for a small cable station. The lunchtime show I was concerned with was called *Around the Kitchen Table*. You can pretty much guess what it involved; but just in case you're in any doubt, I can assure you it was the usual heady mix of minor celebrities plugging anything from biographies to pantomimes; handy hints and tips from a series of incompetent experts; unheard-of charities and appeals and -athons which raised so little money it was embarrassing; and the homespun hour was usually rounded off with a song from a band in the pantry, who you'd never heard of before and knew you'd never have to hear again. You know the sort of thing.

Having just lost my job at the boutique the day before, it would be fair to say that on this particular morning, I wasn't in terrific humour. I was beginning to panic. Would Amber mind if I gave her her Christmas present when she got back, so that I could get something in the January sales? I rifled through the box of freebies that the producer kept under her desk – nothing suitable there: I couldn't see Amber taking kindly to an electric pepper mill, or Heather McCartney's autobiography, for that matter.

Naturally, this week's show had a Christmas theme – and had done since October.

'For god's sake,' I moaned to Wendy, my co-worker, as I held the door open for her, 'when I'm Prime Minister, I'm going to pass a law that bans anybody from even saying the word "Christmas" until the first of December.'

'Really, Charlotte?' she asked. 'Why?'

'Well, you know, we have a tiny summer which is only about five minutes long, then all the shops say it's back-to-school time, then suddenly the tinsel's crept on to the shelves and the world is covered in flashing lights and the festive season is upon us even earlier than last year, for longer than ever before. It'll start before it's finished soon!' I laughed, bitterly.

Wendy looked up at me, completely blank, not understanding how that would be possible.

'I suppose you like Christmas, do you, Wendy?' I didn't know her very well, as we only spent one hour a week together, but we'd already established that we didn't have much in common.

'Ooh, yes,' she simpered, 'I love it. In fact, I've done all my Christmas shopping already.'

'Have you, Wendy?' I drew up my chair and put on my headset. 'How clever of you.' You creepy weirdo maniac freak.

'Well, I have to, before all the shops get too crowded, you see.'

'Oh, right.' Wendy was in a wheelchair.

'Could you –' she indicated her headset, lying on the desk.

'Oh, yeah, I forgot,' I said, as I placed it over her ears for her. She only had one functional arm, and found that sort of thing a bit 'tricksy', as she would say.

'Cheers!' she said brightly. 'Are you going away for Christmas, Charlotte?' she asked, as the producer gave us the thumbs-up through the glass window, and we gave three back.

'Nah.' I passed Wendy the forms we had to fill in, to keep a record of every call, and took the lid off her pen.

'I am.'

I didn't ask, I couldn't face it, I knew she was going to tell me anyway.

'To Jamaica.'

'Great.' The clock came up on our monitor – thirty seconds to go till showtime.

45

'To see my grandmother.'

'Cool.'

'Actually,' she snorted at the prospect of her own joke, 'it's going to be really hot!'

What the fuck am I doing here, I thought to myself, as I watched the presenter rush in from Make-Up to take her seat at the supposedly 'kitchen' table. I'm exchanging pleasantries with a one-armed black cripple, who would probably be a lesbian as well if all kd lang concerts had disabled access. Despite her disabilities I just couldn't like her, and I was sure she'd only been employed in order to fulfil the cable station's legal requirement of being an Equal Opportunities employer, which she did, on about four different counts. So what was my excuse?

One of the phone lines was flashing, even though the programme hadn't started yet.

I flicked the switch. 'Around the Kitchen Table, how may I help you?' I said, in my nicest politest sweetest tone. (I was paranoid now; it was probably the producer's husband, ringing to catch me out.)

'What colour knickers are you wearing?' said a grubby voice.

'What makes you think I'm wearing any?' I flicked the switch off again. 'Wanker.'

Wendy shook her head, in despair. I knew she hated swearing, which only made me do it more.

The signature tune kicked in. On the monitor I watched the opening titles: snippets of nearly

46

famous almost-forgotten people who'd visited the 'kitchen', an ugly baby (the producer's) relentlessly bouncing up and down in a doorway, a hand that had clearly never done a day's work in its life arranging dried flowers in a blue glass vase. Through the studio window, I could see the cameras swooping in on the presenter, like Daleks to Dr Who's assistant. She smiled, and started talking whilst looking Intelligent and Caring. It turned out that today's phone-in was all about coping with festive stress, and the expert at the other end of the 'kitchen' table was a thin, bearded man who'd written a book called *Taking the X Out Of Mas*.

Needless to say, the majority of our calls were about stockings; with the exception of one or two housewives who'd mistaken us for the Samaritans. Wendy and I differed in our treatment of these women; she thought they were sad as in upset, and I thought they were sad as in no life. We dealt with them accordingly.

As usual, none of our callers were capable of being put through to the actual programme, and so yet again a researcher had to pretend to be Colleen from Exeter with a query about her mother-in-law.

'Ah well, another day another dollar,' I sighed, as the end credits rolled and I took off my headset.

'D'you get paid in dollars?' asked Wendy, wincing as I yanked hers off for her.

A young boy with too many piercings and not

enough shampoo, the production runner, poked his head round the Phone Room door. 'Meeting in the Green Room in five minutes,' he lisped.

'Thanks, Justin,' simpered Wendy.

'D'you want a push?' I asked, trying to be helpful. 'I had lots of practice when my daughter was a baby – I'm a bit of a whizz with a pram.'

'No thanks,' replied Wendy, a bit huffily actually, 'I can manage.'

The meeting was to tell us that the show was being taken off the air. It just wasn't getting any viewing figures, nobody was watching it. (More shockingly, people were surprised to hear this.) So tomorrow's programme would be the last one, ever. They were, in TV and life support terms, pulling the plug on us. Some people with kids and mortgages burst into tears. I was just angry. To lose one job in a week may be regarded as misfortune; to lose two looked like carelessness, but was in fact downright bad luck. How much worse could it get?

After an education which left me thinking that the periodic table was the same thing as the menstrual cycle, a few girls managed to go on to university, but I didn't. On our last day at school we all promised faithfully to keep in touch with each other for ever and ever amen, played 'Schools Out' by Alice Cooper on eleven over and over again, and cried loads and loads.

That summer was spent staying at each other's houses, going to parties to drink and smoke and snog other people's brothers, and their brothers' friends.

And then it was September, which became October.

I had no idea what I wanted to do with the rest of my life, I hadn't really thought about it. I hadn't been particularly good at anything at school, but had sort of idly imagined myself going out with a bloke with a Porsche, and so it didn't really matter what I did for a job, did it?

My father had a different opinion. He made me go to the buzzing metropolis that is Leatherhead, in Surrey, to a secretarial college mostly attended by housewives on refresher courses, and one nun. This was not quite glamorous enough for me, but I didn't have any better suggestions and so I went along with his plan, just to get out of the house, really. But the peaceful suburban Surrey village of Ashtead didn't have much nightlife, just the pub, which was full of lecherous real ale campaigners and shabby old ladies in belted raincoats with squiffy hair. The only bad lot to fall in with was the darts team. There were no bikers, just cyclists.

However. I had shorthand and typing qualifications now, so I started temping –

I still didn't want to commit to a proper job, I wanted to be free to go on holiday at a moment's notice, with all the jet set friends I was going to have any minute now. Local jobs were boring, and commuting was getting on my nerves, so I moved up to London, to share a flat with a girl from school called Imogen.

She hadn't been one of my closest friends, in fact she was what we called F&F (fat and friendless). But her father had bought her a flat in Kensington, just like that. She offered me her second bed-room rent-free; the unspoken deal was that I would provide her with some sort of social life in return. Fortunately, most of our year from school were up in London too, doing various courses and crammers and re-takes of their 'A' levels, and so, much to her delight and mine, Imogen's flat became Party Central.

It was cold, very cold, especially for a woman who'd now lost her other glove as well, and Piers wasn't answering the door. He was probably hungover, a bit fragile, as usual. I pressed the intercom again, for an annoyingly long time. It *was* Friday, wasn't it? Well then, why wasn't he in?

I'd seen this job advertised in the local paper about a year ago. 'Fancy working in the British film industry?' had been the attention-grabbing headline. I hadn't seen the small print which said

'part-time' until I was on my way to the inter-
view, but I'd been flattered into taking the job
anyway. Apparently being the sister of a
Hollywood 'development' executive made me a
very worthwhile employee. Piers was very disappointed when I told him (after I'd started working
for him, naturally) that we hardly ever spoke and
was forever trying to get me to make contact with
him, to no avail.

Piers called himself a Freelance Producer, but
it certainly wasn't anything like Matt's job. As far
as I could tell it involved writing a lot of begging
letters to the very wealthy, dodging lots of phone
calls on one line whilst making lots on the other,
and an inordinate amount of photocopying. I'd
been doing secretarial work for him (that is,
pretending to be his full-time secretary) every
Friday for the last year or so, and I'd never known
him do anything remotely filmy, like be 'on set',
or 'on location', he was always 'in the office' – the
walk-in cupboard only an estate agent would call
a second bed-room in his tiny attic flat above the
Goat in Boots on the Fulham Road.

Piers was a bit of a party animal, it has to be
said, a perfect specimen of his posh upbringing.
He was the kind of guy who wears a tie with jeans
and a sports jacket to dinner parties, whose
straggly collar-length hair always needs a cut, the
sort who seems to be there when the trouble starts
but not when it's over. He looked like shit first
thing in the morning, but got better as the day

wore on, the bar downstairs being his natural habitat. He was likeable enough, but in an ineffectual way. He had lots of male friends in motor racing, was very friendly with other people's wives but had no long-lasting proper girlfriend of his own. Bit flakey, bit disorganized, you know the type. Shoes with no socks, even in winter. Probably not so much for style reasons, but more because he couldn't find two that matched.

Come on, Piers! It's freezing out here . . .

I met Sabrina through him. They were old friends and used to have an 'arrangement', which meant that they met up every now and then to have unattached sex, when one or other of them felt like it. (She was a bit of a maniac, apparently; he once confided in me that he was too scared of her to say no. But he did add that she was very good at what she did.) Anyway, one Friday about three months ago, just as I was leaving, she rang to remind him that he was accompanying her on a client outing to see that Abba tribute band, Björn Again, that evening, he hadn't forgotten, had he?

Not only had he forgotten, he was already in Amsterdam for the weekend, trying to raise funding for a film about a man who marries a penguin, yes, really, and so she went ballistic. 'That bastard! I can't believe he's done this to me, what a c**t' – the works.

It didn't take her long – I ended up going instead.

You know when you meet someone, and you just click, instantly? Well this was like that. We'd spent the first part of the evening laughing at the saddos in the audience, so proud of their satin knickerbockers and boleros, and then as soon as was decently possible we'd left and shared a cab home. Then we'd sat in her elegant single person's pale-carpeted apartment until two o'clock in the morning, drinking lots of wine and laughing about Piers' skinny willy and exchanging romantic histories, y'know, the way you do. She lived within walking distance of my house, and I staggered home that night pissed as a fart and happy to have found a kindred spirit. And staggered back again when I realized I'd left my handbag behind.

But Piers had been rather put out by our new-best-friendship, as he felt we were ganging up on him. Well, that was our diagnosis of the problem anyway. The problem being that he hadn't been available for sex with her since then, and neither had he paid me a penny. It wasn't a massive amount, but enough to see me through Christmas – I was due about twelve weeks' wages now. (Piers' payments had always been sporadic; it was the way he worked. I'd come to see it as a way of saving up, actually. The lump sum usually went towards paying off a lumpy bill.) I hated talking about money and hadn't mentioned it to him yet, but had promised Sabrina I'd Say Something today. In fact, I'd promised myself I

53

wouldn't leave Piers' flat until I had a cheque in my hand.

Now I had my finger firmly pressed down on the buzzer, making one continuous ring. Even if he was still in bed, it was bound to annoy him enough to get up and do something about it.

Still no response. Maybe he'd popped out for a pint of milk or something. I looked behind me, straight into the bulging eyes of a ginger-haired man in a woolly hat.

'Shit, you gave me a shock!' I spluttered, hand on beating heart.

'Where us 'e?' said the man, in a thick Irish accent.

'Who, Piers?'

'Yes, hum.' He stared at me, as if it was my fault that the door wasn't being answered.

'I don't know, he's normally in,' was all I could say.

'Who're you?' asked the man.

I decided not to give my name. 'I'm his secretary.'

'Really?!' the man laughed, and spat a glob of something nasty on to the pavement.

'And you are . . . ?'

He stepped back to squint up into the grey sky at Piers' window. 'A friend.'

He certainly didn't look or sound like Piers' usual mates, who were all called Quentin and Nigel and who were all, without exception, not like this man.

My finger on the buzzer was getting tired. I stopped and squatted down to look through the letterbox. Masses of circulars and property magazines and pizza flyers on the floor, but no sign of life.

'This is my thord day of trying to get hold of the focker,' said the ginger man. 'A'm sick to the back teeth o'thus.' And he pulled a crowbar from the inside of his donkey jacket and started to smash the door in.

As I had now placed his accent as being Northern Irish, I decided not to protest. He was probably in the IRA and I didn't fancy being tarred and feathered and dumped outside some smart wine bar full of school parents on the Fulham Road.

One more bash and we were in. I let him go up the stairs first.

It only took one blow to break the lock on the door into the flat. There had been a party, that was evident. There were wine bottles and champagne glasses everywhere, and the whole place reeked of stale cigarette smoke and sweaty armpits. The ashtrays were full of roaches, a Dire Straits CD cover was still speckled with grains of white powder; beside it lay a Blockbuster video rental card and a rolled-up £20 note.

'Bollocks!' exploded the terrorist, as he came back from checking the bedroom. 'Looks lake he's done a ronner,' he said, scanning the mantelpiece and picking up a brown envelope. 'Are you Charlotte?'

It was an unopened gas bill, a Final Reminder. On the back of it was written:

*Charlotte*
*Sorry to do this to you, etc, but I can't do this any more. I know I owe you a shitload of money, but I just haven't got it at the moment. I promise I'll pay it back to you, honestly.*
*I'll call you as soon as I can. Don't worry about me, I'll be fine.*
*Piers*
*PS Happy Christmas, etc.*

'"Don't worry about me?"' I said out loud, to the walls. 'I'm not worried about you, Piers, I'm worried about my money, you little shit!'

The flat door slammed open and shut again, and I realized the IRA man had gone.

I flumped down on the sofa and held my head in my hands. At the beginning of this week, I'd been working in fashion, television and the film industry. Not any more. And now that it was Christmas, the world would grind to a halt, and I wouldn't get another job until at least the middle of January. How the hell was I going to get through the next few weeks?

Just as I was tucking the Blockbuster card and the rolled-up £20 note into my pocket, two policemen appeared in the doorway.

They accused me of breaking and entering; there was even talk of getting a policewoman over from the station, to search me for drugs. It took me a long time to convince them that I was just a house-wife from Fulham, or Hammersmith, depending on who you were talking to. Fortunately they recognized the IRA man from my description – apparently he was a well-known debt-collector for a local drug dealer.

So in the space of a week I'd lost three jobs. I suppose someone in their right mind would be deeply upset by that; I just thought it was boring.

# CHAPTER 3

'It has lately been drawn to your corre-
spondent's attention that, at social gather-
ings, she is not the human magnet she
would be. Indeed, it turns out that as a
source of entertainment, conviviality and
good fun, she ranks somewhere between a
sprig of parsley and a single ice-skate.'

Dorothy Parker, *Review of the Technique of
the Love Affair*,
November, 1928

There can be no sound more delicious than
the glugglug of dark-red wine being
poured into huge glass goblets by a gossipy
friend on a frosty winter's night, real fire a-
cracklin' in the grate. Amber was asleep upstairs,
oblivious to the fact that we were burning the little
kiddie chairs and table that she hardly ever used
any more. In fact, I was surprised the noise hadn't
woken her up; we'd just been hysterical, attacking
the baby furniture on the kitchen floor with a now

blunt carving-knife and a hammer, trying to split them into fire-size pieces, singing 'I'm a lumberjack and I'm OK' at the top of our voices, artificially warmed inside by the previous bottle of white.

'So where d'you think Piers has gone?' I asked, as I lit another fag.

'Fuck knows,' said Sabrina, helping herself to another one from my pack, 'silly sod.' (She doesn't smoke, but neither is she a non-smoker, which means that she never buys her own cigarettes but relies on other people to provide them for her.)

'I'm never going to get my money, am I?'

'Doubt it.' She exhaled with passion. 'He's a man, isn't he? No fucking morals, spineless bastard.'

'Yeah, you're right.' We both drank a little more.

Sabrina's mobile vibrated and whirred and diddly-dee'd its way around the coffee table. She picked it up and looked at the little screen. 'It's him!' She cleared her throat, licked her lips. 'Hello?' she said, in a dark-brown velvety voice that always made men want to marry her. (I'd tried it myself, but it always made people ask if I had a sore throat.)

As she billed and cooed her way into yet another man's heart, I looked across at my friend and wanted to shake my head, but didn't. She'd talked of little else since she'd arrived, so I knew all about him, but I didn't bother to commit any of this information to memory. Just in the few months

59

I'd known her, a pattern had already emerged: Sabrina meets man of dreams, man of dreams turns out to have something-terribly-wrong-with-him, man of dreams is dumped and replaced by new man of dreams, who turns out to have a different but equally untenable something-terribly-wrong-with-him and so he too is dumped and replaced by yet another man of dreams.

But don't get me wrong, Sabrina was fantastic. She was really together, really sorted. I couldn't quite believe I had a friend like this. I kept thinking she was going to go off me any minute now, when she found out that I really wasn't the person she thought I was. She was so alive, so vibrant, so clever – what on earth did she see in me? I didn't dare try to answer that question, I was too busy just hanging around her for as long as she let me, hoping that whatever she had might rub off on me.

And she had a lot. She had an incredibly well-paid, high-powered job in Financial PR (whatever that means); she drove a very fast sports car very fast; she drank like a fish but never got drunk, and was incredibly focussed and driven in every-thing she did. Failure was quite simply not an option.

'Ooh, don't say that, you're turning me on . . .' Sabrina smooched into the phone, and winked at me.

But she had one fatal flaw. Men. Any wisdom, life strategies or formulae for success that she had gathered over the years and used to great effect on other areas of her life, she promptly forgot when it came to men. It was ridiculous, tragic even. Pathetic, actually. She just went to bits if there was even a sniff of romance in the air, and would go to any lengths, the more extreme the better, to secure herself the object of her desire. And worse than that, she kept trying to involve me in her antics, in the comic belief that all I really needed was a good man to make everything all right again. (I went along with it, just because I liked her. But I wasn't holding my breath until a man came along in a dashing white Porsche to rescue me.)

In fact, only two weeks ago, she'd dragged me and Amber (our main asset, apparently) to the open-air ice skating rink outside Somerset House. She reckoned we stood a good chance of falling into the arms of a supportive man, quite literally. Amber and I had just got cold and cross, and ended up sipping hot chocolate behind the barrier, watching Sabrina throw herself on to the ice, into the path of any oncoming male (and quite a few accident-prone females). So after witnessing several pileups, we'd gone home; Sabrina had gone out for a drink with a bruised banker from New York called Bill.

'Bye bye, darling. Yes, I love you too . . .' she raised her eyes skyward for my benefit, 'see you later then, can't wait.' She ended the call and stubbed her fag out in the ashtray she'd nicked for me from some chic Mayfair restaurant the week before.

61

'Who was that?!' I exclaimed. She'd just said you-know-what, I.L.Y! It can't have been this Bill she'd been talking about, she'd only known him a couple of weeks.

'Bill, of course,' she said, as if I needed an explanation. 'Have you got any mints?'

'Er, no,' I lied. (I did, but they were kicking around the bottom of my bag, loose, gathering grime. Not for public consumption, for my mouth only. I'd have thrown them away, but I didn't think I could afford new ones.) 'Listen, Sabrina –'

'Yes?' She was scrabbling around in her handbag.

I took a deep breath. 'What are you doing for Christmas?'

'Funny you should say that,' she pulled out her make-up bag, 'I was going to ask you exactly the same thing.'

'Really?!'

'Yeah.' She studied her immaculately made-up face in a tiny mirror, and frowned. 'Mum's going with her sister to Miami again this year, they're going husband-hunting apparently, so I'm off the hook.' She got out some expensive-looking make-up in shiny gold casing. 'Why, what're you up to?'

I explained, while she titivated.

'Great!' She snapped her compact shut. 'Well if we're both going to be on our own, let's spend it together!'

'Really?!' I couldn't believe she'd said it, I held my breath.

'Yeah – hey, I know,' her wide eyes lit up, 'let's go away! Let's just bugger off and lie on a beach for a couple of weeks . . .'

'Oh.' God, I hated my life. 'I can't.'

She looked up, puzzled.

'My three least favourite words in the dictionary – "can't", "afford", and "it",' I explained.

Sabrina laughed, she thought I was funny. 'Oh come on, Lottie, it can't be that bad, can it?' (She was the only person in the world I let call me that, I hadn't quite managed to tell her when she first did it that I hated it, and now the moment had passed.)

'I'm afraid it is.' I sighed as I drank. 'I mean, I've got money, of course,' I tried a light-hearted laugh, I didn't want her to think I was the complete financial buffoon that I was, 'but I've got more urgent things to be spending it on than a holiday.' Like the rest of the credit card bill for the last one I had, two and a half years ago.

'Oh sod it, I'll pay!' she said.

'Oh no.' Yes! But no. 'No no no no no, I can't let you do –'

'Oh shut up. Look, Lottie, I don't want to go on my own, and so if I have to pay for you to come with me, then so be it!' Finished now, she zipped up her make-up bag. To me, she looked exactly the same as before – big eyes, big lips. Sabrina wasn't beautiful, but she was striking. 'OK – here's the deal. I'll pay for the flights and accommodation, if you'll sort it all out, y'know, book it,

63

do the boring bits. I just haven't got the time to do anything at the minute, work's frantic.' She messed up her hair. 'Come on, it'll be fun!' She knocked back the last of her wine, just as the doorbell went.

'Who on earth can that be?' I wasn't expecting anyone, it was nearly midnight. Do bailiffs work this late?

'It's Bill. We just can't keep our hands off each other at the moment, so he's come to whisk me away . . .' She stood up and looked in the mirror above the fireplace. She messed up her hair again. 'How do I look?'

I wanted to say 'like a blow-up doll who's been dragged through a hedge backwards', but didn't dare. So I said 'D'you have a favourite travel agent?' instead.

'No – try the internet,' she said, as she pulled her faux fur coat on, 'lastminute.com, something like that.'

I didn't bother to go to the door to meet this Bill, what was the point? He'd be dumped in a few weeks. As I air-kissed Sabrina goodbye, I said, 'Thank you so much, I'll get on to it right away,' and really meant it. At last, things were looking up!

My virginity had become a bit of an embarrassment. I'd always said that I wouldn't sleep with a man unless I knew he loved me (I'd read that at school, in an illicit

*Jackie* magazine, it was Cathy and Claire's No. 1 rule) but everyone else had lost theirs ages ago, and I was nineteen now. If not actually on the shelf, then certainly down at B&Q buying one.

I'd snogged, of course. I'd been pinned into the corner by somebody's tongue at parties, oh yes. And I'd had my poor bosoms pinched, bitten and tweaked, all in the name of passion. I'd heavy petted too, lots. Well, you know, a bit. Enough. I'd lain on top of coats on top of beds, I'd left my tights under grand pianos, I'd felt and held my fair share of willies (but never seen one eye to eye, so to speak, because that would be disgusting).

But nothing ever came of it. Other girls would get off with a boy at a party and be going steady with them the next day, thereby securing themselves A Boyfriend. But it never worked out that way for me. It seemed that I could have one person's hand in my knickers on a Friday night, and another one's up there of a Saturday, without so much as a request to repeat the experience from either of them when the lights came back on.

I took to keeping a little pad of paper in my handbag, with my name and phone number already written out on the top three pages, to bypass the no pen excuse.

We didn't have answer machines then, and it turns out that a watched telephone works on the same principle as a watched pot. So I took the precaution of adding my address underneath my number, just in case. And my surname.

I didn't really know what I was doing – I didn't have the sort of mother you could ask. I thought it was a good idea to use a vaginal deodorant, for maximum freshness. I remember an Italian boy licking his fingers for fuller sexy satisfaction, and then accusing me, loudly, of trying to poison him.

I went on The Pill because I'd heard it made your tits bigger. It didn't. I still had the same bosoms, but I did grow a bigger bottom.

I stopped wearing a bra, for easy access. The boys seemed disappointed not to have the chance to show off their finely honed unclasping skills.

Everyone else was going steady, why wasn't I? Much research into women's magazines told me that I must be some sort of freak. I followed their advice; I changed my hairstyle, I flattered my fuller figure, I went to the theatre and sat through dreary productions of worthy plays in order to have something to discuss with Erudite Man (my type, according to *19* magazine) at the next party. All to no avail; I ended up with hair shorter than Judi Dench, the diaphanous wardrobe of Judi Dench and a full working knowledge of Judi Dench's most recent theatrical triumphs.

It did happen eventually, of course. I was nineteen and it was Valentine's night. I came back from a quick trip to the off-licence to find a man slumped on our steps. Assuming him to be an alcoholic, I ignored him and put my key in the lock.

'Hi,' he said, I think he'd been asleep, 'd'you know Imogen?'

'Imogen who?' I asked, as if the whole building was chock-a-block full of Imogens.

'Imogen Hartington-Clark,' he said. I realized he wasn't a drunk at all, even though he was quite old. In fact, he was rather good-looking, in a crumpled corduroy flunked-Oxbridge sort of way.

'Yes, she's my flatmate!' I said, with more excitement than that statement deserved.

'Great,' he said, standing up, he was nice and tall, 'is she in?'

'No,' I said, trying not to sound too bitter, 'she's out with her boyfriend.' (I know, don't.)

'Oh.' He looked crestfallen, like he could do with being held in the arms of a good woman, maybe even one with small tits. 'Can I come in and wait for her?'

'Yes, sure!' I said, and even carried his rucksack up the stairs for him.

The phone was ringing when we got in. (I didn't answer it because I didn't want anyone to think I was in on Valentine's night, and because it might be my mother ringing up to remind me not to forget to get married and have children, although she cleverly disguised her underlying theme with questions like 'how are you?' and 'done anything interesting?') So I just let it ring, muttering something about it probably being Imogen's dad, who was a complete and utter bastard.

'Yeah, I know,' he said, putting his feet up on the sofa (without taking his shoes off, he was very bohemian) as I uncorked the wine, 'he's my dad too.'

Imogen was so posh that her family was very, very extended, almost to breaking point. She had step-everythings, hundreds of them, all over the world. She had half-siblings ranging from three to forty, and more aunts than you could shake a wedding at. They all had ridiculous names like Peregrine and Lettice, and yet their dogs were called Dave or Bob. The women ran the family while the men talked about it. They all fought over money, but nobody liked to mention it. The children either spent their inheritance or earned it all over again, only to see it squandered by the next generation.

I was quite used to unexpected visits from her relations, although I can't say I liked it – they seemed to think our flat was their flat, but we never got invited back to stay in rambling stately homes in Ireland or luscious plantation houses in the Caribbean. But at least none of them tried to move in; they just came to stay overnight, mostly, on their way to Heathrow or down to see the dentist in Harley Street the following morning, that kind of thing. The family's properties formed their own private network of crashpads, basically. I suspect it was only bricks and mortar that held this lot together.

'What's your name?' I asked, as I handed him his wine in a mug – neither Imogen nor I liked doing the washing-up and we were in the middle of yet another Mexican stand-off about it. I'd had soup out of a vase before now.

'Jonty,' he said, 'first wife, third child,' he explained. (They all identified themselves in this way, I was used to it, and had given up trying to remember names – as, it seemed, had they.)

Jonty was thirty-three years old. He'd just got back from a year in India, which explained the striped cotton waistcoat and the cheesecloth shirt and the sandals and the filthy feet. And the slightly wasted look, probably brought on by amoebic dysentery, but all covered up with a beautiful tan and a very sexy smile.

'Were you working over there?' I asked, without thinking.

'Er, no,' these people didn't work, 'I was just looking at the poverty, you know, seeing what it really means to be literally dirt poor.'

'Wow,' I said.

Anyway, he talked and I listened and we drank and drank and I listened and he talked some more, and we ate Imogen's secret stash of fig rolls and cashew nuts and we drank some more, and by about nine o'clock I'd decided that he was the most interesting person in the world and that I was the most boring. By ten o'clock, I'd decided that nineteen to thirty-three wasn't that big an age gap after all, even though I couldn't actually work out how many years it was without using a calculator. By eleven, I was madly in love with him and was picturing us in an ashram just outside Calcutta, with seven beautiful children of our own and a few lovely brown ones that we'd adopted out of the kindness of our hearts.

By midnight, he was throwing me around

my bedroom, having sex by, with and from me, grunting and oofing and just not stopping for quite long enough for me to say 'by the way, I'm a virgin'. It kind of just didn't come up in the conversation, probably because there wasn't any, our mouths were otherwise engaged. But although my pissed head was willing, and my lonely heart was desperate, my poor body was having none of it and went into a distinctly unattractive tremor – I was shaking like a leaf, from head to toe. I told myself at the time that it was because he kept stripping the duvet off me, I was just cold, that's all. I know now that it was sheer fear.

But he probably didn't notice, he was too busy performing his impressive repertoire of sex displays, swinging from figurative chandeliers, jumping off imaginary wardrobes. I think he thought he was quite a 'sexpert', and that I needed to be shown that, so he moved me around to accommodate his expertise. I can remember one very complicated manoeuvre involving him in the lotus position and me crouching over him like a female dog about to have a wee, which still makes me cringe to this day.

It wasn't horrible, I mean it wasn't rape. But I think it would be fair to say that he enjoyed it more than I did. He was kind enough to kiss me before he rolled off, and then he put his head on my breast and went to sleep. I could hardly breathe under the weight of him, but I didn't ask him to get off because it didn't seem very romantic. I didn't sleep a wink that night; not only was I waiting to feel like A Woman now, but I was also worrying about how to get the stains off the sheets.

I had to go to work in the morning – he didn't, of course. I turned my alarm off before it rang and crept out of bed and got ready very quietly. I didn't want to wake him up, and I don't think he wanted me to either. When I got home that evening, he'd gone. I cried – not because I'd lost my virginity to someone who didn't love me, but because he hadn't left a note to say goodbye.

It was all very well Sabrina telling me to find a holiday on the internet, but didn't she know I didn't have a computer? Probably not. She'd given me her email address when we'd first met; I'd said that my computer was being mended. Then we'd both launched into a rant about the unaesthetic values of moulded plastic and she hadn't mentioned it again.

The next day I didn't do anything about the holiday, because I thought she probably didn't mean it, she was just being nice. (It seemed too good to be true – a holiday in the sun, paid for by somebody else. Although, quite where I was going to get my spending money from, I didn't know.)

The day after that she rang, and asked how I was getting on. 'Great,' I said, 'it's just a question of ploughing through them all.' She seemed to know what that meant, even though I didn't. We discussed the Caribbean, and South Africa and Morocco – I said I'd find out what I could. Which was very little – my TV was so old it didn't even have Ceefax.

The next day, I had to go out to the cashpoint, which was right next door to a travel agent's. They laughed me out of there, they didn't have anything left for Christmas except either four days in Malta, or a fortnight at the most expensive spa in the world, in Mauritius, if you please. I couldn't possibly ask Sabrina to fork out for something like that. The travel agent suggested I look on the internet.

Getting a little desperate now, I splashed out on a *Time Out* magazine. The holidays looked a bit weird, mostly involving camels and magic buses and flights to Australia for peanuts. I phoned one, but they kept me on hold, forcing me to pay to listen to an electronic 'Greensleeves' until the girl came back and said, 'Have you tried our website?'

Normally, I would have made Arthur look it all up for me, but I still hadn't heard back from him. Probably still in a huff about that wretched dog. I made a mental note to send him a gloating post-card from wherever we went.

'So – where are we going?!' asked Sabrina, four days after she'd made her kind offer.

'Oh god, the au pair's left the bath running again,' I said. 'I'll call you back.' I knew she wouldn't remember that the new au pair had gone the same way as the Helga/Anya one before her, this one had been fired for letting the bath overflow, twice. I replaced the receiver and snuggled back down under the duvet. I was fully dressed as the house was freezing – I only had the heating on when Amber was home. Bed was the best place for me.

A couple of hours later, she rang again. 'You sound like you've been asleep,' she said.

'I haven't,' I lied, 'I just don't feel very well, that's all. I think I'm coming down with something . . .'

'Oh dear,' she said. 'You definitely need a holiday in the sun. Any news?'

'Yes!' I said, I don't know why.

'Ooh, what?!' She was verbally rubbing her hands with excitement. 'Go on, hit me with it!'

'Well,' I said. Um. Fuck. 'We've got a choice . . .'

'Cool!' she said. 'Oh, hang on, bloody work getting in the way of my personal life again – no, no, Hugo, that's completely wrong, you don't do it like that – shit – sorry, Lottie, I've got to go, I'll call you back.'

I pulled the phone out of the wall and tried to get back to sleep. I heard it ringing downstairs. I ignored it. I picked up Amber from school. 'Ooh look, Mum, five messages!' she said when we arrived home. I didn't listen back to them, I knew who they were from.

I spent that evening pretending to be out when Sabrina came knocking on my front door, not once, but twice. She even called my name through the letterbox. I felt like I was being nagged now, stalked even. Jeez! I turned all the lights out and read a book in bed, by torchlight.

This is ridiculous, I thought, as I was still awake at 3.12 a.m. Do you want to go on holiday, or not?

There was a terrible wailing noise – I thought it was the local over-crowded cat population doing their bad ghost impressions outside, and so I grabbed the jumbo Uzi Schwarzenegger water gun I kept by the bed for exactly this purpose, flung open the window and shot out into the dark. But still the noise continued.

'I've got an earache,' Amber was crying. 'I need some Calpol, Mummy, please . . .'

We didn't have any. We didn't have anything that would do instead, either. Not even an old aspirin. I made her some hot Ribena, but it didn't really help. I gave her a hot water bottle, wrapped up in a towel, to hold to her ear. She got into my bed, we snuggled up together, and I hummed her baby songs to her until she nodded off again, but she soon woke up, screaming with the pain.

'Shh, Amber!' I hissed, half-asleep. 'You'll wake up the whole street!'

'It hurts, Mum,' she wailed, 'it really hurts!'

'Well, what the bloody hell d'you want me to do about it?' I know, I know; I was snappy, I felt helpless, I was at my wits' end. Where was her father at times like this? 'Look, we haven't got any medicine, all the shops are shut and so is the doctor's – you'll just have to wait until the morning, I'm sorry. Shall I turn the TV on?'

Not surprisingly, Open University didn't keep her attention for too long, and neither did the Australian Grand Prix, and so in the end I had to call a cab and take her to casualty. They gave her antibiotics, eventually.

We got the bus home, at 7.30 in the morning. We were cold, we were tired, we were miserable. Amber didn't want anything to eat, which was lucky because there wasn't really anything to eat, and so we got back into bed and snuggled up to each other.

'Mu-um?'

'Yes?'

'What are you doing?'

I smiled, this was an old game of ours. 'I'm baking a cake.' I waited the obligatory three seconds. 'Amber?'

'Yes?'

'What are you doing?'

'I'm riding an elephant.' One, two, three. - 'Muum?'

'Yes?'

'What are you doing?'

She fell asleep, I couldn't. My brain wouldn't shut up.

Anxiety is a terrible thing. It's different from good old-fashioned worry, it's much worse. It's more brittle, it's more damaging. It eats you up, it becomes part of you, it takes over your life. You don't know where to begin, what to start dealing with, because it seems that every single thing is urgent, needs sorting out immediately, right now. All your problems are part of each other, they're stuck together, in one big cancerous lump which grows in the pit of your stomach. 'But if I do this, that will happen. And if I don't do that, this will happen.' There's no way through. Anxiety is a kind of madness, an insidious kind, the kind you can't see.

It never goes away, it's always there. So you try to escape. You run to the wine bottle, the joint, the man, the weekend away in a concerned friend's country cottage, the health farm that you can't afford, you can even hang a total geographical and move house, but you still can't run away quite far enough. And even if you're lucky enough to be having quite a good day, you suddenly remember something bad that stops you in your tracks and slams you right back against that wall. Trapped, desperate, you start to look differently at your friends, picturing their easy lives, furious if they dare to complain. You know that no one will ever understand how hard it is for you. They may say they do, but they don't. Not that you'd ever ask them for help anyway. You got yourself into this, you can bloody well get yourself out of it. Perversely, you want to punch anyone who offers advice.

So you start to get creative. You go further and further into the problems, looking for the solutions. Even though you know you're under a lot of pressure, you convince yourself that you're making the right decisions. You come up with yet another way of dealing with it, you think you're doing the right thing. You're not. But you don't know that.

Which may be why I thought it was OK to leave my eight-year-old daughter asleep in the house that day, on her own, while I quickly popped out to investigate my latest bright idea.

'You're lucky, it's Happy Hour,' said the gurning clown behind the counter.

'What exactly does that mean?' I asked. 'It's only ten o'clock in the morning and this is an internet café, isn't it, not a cocktail bar?'

He then launched into a really tedious explanation, something about if you come in before 11 a.m.

and after 4 but before 7 it's only 50p for fifteen minutes otherwise it's £1, £2 for thirty minutes, blah blah blah.

'Yes, yes,' I said, quickly, to let him know I was a busy person in a rush, 'I'll have a coffee and a computer, if you don't mind.'

Picking up a felt pen, he wrote some numbers down on what looked like a Perspex photo-frame. Pretending to know what he was doing, I allowed him to lead me to the one remaining seat, next door to what looked like Hugh Grant.

'D'you need any help?' the assistant asked, as I peered at the screen in front of me. He was a bit too close for comfort, a personal-space invader. He was evidently Australian, the shiny happy irritating kind, complete with loud surfy shirt and wild scurfy hair. Quite nice twinkly ocean-blue eyes, but definitely not handsome. He had an open, boyish face but muscly, hairy arms. He seemed to be the sort of guy all the girls loved, but would never be in love with – ugh, you just couldn't. 'It's no trouble, really,' he grinned. Over-helpfully. 'Shall I start you off?'

'No!' I snapped, not really meaning to, but it was too late. 'I'm fine. Really.'

Smiling, he put the Perspex stand beside the monitor. He'd written the time on it – ah, right. 'I'll get your coffee,' he said. 'Milk? Sugar? Or organic Australian honey, how 'bout that?' He was obviously keen on the theming thing; there were supposedly Aboriginal-style daubings around the

79

walls (but they looked more like an IRA smear campaign), and didgeridoos of all shapes and sizes proudly displayed around the place, a little like the guitars at the Hard Rock Café, but not much.

Having answered all those questions to the best of my ability, I set to it. I'd seen people work computers before, obviously, so I knew to take hold of the mouse and do some clicking.

Five minutes later, I was forced to tap Hugh Grant on the shoulder and say, 'Excuse me, you don't know how to get into the onternet, do you?'

He looked across at me. God, he was gorgeous! He was much more handsome than Hugh Grant. I had the strange sensation of my rusty old sex machinery starting up again, clanking into action after a very long sleep. 'Er, yes, but maybe you should ask that guy to show you.' He went back to his screen.

'D'you need some help?' Oz was right beside me before you could say 'rejected'.

'Well, um . . .'

He looked at my screen and grinned. 'Looks like you've got yourself into a bit of a mess here,' he told me, like I didn't know, 'we'll get you out of this and on to the net in no time, no worries.'

I sat back in my chair and let him click his way out of my trouble. Hugh Grant was engrossed in his computer. He knew I was looking at him though, because he shot me a furtive look back before smiling at something that had just popped up with a 'ding' on his screen.

'There you go!' said Oz, triumphant.

'Right, that's it, is it?' I said.

'Yip,' he smiled. 'D'you know what you're doing now?'

'Oh yes,' I said, too loudly. 'Yes yes yes.' And wanting to seem like a nice person, for Hugh's benefit, I said 'thanks' as well.

Five minutes of inactivity later, Oz was showing me how to set up an email account, even though I just wanted to find out where me and Sabrina could go on holiday. 'What name d'you want to use?' he asked.

'I have no idea,' I said, as I watched Hugh put his coat and scarf on, and a rather cute woolly hat too.

'What about beautifuleyes@hotmail.com?' said Oz.

'What about fuckoffanddie.com?' I said, distractedly, as I watched Hugh pick up his rucksack – nice bum – and leave.

Oz was really laughing, he thought that was hilarious. He obviously didn't realize that I meant it.

'Does that man come here often?' I asked, as I watched him through the café window, crossing the road.

'Oh yeah, most days, he's one of our regulars,' Oz replied. 'Right, that's you all set up now. Is there anything else I can help you with?'

It turned out to be quite good fun in the end. After an hour's tuition from the over-attentive Oz,

I was right-clicking and double-clicking and really rather proud of myself for learning something new. Maybe I could get a job with computers in the New Year.

I left the Down Undernet Café (yes, really) happily clutching a printout of the winter-sun holiday I'd booked online to show Sabrina. I popped into a couple of shops to do some Christmas browsing, bought some mince pies instead, and even found myself humming along with the charity carol singers as I waited for the bus home.

It wasn't until I turned into our road that I remembered. I'd been so preoccupied, I'd actually forgotten Amber wasn't at school today. I'd left my daughter home alone.

Having lost my virginity to Imogen's step-brother, I duly got my notification from Mother Nature that I was now officially A Woman – a severe bout of cystitis. Undaunted, I determined to find myself The Perfect Relationship, which meant getting, someone to stay with me for longer than one night.

I managed to hang on to one guy for eight months, and then he 'accepted a transfer' to Paris. So I began to commute to see him every other weekend, at great expense, but in my mind I was investing in my future. Then one Friday night I surprised him and he surprised me. He was writhing around with some French girl, right there on the sofa. Obviously I was upset, but I decided that if that's what worked for him then fine – I'd accept his mistress, as long as she knew she was just his *pièce à la côté*. I made him promise me we'd get married when he came back to London. He's still there, as far as I know.

I kept looking though. I had to. I wanted what all my friends were getting – the big house, the big car, the lovely husband and adorable kids, and one of those industrial-looking Dualit six-slot toasters. (For some reason, I was obsessed with having one of those – not only because it was a design classic, but also because it would be concrete proof that this was a family home with lots of children, 'we' ate a lot of toast.) I studied the art of seduction, I learned all the techniques to ensnare any man I wanted. But even though I could get the men in all right, I couldn't make them stay.

It was a painful time. I have memories of chasing after men who'd just rejected me, demanding to know why they weren't interested. Without listening to the answer, I'd promise to change my behaviour, and during long tearful phone calls I'd beg them to give me another chance.

The 'nice' ones did, only to discover that I hadn't changed at all, and that they should have walked away when they could. By the time they did manage to get out of the relationship, I'd made it my business to strip them of any remaining self-esteem. 'Loser!' I'd shout, 'and by the way, you're a lousy shag/my friends never liked you/don't forget to work on your personality!' – whatever their biggest fear was, I'd find it and whip them with it.

The 'nasty' ones just left me to figure it out for myself.

I was out of breath from running. My heart was thumping loudly; I opened the front door very quietly, hoping it wouldn't wake Amber up. She was probably still asleep, I told myself, she wouldn't even have noticed I wasn't here.

'Mum!' A very distressed Amber flew out of the sitting room and attached herself to my legs. 'Where've you been? I missed you,' she began to cry again, 'I didn't know where you were, Mum, where were you? Why did you leave me here on my own?' She began to sob, pitifully.

The TV was on, far too loud; I went into the sitting-room to turn it off. 'I'm so sorry, Amber, I really really –' I stopped dead in my tracks.

Sabrina was sitting on the sofa, bolt upright, staring at me. She was dressed for work, her laptop was open on the coffee table.

'Hi, darling,' I tried to sound breezy, 'how are you?'

'What the fuck do you think you're playing at?' she replied.

'I'm sorry?' I said, shocked.

'Are you?' She was white with anger. 'Where the hell have you been?'

'Researching our holiday, actually,' I said, fumbling around in the overflow of my handbag for the internet pages I'd printed off. 'I've found a great hotel in –'

'Have you any idea how it feels to wake up and find your mother's not there? Not knowing when she's coming back? If she's coming back? D'you know how frightening that is for a child?' She stood up, hands on hips. 'Do you?'

'But I only popped out for –'

'I've been here for' – she looked at her watch – 'just over two hours. That's hardly a "pop", is it?' she spat. 'Anything could have happened – the house could have burned down, someone could have broken in –' Amber began to cry again. 'She could have electrocuted herself, anything!'

'Yes, but she didn't, did she?' Admittedly, I was flailing.

'THAT IS NOT THE POINT!' I'd never seen Sabrina like this before, she was quite literally shaking with rage. 'You abandoned her, you left her on her own! How *dare* you do that?!'

I began to see that perhaps this wasn't all about me. Sabrina never mentioned her father, maybe that was it. I thought I'd change the subject. 'How does the Dominican Republic sound?' I said, brightly enough to make it sound divertingly attractive. In fact, I wished I was there right now.

'I'm not going away for Christmas with you any more.' She snapped her laptop shut and zipped it into a black leather case.

Silence. Zip, zip.

'What, because of this?' I asked, staggered. No, she couldn't. Could she? 'Look, it's the first time I've ever done it, I wouldn't normally but –'

'No, that's not the reason, although I have to say, I don't think I'd feel comfortable on holiday with a woman who thinks it's OK to leave her child at home on her own.' She shagged up her hair in the mirror above the fireplace. Turning to go, she didn't even bother to look at me as she said, 'Bill is taking me to a luxurious spa in Mauritius instead. I've been trying to get hold of you for the last couple of days, to tell you, but couldn't seem to get through. Which is why I called round this morning, on my way to work.' She suddenly looked at me, her eyes narrowed. 'Amber told me all about her trip to the hospital, it sounds awful. Did you leave her home alone last night as well?'

'No, no!' I protested, but she'd already swept out of the room. Bending down to kiss Amber who was sitting sniffing on the bottom step of the stairs, Sabrina handed her her business card and said softly in my daughter's ear, 'Just call me if you need me, sweetheart. OK?'

'OK,' said Amber, with a smile normally reserved for me.

Standing up and spinning round, Sabrina said, 'Charlotte. If I ever, ever catch you doing that again, I'm going to ring Social Services, OK?'

But before I could reply, she'd gone.

Without thinking, I rounded on Amber. 'Don't you know not to open the door to strangers?!' I exclaimed, knowing perfectly well I hadn't actually ever told her this one, but it didn't matter now, I was furious.

'But Sabrina's not a stranger,' she said, quietly. 'And I didn't know where you'd gone . . .' She looked up at me. 'I was scared, Mummy.'

I sat down beside Amber on the stair, to try and explain, but she ran up to her bedroom and slammed the door.

I held my hands over my ears, to drown out her sobs. I'd just paid the non-refundable deposit for our holiday over the internet with the last bit left on my new smash-glass-in-case-of-emergencies credit card, which I'd only got a couple of months ago. I'd just lost my best friend. And now I was going to have to spend Christmas all on my own. I buried my head in my knees, I curled up really tight, but I couldn't drown out my sobs either.

It was that awful bit in the service that makes everyone cringe.

'. . . if any man can shew any just cause, why they may not lawfully be joined together, let him now speak, or else hereafter forever hold his peace.'

There was an awkward shuffling in the Abbey, a cough, one of the bridesmaids tittered. I half expected Gladys Knight to come screaming down the aisle singing 'It Should Have Been Me!' at the top of her voice, with The Pips right behind her, entertaining the rest of the congregation with some nifty footwork.

But nobody said a word.

My dress was digging into me, it had never been comfortable, right from the first fitting. And the thing on my head felt like a crown of thorns, which I suppose was appropriate for a martyr to the matrimony cause.

'Wilt thou have this Woman to thy wedded wife, to live together in God's ordinance . . .'

Gus looked across, his face full of love and adoration, with just a hint of a smile playing around his lips. 'I will,' he said.

That was it. Two simple words. It was that easy.

'. . . forsaking all other, keep thee only unto him, so long as ye both shall live?'

'I will,' said Imogen.

Of course she bloody will, I thought, no one else would have her. And yet it had taken three of us bridesmaids and her father and the horse-drawn carriage driver to push her into the church, because she was 'scared'.

Of what?! She should have got there early, just in case Gus changed his mind!

The reception was in one of their stately homes, which meant that there were plenty of places to hide from Jonty, and Gus's flat-mate, and all the other men I'd met through Imogen and consequently slept with. The house being hundreds of years old, there was no smoking allowed, as one careless flick of ash could mean the whole place going up in seconds. After the wedding breakfast, which included a series of interminable speeches from people so posh they'd stopped using consonants completely, I was gagging for a fag. It was too bleak to go outside, and my bridesmaid upholstery was no defence against the English country house chill factor, even though it was July. Eventually, after much getting lost, I found what looked like a little study in the west wing, which also contained a silver tray of glinting crystal decanters filled with deliciously dangerous drinks. Perfect! So I was actually hanging out of a Norman window when he came in.

'Wow,' he said, 'that's a sight for sore eyes!'

I guiltily threw my fag away (it just missed a passing peacock down below) and squeezed myself back into the room.

What is it about men in uniform? No really, what is it? Well, OK, he wasn't exactly wearing the costume of a fighter pilot but he was in a morning suit, which was one up from black tie, which was ten up from jeans and a T-shirt. Anyway.

'You're one of the bridesmaids, aren't you?'

'No, this is my dress of choice,' I retorted, probably out of nervousness.

He smiled at my feeble joke, and so I instantly liked him. 'So how d'you know these people?' He walked over to the citadel of alcohol and poured himself a large brandy. He moved with ease, almost gracefully, he had a liquid smoothness and a really nice arse. The shaft of strong sunlight filtering through the ancient panes of distorted glass gave him a sunny sheen, and I was caught.

He'd been brought here by a work colleague, whose date had let her down at the last minute. It wasn't even his suit. He'd never met Imogen, or Gus. He hated weddings, too.

'Love is for losers!' We clinked our heavy cut glasses together and drank a toast to the unhappy couple. He was an outsider, and I felt like one. Nobody came to find us. And we didn't bother to find them. We stayed in that room, chatting and drinking and laughing, for the rest of the afternoon, and the evening, and the night.

His name was Joe. He was five years younger than me, and he didn't have a girl-friend (or a boyfriend, I checked that one out too); he lived in a shared flat in south London, he was a musician really but was working in an office at the moment, just to pay the bills. His parents had divorced horribly when he was nine, he had an elder sister who was a single parent and exhausted; she made him Sunday lunch in return for taking the kids to the park afterwards. He hated celery, he loved *Coronation Street*. He wasn't classically handsome, but he was beautiful when passionate. He was much better-looking than me. He had a certain 'bad news' air about him, but when he spoke about his music, his whole face lit up. I thought he had nice hands, he thought I had nice eyes.

We didn't have sex, we were both too drunk. But we didn't need to, not yet. As I snuggled up to him on that big squashy sofa covered in old tartan rugs and white dog hairs, I just knew that we would make something beautiful together one day.

And we did. Amber.


'Right, that it?' asked my father as he slammed the car boot shut.

'Yes, that's everything,' I replied, as I folded my arms tight and wiggled my legs to keep warm, it was freezing out there on the pavement. 'That's everything I've got,' I wanted to say, looking at Amber's excited little face strapped into the back seat, but I didn't.

'Right.' He went to open the driver's door, but suddenly looked up at me. 'You going to be all right?'

For fuck's sake. 'Yes, I'm a big girl now, Dad. I even got myself dressed this morning.'

He smiled. 'Quite.'

Awkward pause.

'Right then, better get your mother to the airport. Don't want her to catch cold, do we?'

'No, no, perish the thought,' I said, shivering. She hadn't said a word since they arrived; apparently she was cross that I hadn't sent Christmas cards to her relations. So she'd stayed in the car.

'Phone on Christmas Day, that the plan?' he asked, as he lowered himself into the driving seat.

'Yes, Dad, it is.' As you well know. Now bugger off. 'Shouldn't you get going? You know how Mum hates to be late . . .'

'Yes, right –' He shut the door, turned the engine on and wound down the window. 'Happy Christmas then, Charlotte,' he said.

'Merry Christmas, Dad,' I said, through the inexplicable lump forming in my throat.

'Happy Christmas, Mummy!' piped up Amber, 'and thank you for letting me go!' She blew me lots of kisses, lots of sweet bye-byes.

'Am I letting you go or are you being taken

away?' I wanted to say. But I didn't. 'Have a lovely time, darling!' I managed to call to her, as the car pulled off.

I'll never forget her little face, bright as a button as it waved at me excitedly through the back window of my parents' car, right up until the last moment, until they disappeared out of sight. I stayed out there on the pavement for a while, just staring at the place they'd disappeared from. I was frozen to the spot, not because it was cold, but because I didn't want to go back into the house. I couldn't. I felt as if I was standing in a pool of setting concrete.

It was as if I knew that something terrible was about to happen, and that I was absolutely powerless to stop it.

# CHAPTER 4

'The truth about loving is that if you put each other first, you come up with a kind of balance. I think I believe this, but you have to make sure he is putting you first too.'

Jill Robinson and Stuart Shaw,
*Falling in Love When You Thought You Were Through*

At first, I liked Joe because he wasn't like all the others I'd tried to fit in with. He hadn't been to private school, he was from Twickenham but his family didn't own it, he wasn't motivated by money and status. He was a musical poet, I suppose, words and flow and rhythm were his thing. He was a gifted musician, he had an exceptional talent. He hated dinner parties and drinks parties and point-to-points and polo and all those other posh pursuits – and so, quite frankly, did I. I wanted to live in another world, and Joe provided one for me. It was easy to get involved in his world and forget about your own. I couldn't believe he liked me, it felt too good to be true.

After Imogen's wedding, we were inseparable. We spent every waking moment we could together, and we slept spoon by spoon every night. We didn't see anybody else, because we didn't want to. I left little notes in his pocket for him to find during the day, he would spend his lunch hour finding the perfect strawberry for me. We were special, really special.

We spent an entire weekend drunk and stoned in bed, two whole days and three delicious nights, completely naked, accompanied only by his guitar and my unanswered phone.

We both developed fictitious illnesses for our employers, so that we could have lots of time off for 'tests'.

He laughed at my jokes, and I cried at his songs.

For the first time in my life, I was – and I don't use this word lightly – happy. I felt better with him than without him. He was kind, he was good, he was generous with his heart, he lived life on his terms – and he made me want to be like that too. My search was over, I could relax. I had found the other half of my orange.

A month later, Imogen and Dr Gus came

back from their honeymoon, and I had to move out. So I moved in with Joe, into his tiny bedroom in Alexandra Palace, which was a bit of a squeeze, and the rest of the household shouldn't have minded as much as they did, because at least I made sure the place was clean and tidy.

We had a few little arguments then, probably because we were living on top of each other, sometimes literally – and so I found us a place of our own slightly nearer to civilization, in Swiss Cottage. The rent was bigger than the flat, but I knew it would be worth it.

I hired a van and moved us in on my own, as Joe had promised to take his sister's kids swimming that day.

I worked in the local wine bar three nights a week, to help with the bills. Joe's band was about to get a deal and so he had to rehearse. This was fine by me, I wanted to help, I wanted the best for him.

Eventually, the band's manager (someone they'd hired purely on the basis of looking like Danny the drug dealer in *Withnail and I*) advised them to give up doing anything else completely, so that they could concentrate on songwriting.

Which meant that our tiny flat was filled with the carcasses of all-drinking, all-drugging musos and their guitars, morning, noon and night. I'd get home from a very long day at work with dinner for two in a carrier bag; I'd have to stretch it to dinner for seven, without looking churlish.

I tried to Say Something about it, but Joe accused me of being bourgeois and suburban and boring. He understood, of course he did, but if I could only hang on a bit longer, they were going to be rock stars in a minute . . .

I felt ashamed for complaining. Of course I would support him, it was the least I could do. And then, when he was Sting, he would support me. That's how it works.

Isn't it?

So Amber had really gone, it had really happened. I shut the front door behind me and leaned back on it, like they do at the end of soap operas, but I didn't bother to do the Look of Anguish because there was nobody there to see it.

Right.

Right then.

Right.

Now what?

What are you supposed to do when your daughter's gone abroad with the rest of your family, you have no job, no money, no future and, come to think of it, no friends? No one's written a self-help book about that, have they? There's no *Dummies Guide to Having No*

*Life*, as far as I know, no *Chicken Soup for Pointless People*.

That's how I felt. Pointless. With no purpose. Well, what was I for? I had no one to look after, nothing to do. No one to look after me, either. No friends, no family. All gone off without me. Nobody.

I had no excuse now. This would be the perfect time to commit suicide, I thought. And what with it being Christmas, I'd not be found until it was far too late. Amber was safely tucked away in America, the nosey nurse opposite would alert the police . . .

Yes, that's what I'd do. It was perfect. Phew, what a relief, to have a proper plan at last. But I didn't want to be selfish about it, I'd better leave everything in order. Now then, where to start?

I know, I'll put a wash on. Clean something. Tidy up. De-clutter the house. Reclaim the spare room! Decorate from top to toe! Sell up, move to Australia, get a tan, meet a husband on the beach, live happily ever after . . . No, no, that's not the plan. The Plan is to leave them, so that they can live happily ever after. Time to take myself off.

There was a little note stuck to the front of the washing machine. It said 'hi Mum hope I am hellp-full x x Amber'. She'd put a load of washing in there, bless her. That pile of whites which had been sitting by the machine for days now, and she'd also put in her favourite dolly's jumper. Which was red.

It's the little things, isn't it? I didn't want to deal with it right now, it wasn't important. So I took the load of wet PINK washing and just threw it out of the back door. I didn't want it in the house any more.

The kitchen was full of RUBBISH too. Unnecessary. I chucked all that out into the garden, I ended up with just what I needed until I was dead, and no more. One saucepan, one knife, one fork, one spoon. One tin-opener, one corkscrew, one wooden spoon, one carving knife. One glass, and a mug. The rest of it could all FUCK OFF.

The dining-room/study/bike-park/ downstairs-dumping-ground looked great, once I'd thrown everything out through the French windows. I pulled up the carpet too, it made the room feel CLAUSTROPHOBIC, it all had to go. It was a bit unwieldy, but I managed somehow. Out, out, out. Get OUT! It felt good to be in control, at last.

Outside, all the crap in my life was scattered over the frozen ground. There was paper everywhere, bills, circulars, letters from the bank, final demands, parking ticket demands, demands from everyone demanding me to do what they demanded. Hundreds of receipts and chitties blew around the tiny garden, fluttering over mounds of ring binders with nothing in them, piles of brochures about starting your own business, teaching yourself tarot, winding yourself up. There were countless Works of Art painted by Amber, and countless newspapers kept by me. A lamp that didn't work, that picture frame that needed mending. My mother's old sewing machine, my father's old beer tankards. Those bits of dining table I'd bought from Ikea and given up on, those horrible old junk shop chairs I'd bought for £20 and never got round to painting.

Rubble. Jumble. Clutter. All getting in my way, I had to get rid of it. IT HAD TO GO.

We loved being together, but we hardly ever were. He'd be out all night, I'd be out all day. We still spent weekends in bed, but asleep, recovering from the excesses of the week. We were grumpy, we were exhausted, we didn't feel sexy any more. We were both working really hard, for the good of each other, or so we thought. In fact, we were pulling ourselves apart.

I thought we were going to get married and have a baby.

He thought we were going to see the world through rock'n'roll shades.

We both thought we could glue ourselves back together again.

I don't know what time of day it was, but after this burst of intense activity, I reckoned I deserved a fag and a drink. I marched round to Sandip's.

'Please leave the magazines alone,' he pleaded. (I had recently taken to angrily emptying out those annoying loose leaflets they put inside, leaving them scattered across the floor of his shop. It was still a one-woman campaign, but I reckoned that if every newsagent in the country complained about this, the magazine publishers would stop doing it.)

'Twenty Silk Cut.'

He handed them over, I remember his hand was shaking.

'I haven't got any money, you can put them on my bill,' I announced. 'And I'm taking a bottle of wine.' I grabbed one with a fluorescent orange starcut sticker on it saying '£3.99' off the shelf. And the one behind it. 'Two, actually.' Fuck it, I was about to kill myself, I wouldn't be around to pay him back. 'Three. Goodbye.' He didn't argue with me, I think I scared him.

I drank the first bottle in one go, locked in the downstairs loo, picked up that same copy of *Elle Decor*, ripped up every page. I took another bottle with me upstairs, we would tackle the spare room together.

The band got a recording contract.

I got pregnant.

We were too busy to get married properly, so we did it one rainy Saturday afternoon at the local Registry Office, with a couple of Joe's bandmates as witnesses.

Apparently, my mother still cries about that.

It was what's known as a box room, only there were no boxes in it. Except one. The one I had to find. I was on a mission.

I could only just open the door. Once I'd managed to get my head inside, I could see exactly how many obstacles I had to deal with. The flotsam and jetsam was waist high, there were things in the corner piled right up to the ceiling. Undaunted, I clambered over the squashy mountains to the window and tried to open it.

It was locked, or stuck, or both. It just wouldn't budge. But I had work to do. I wasn't going to let a Victorian sash window get in my way. I grabbed one of the brandnew but too big ice skates which I'd bought for Amber ages ago from a car-boot sale, and put it inside a yellowing pillow case which had been lying around for years, waiting for something to happen.

It's quite satisfying breaking a window; it makes a lovely noise. I punched out the flimsy wooden bits too, to make a bigger space. There was an icy blast as the December frost rushed in, I found it invigorating.

I didn't bother to go through everything. Well, if it's been in there that long you don't really know you've got it, do you? Which means you don't need it. So out it went.

Bundle upon bundle of unidentifiable clothes, a shower hose from the bathroom that had split long ago, an entangled nest of wire coathangers clinging on to each other for dear life – everything was thrown out of the hole that had been the window.

Eventually, I began to see the bed. Books that I'd never read and was never going to, offcuts of spare carpet just in case, a dented lampshade with a hole burned out of it. That Dualit six-slot toaster, still in its box. Why was I hanging on to this stuff? Go, go, GO!

I took the duvet off the bed and chucked that out too; beneath it, laid out carefully on the mattress, were Amber's little baby clothes; vests, babygros, tiny pink cardigans and hats and matching bootees. A groovy little T-shirt with 'Daddy's girl' written on it in glitter. Unworn. A tiny little red romper suit, surely too small for a human being? Underneath the bed I found her baby bath, inside it that bloody sterilizer, the bottles, the teats, all the baby hardware you think you need, but don't. And her Moses basket, still covered in white broderie anglaise, filled with her muslins, her dummies, her cuddly toys. Her little music box that played John Lennon's 'Imagine', which used to soothe her to sleep. Her tiny hospital wristband, from when she was born. The soft peachy blanket I wrapped her up in, to bring her home . . .

It all HAD TO GO, to join the big SHIT-HEAP down below that had become my life. Satisfied with the space I'd cleared for myself, I sat down on the bed and took a large glug of wine from the bottle. Just one more thing to do, then I could rest.

I carried on working, right up until the last minute.

So did he.

I thought my hippie had turned into a bread-head.

He thought I was trying to kill our baby.

It became a competition to see who could give the other the better life.

It was underneath the bed, tucked behind the baby bath, almost out of sight. Almost, but not quite. I knew exactly where it was, it was as if this box had a flashing red light on it, a transmitter that sent a bip-bip to my brain all day and all night. Sometimes I forgot about it, if I could get drunk enough. But never for very long.

I dragged it out from under the bed and stared at it for a bit. It said 'Salta Grapefruit' on the side, and it looked quite harmless. When I'd sealed it up, I hadn't labelled it, because I realized I would always know what it contained.

I drank some more wine.

I went out to the loo, and the box was still there when I got back.

I sat down on the bed and said to myself 'go on then'.

I didn't move.

'Come on!' I actually said the words out loud, my voice rang around the empty room. 'Throw it away!'

'I can't,' said my head.

'You can,' said my mouth, 'you must.'

I moved down on to the floor.

We eyeballed each other, the box and I, for quite some time. It had a defiant air, like it knew it had the upper hand. It was cocky, that box.

I knew what to do, of course. If in doubt, have a bath. I went next door and turned the taps on. Not wanting them to go to waste, I emptied all those last bits of bubble bath from expensive gift bottles into the running hot tap. It was an assault on the nosebuds; the foam was already waist-high by the time I left the room.

I nudged the box with my toe. It didn't move. Too heavy. Too much in there. Bastard.

I just about managed to get the mattress out of the window. The bed was too big.

The box was next.

The box was the only thing left.

THE BOX HAD TO GO. Then I'd be clean.

I was exhausted. I was tired, I was weak, I was just one little person struggling to get some control back from the rest of the world. But somehow, somehow I found the strength to pick up that box with both arms and walk the last few steps towards the window.

As I did, the bottom fell through, and the contents came spilling out, all over my feet.

I smiled. 'Hey, Joe,' I said.

'Is it true your mother slept with Jimmi Hendrix?' asked the pretty girl reporter, sitting on my sofa, drinking my tea.

'Yeah,' said Joe, smiling at her in the way he used to smile at me.

'Wow,' she said, visibly impressed.

Danny the Manager made up all that stuff, to make them sound more interesting. 'Got to get an angle,' he'd said, over and over again, 'bit of spin, give it a USP.' Apparently this stood for Unique Selling Point.

My USP was that I was having a baby and nobody seemed to have noticed. Except my father – he paid the deposit for the house in Fulham. 'Got to give the child a proper start,' he said, eyeing the bump.

My mother's look said it all.

It was all there. All the letters and cards and photos and silly bits and bobs that only mean something to the people who keep them. Every single bittersweet moment, a life together captured in a picture or an object or just a sentence. Not in the box any more though, out now. Spread out on the floor in front of me, like a map of our life. Joe and me, me and Joe. Us. We.

I had to look, I had to. On holiday in Cyprus.

The Chinese takeaway menu with 'I love you' in his spidery writing, squeezed in between the prawn crackers and the seaweed. A cassette of the first song he wrote for me, which was a bit shit, but that wasn't the point. The champagne cork with a 20p piece stuck in it, and the words 'one month, one love' written in biro around it. A lock of his hair which I stole when he was asleep. A photo of me, holding up my maternity top to reveal the smiley face he'd drawn on my bump in lipstick. A little note saying 'Sorry I was cross on Tuesday 14 October', when I was about four months pregnant with Amber.

And then a photo of us three. At the hospital. Me smiling, her sleeping, him grim. Sad. For the first time, I noticed that Joe looked sad in that picture. Haunted. Like it was his life that was about to end, not mine. Ah, was it a bit hard for you? Bastard!

I could feel the old anger rising in me, it was white cold, it was running through my veins. My chest constricted, my jaw set. I was back in my old position, ready to kill. Steely, strong, mad.

I was ready to THROW HIM OUT of the window too, but then I saw it, the last note. The one I'd found on the kitchen table when I'd had to put Amber and all those flowers in a taxi, my heart full of hate, because he hadn't turned up at the hospital to bring us home.

'I'll be back' it said. 'J', and three kisses, one for each of us.

He didn't come back. Not that night, and not the day after.

I'd had a caesarian, I wasn't supposed to lift anything heavier than a kettle. I felt as if I'd been sawn in half by a crap magician who'd produced a baby as a surprise, and now I had to look after it. But I didn't know how to; the first baby I ever held was my own.

I moved my duvet on to the sofa downstairs, so that I could hear him if he came in. I didn't sleep a wink, but neither did Amber.

On the third day he returned, tired and very sheepish. I didn't ask where he'd been, I didn't want to know. I was just glad he was home.

But when I woke up the next morning, he'd gone again.

'That was eight years ago and we haven't seen you since!' I shouted at the note. 'And I'm still waiting! Where are you, Joe?!' I screwed it up into a little ball and threw it out of the window. As I watched it fall in slow motion, down on to the dump below, I screamed, 'You left me to look after her! You just left me to do it. You were supposed to *help me*, you were supposed to *look after me*!' I spun round and kicked him all over the room, 'You selfish bastard! You bastard!' I ground him into the floor, I stamped on his face. 'You bastard!'

I ran downstairs, to check it was still there. It was, in its usual place behind the hall radiator, just by the front door. God help him if he ever came back, I'd be ready for him.

There was an almighty crash. It seemed the kitchen ceiling just couldn't take the bath over-flowing for a third time. Most of it had collapsed on to the table beneath. I remember being too tired to do anything about it, I didn't even have the energy to get upset. It didn't occur to me to go back upstairs, to turn the taps off.

By now, I'd forgotten I was supposed to be committing suicide. I lay on the sofa and watched TV instead.

> They were a one-hit wonder, they got to number 7.
> A novelty band.
> Not really worth leaving your wife and child for, is it?

Ant and/or Dec introduced the band, there to provide a much-needed break from their festive mayhem. It was the usual rubbish, a nursery rhyme with a beat, a child singing to other children about stuff they hadn't yet experienced.

'I'm a sweet little thing,' sang a teenage girl in the porn version of a school uniform, her backing band dressed up like teachers.

'She's a sweet little thing,' sang the lead guitarist, with a school cap askew on his head.

Joe! It was Joe! He looked just like Joe! Older, greyer, but Joe!

Get out of the way, you stupid girl, let's see him again. 'Move!' I shouted at the TV. Was it Joe?

The screen went black. I grabbed the remote, pressed every button. Ripped off the fiddly front panel of the television, pushed and twiddled all the buttons. The video started to flash 00:00, a red light said 'BATT'. Power cut. Must have been the bath and the electrics or something. I'd never know if it was him. Threw the remote at the telly. It bounced off. How annoying. I'd wanted to see it leave a cartoon shape of the smash behind it.

I stared up at the ceiling, in the dim grey light of early evening. Was it him? Why hadn't he come to see us? Tears filled my eyes and ran down my temples, into my hair. What had I done to make him go away? It was a question I'd asked myself every day since he left us, but I still didn't know the answer.

'Doesn't he even want to see his daughter?' I asked.

'He's busy,' his sister replied. 'He's not even in the country. He's in Germany, promoting the new single.'

'But –'

'I'm sorry.' I could hear her kids screaming in the background.

'Is it me? Is it something I've done?'

'I don't know, love, he doesn't talk about it.'

'Well, can't you ask him?' I couldn't help the irritated tone that was creeping into my voice. I'd tried to be patient, I really had.

'Look,' she sighed, 'I've got enough on my plate. This is between you and him, it's nothing to do with me.'

'Yes, I know, but –'

'Bye, love.' And she put the phone down, just like that.

I'd only been there once before, but I remembered where she lived. I turned up on her doorstep, in Twickenham, with Amber in the pram. I hoped that the sight of his adorable daughter would melt his heart, but there was nobody in.

So I just stood there, banging on the door, until a neighbour told me they'd moved.

And we haven't seen him since. He'd sent a few postcards from glamorous locations all over the world, but they didn't say much. Just things like 'love Joe xxx' or 'it's freezing here!' About two years ago, one from Tokyo said 'will come and see you when we get back'. But he never came. The postcards had kept coming though, from all four corners, each one saying less than the one before. The last few had had no message, just my name on the address. Not even a kiss.

Bastard.

Bang bang!

I must have fallen asleep. Through the sitting-room window I could see that it was snowing outside, the streetlight made the silent blobs look big and orange, like they'd been Tango'd.

Bang bang bang!

Someone was knocking on my front door.

'Fuck off!' I called out. What time was it?

'Charlotte?' said a man's voice.

It was him! He'd come to get me! I knew it!

I crawled to the doorway on all fours, and looked out into the hall. I could just pick out a man's face, looking through the letterbox.

'Are you going to let me in?' it said.

I stood up, and walked as normally as I could into the hallway, grabbing the knife from the radiator with one hand and slowly opening the door with the other.

'Why are you all in the dark?' he said, backlit by the porch light from the house opposite. Almost gave him a halo.

I didn't reply, it was none of his business. Behind my back, I swapped the knife from one hand to the other.

'Look, I'm here because it's Christmas Eve and I just thought this was silly, I couldn't stand it any longer,' he said. 'Here,' he held out something in a Marks & Spencers bag, 'peace offering.'

I didn't take it, I didn't have any spare hands. He bent down and put it on the floor, just inside the door. I could see the snowflakes melting on his coat. 'Shall I come in?' he asked.

'*No!*' I said, stiffening. After all these years, now that I had my chance, I didn't know what to do with it. I was shaking from head to toe. 'Stay there!' I said.

'OK, OK,' he held up his hands. 'It's just that –' he shifted his weight on to his other foot, 'well, I've missed you.'

'Really?' I said, my grip tightening around the knife's handle, 'well I've missed you too. So,' I said, 'has Amber.'

'Aw, bless her,' he patronized, 'how is she?'

'Oh, she's great,' I replied, 'no thanks to you.'

'Oh. Well, there's a little present in there for her –'

'A little present?! Is that it?' I laughed. 'You're incredible!' I could feel my hand getting sweaty now. 'You think you can just waltz back into our lives with "a little present" and everything's going to be fine, do you? Where the fuck have you been?'

'Look, Charlotte, I –' he took a step closer.

'Don't you dare come near me!' I showed him the knife now. 'Don't you bloody *dare*!'

But he didn't need telling twice. He turned and ran. Oddly, he shut the gate behind him.

Bloody coward, I thought, as I replaced the knife behind the radiator. I should have stabbed him. God I was crap, I couldn't even do that properly. Now, where was that third bottle of wine?

I hope Amber isn't one of those freaky people who remembers being a baby. I hope she won't remember my endless tears of rage and hurt and pain, how I hated seeing her father's spirit living in her eyes, how I wasn't able to look after myself at all.

Instead, I hope she remembers that I gave her everything I could. It wasn't much, but it was all I had.

I lost track of time after that. I think I spent what must have been Christmas morning clearing out the sitting room, throwing most of our belongings out on to the snow-covered front garden, and the rest on to the pavement, on to parked cars, on to passing pedestrians, I just didn't care. I was pleased to see that the overnight blanket of snow had completely covered the junk in the back garden, it was invisible now, wiped out, obliterated. And I remember the phone ringing and ringing and ringing, but it didn't really bother me.

I don't know who called the police, but apparently they found me lying on my back under the Christmas tree, with an empty bottle of port and a half-eaten lump of Stilton beside me. I'd carefully hung all the snowman sweeties he'd brought for Amber on the tree – I wanted it to look pretty for her when she came home.

I do remember staring up at the branches, hearing that stupid au pair's voice going round and round in my head. 'You heff no love,' she kept saying, 'you heff no love.'

'I don't need love,' I kept saying back to her, 'I can do this on my own.'

Mad.

# CHAPTER 5

'It is invariably saddening to look through new eyes at things upon which you have expended your own powers of adjustment.'

F. Scott Fitzgerald, *The Great Gatsby*

'Is it all right if I sit with her for a bit?' asked Arthur.

'Yah, of course,' smiled the South African nurse, the cheap tinsel she'd wound round her cap glinting festively, a light scent of sherry on her breath. 'I'll be in the nurses' station if you want me.'

Arthur sat down in the comfy chair beside the bed. Charlotte was lying almost comatose on her side, her back turned to him, eyes closed but facing the window. 'It's quite nice here, isn't it?' he said as he settled in. 'Floral drapes, carpet, telly, en suite bathroom; bit like having a nervous breakdown in a Holiday Inn!'

Nothing. Perhaps he shouldn't joke about it, maybe she was feeling a bit sensitive for once. Yeah, right.

'I know you're not asleep, Charlotte Small, you can't fool me.'

Nothing.

'Oh well, suit yourself.' He pulled out a magazine from the carrier bag he'd brought with him and began to leaf through it. 'Ah, the Beckhams having a family Christmas at Beckingham Palace; the Windsors having a formal Christmas at Buckingham Palace; and a couple of queens are reunited in Crystal Palace.' He smiled at his own joke, he was on good form at the moment, he was always funnier when he was in love. 'Charlotte? Did you get that? Me and Jimmy are back together again. Isn't that wonderful?'

Nothing.

'And it's all thanks to you! If you hadn't killed our dog, I would never have phoned Jimmy to tell him, we wouldn't have met up to share our grief together only to realize how much we'd missed each other and discovered that even though McQueen was dead our love wasn't.' Even now he felt his heart skip with joy, he was excited about the future once more. 'So he's moving out of that hovel in Crystal Palace and he's coming to live with me in the lifestyle cell-block in fashionable east London, isn't that brilliant?!'

Silence. Honestly, you'd think she'd be pleased for them. Maybe not.

Arthur got up and walked towards the window. 'He's sitting outside in my car now, bless him. We're on a double yellow line, in fact. Do traffic wardens work over Christmas?' He peered through the slatted blind out on to the cold grey London street. 'Ooh yes, look, there he is!' He began to wave frantically. 'Don't think he can see me.' His eyes filled with tears. 'I love that boy so much, you know. God, love is such a powerful thing, isn't it? I just wish you had someone to – anyway.' He just stopped himself in time, he didn't want to set her off again. Arthur glanced nervously at Charlotte in the bed. Her eyes were open now, but she had nothing else on her face.

He smiled at her.

She didn't smile back.

'Jimmy and I are very worried about you, Charlotte.'

She wasn't even blinking.

'Well, OK, I am.' Arthur was struggling to contain himself, he knew she hated it when he cried. 'Don't you dare give up, Charlotte Small – we've been through far too much together for you to drop out now.' He laughed without a trace of humour. 'Listen, it's not been easy being your friend for the last few months, you've been monstrous. And I know, even if you don't, that inside that spiky nightmare of a woman is one of the kindest, most caring people I've ever had the good fortune to call a friend. So bloody well stop all this and as you say to me all the time, pull yourself together, woman!'

No, it was all too much for him, here came the tears. Arthur wept silently, as he pulled several tissues out of the box on her bedside table. He dabbed his eyes and blew his nose.

'Just in case you're wondering how you got here, by the way,' he said into the tissue, 'I rang the police. I'm sorry, I know it was a mean thing to do and they did make a terrible mess of your front door, but it was all I could think of. I mean, you know, you just weren't right. Your face looked horrible, your hair was all sort of matted, you'd really let yourself go. Honestly, darling, it was a bit *Planet of the Apes*.'

Surely that would provoke a reaction? Had her sense of humour gone the same way as her marbles?

'And when you went for me with that knife, well . . .'

He trailed off. Maybe she didn't remember that. God knows, he wanted to forget it, he'd never been so frightened in his life. Maybe it's best to gloss over that part for now.

'So, apparently, when they broke in, your phone was ringing non-stop. It was your dad and Amber, calling to wish you a Happy Christmas. Thank god your father had some connections in the loon –' he stopped himself just in time, 'mental health world, and so he rang some posh doctor friend of his who got the police to bring you here. Y'know, you're bloody lucky your dad's got the money for this – if you'd gone National Health you'd probably have ended up on a ward full of Napoleons.'

There was a tiny flicker, perhaps it was a nervous twitch. Arthur sighed, he wanted his friend back.

'Anyway, that was yesterday, and now you're going to be fine, aren't you?!' Silence. 'Of course, I'm only really hanging around in case your brother comes to see you. I just know that it'll be love at first sight, and he'll never look at another woman again – ooh, Charlotte, imagine, you'll be my sister-in-law!'

Nothing.

'It's Boxing Day today!' he announced, for lack of anything else to say. Arthur checked his hair in the mirror above her basin, adjusted it, went back to the chair. 'We've had such a good time, Jimmy and me – we actually found a warehouse club in the East End that was open on Christmas Day, we came home at 4.30 last night! It was fucking mad!'

Thank god she's not with it, he thought; what am I like, saying 'mad' to someone in a psychiatric ward.

Saved by the nurse. 'Right then, Charlotte,' she breezed, 'the RMO is here to see you, for today's assessment.'

'RMO?' asked Arthur.

'Resident Medical Officer,' said the handsome man behind the nurse. Arthur immediately recognized him in an oh-mi-god way, as befits those who indulge in casual sex. He left the building as quickly as he could, before the RMO could remember what they'd done together only a few weeks before.

'She'll be fine,' he said to Jimmy as he drove

away, a little hot under the collar, 'I happen to know she's in very good hands.'

It was like looking at an old black-and-white television with the sound muffled. But for some reason, the fact that I could look without seeing, and hear without knowing, didn't bother me. I enjoyed the paralysis, it meant I didn't have to move. I didn't have to join in any more. It was great.

If you were casting a shrink for a cheesy movie, you would definitely have chosen this man. He was small in places, but big in others. He was short, frail-framed and lightly hunched. His expressive hands were bony but strong, his eyes were tiny but bright, and an enormous pair of Joe 90 black-framed spectacles were clinging to his beaky nose. His silver crinkle-cut hair was oiled back off his face, and his suit hung off his broad stooped shoulders, tie swinging in the breeze. He looked exactly like a middle-European intellectual, which was exactly what he was.

'Good morning, Charlotte, I'm the Consultant Psychiatrist here, my name's Doctor Lichtenstein. Some patients call me Edwin. What will you call me?'

Nothing.

'How long has she been like this?' he asked the skinny nurse standing beside him at the end of Charlotte's bed.

121

'I dunno, I've only just come on duty.' She yawned. 'I prefer nights, there's less to do.'

He sighed. 'Get Sister for me, will you?'

She sighed, and left the room.

'So, Charlotte Small,' he put her file down on the table over the bed, 'how do you propose we get you up and running again?' He walked over to the basin and began to wash his hands. 'What makes you tick, hmm?'

He didn't expect an answer, and he didn't get one. He dried his hands on the small towel as he spoke.

'I'm in charge of you, you see, while you're here. It's my job to restore you back to some sort of order, and it's your job to resist all my efforts. It's a battle really, between you and me. Only it's not a very fair fight; I've got staff and drugs and straitjackets and padded cells and patient paranoia on my side; you've only got bloody-mindedness.'

He stood at the foot of her bed, jangling the loose change in his pocket.

'Which can be very effective, of course. Only it's not much fun for you, because the more stubborn you are, the longer you have to stay here. Which suits me fine, because the longer I've got you, the more chance I have of winning. I'll get to know all your weak spots, you see. It's my job to find the chinks in your armour.'

And this one looks very well-defended, he thought to himself. She might be a hard nut to crack. Good, he liked those best.

'However. The one thing you're not allowed to do is to kill yourself, because that's cheating.'

'Cup of tea, Doctor?' asked a big black nurse with an ear-splitting smile as she entered the room.

'Ah, Sister Ellen, I was hoping it would be you!'

'Did you have a good Christmas?' she asked, as she bent down to smooth Charlotte's brightly coloured duvet, tutting internally. Hospital corners belonged in hospitals, duvets didn't.

'Yes, very good, thanks – you?'

'Fine, Doctor, fine. My sister Millicent came over and we had a big Caribbean cook-up, my husband passed out in front of the television after Her Majesty's speech and the kids were nowhere to be seen – it was the usual thing!' Her expression changed. 'How is Mrs Lichtenstein?'

'Yes, um, thank you for asking, yes, she's – er – getting better, thanks.'

'Now that's good news.' Sister Ellen beamed. 'I am so glad to hear that! And the grandchildren?'

'Far too demanding, as usual. I was rather glad to be coming back to work this morning, for the peace!'

Charlotte turned on to her back and stared up at the ceiling.

'Anyway, Sister, back to business. How long has she been catatonic?'

'Since she came in, I believe, Doctor.' Ellen reached for the chart at the end of the bed. 'Yes, she's not said a word since she was admitted on Christmas Day. We've only had the RMO's obs to go on – we don't even know the name of her GP.' She scowled. 'She's not eaten anything, not a scrap.' She lowered her voice. 'And there has been bed-wetting, Doctor.'

'Hmm, that's quite impressive. On strike for three days.' He looked down at Charlotte's face. 'Well done!'

She shut her eyes.

'Any visitors?'

'No. Just one man on the first day, no one since then.'

'Boyfriend?'

'Apparently not, according to the RMO . . .'

'Right. I promised this patient's father that I would have her up and out of here as soon as possible.' He cleared his throat. 'We're going to have to step up our campaign, Sister. I think you know what that means?' He winked at her.

She winked back. 'Oh yes, doctor.' She looked down at the patient, whose eyes were clamped shut now. 'It's come to that, has it?'

'Yes, Sister,' he said, in a very serious tone, 'I'm afraid it has.'

They smiled at each other across the bed, and left the room.

I didn't want to come back.

'Right then, Charlotte, time for a bath!'

'Sister asked me to make you some banana custard. I'll just leave it here, shall I?'

'We've come to change your sheets – you're going to have to get out of bed, I'm afraid.'

'Why don't I show you the kitchen, then you can make yourself a cup of tea whenever you like.'

'All right if I vacuum in here?'

'Here's your anti-depressant. No sleeping pill tonight, I'm afraid – doctor's orders.'

'Sister's bought you a new nightie, and a dressing gown, and some slippers from Marks and Spencer. Who's a lucky girl?'

'Maintenance. I've come to take the TV away, routine inspection. There's another one in the communal sitting room, just down the end of the ward.'

'Your father rang to see how you are. Your daughter's really missing you.'

But I knew I couldn't stay away for ever.

'Hi! You're new, aren't you?' A chirpy young Asian girl came into the kitchen and opened a cupboard door. 'I'm Amira, I'm in the room just across the corridor from you, I saw them bring you in; what's your name?'

Charlotte didn't answer. She reached into her peach and green striped velour dressing gown for a tissue and blew her nose.

'Oh bloody 'ell, look at that, no clean mugs again! 'Scuse me.' Charlotte pressed herself up against the wall as the young girl moved over to the sink. 'Honestly, just because people are

125

mentally ill, doesn't mean to say they can't do the washing-up, does it?'

The kettle began to rumble.

'What you in for?' asked Amira, as she rolled up her pink housecoat with Maribou trim sleeves. She was pretty, petite, bird-like with big brown eyes and long dark lashes and a tickle on her lips. The sort of girl you see queueing with friends outside nightclubs, over-excited, shrieking.

Charlotte didn't answer.

Amira turned round and looked at her as the sink was filling up with water. 'Ah, are you a bit shy?' She crinkled her nose. 'Don't worry about it,' she had a faint Midlands accent, 'I was like that when I come in the first time. Horrible, isn't it? You feel so stupid, you think "what the hell am I doing in here?" Then you think "they must be mad" and then you realize you're the mad one!' She laughed loudly as she began to clean the cups. 'I'll wash, you dry,' she decided, pointing at a greying tea towel hanging on a hook underneath a label that said 'Tea Towel'.

The kettle got louder. So did Amira.

'Have you been to any of the therapy sessions yet?' Not waiting for a reply, she carried on. 'I don't think you have, have you, because I haven't seen you there. They're not as bad as you think – in actual fact, sometimes they're quite funny. Honestly,' she laughed again, even louder this time, 'some of the nutters we get in here, the things people come out with . . .'

A nurse poked her head round the door. 'Everything all right?'

To Charlotte's confusion, Amira began to open and close drawers frantically. 'I'm just looking for a really sharp knife, nurse, have you got one? Please, please?'

'Ha, ha, Amira, very funny,' chirped the nurse, 'it's Support in five minutes, you'd better get down there sharpish.'

'Sharpish,' shrieked Amira, 'that's very funny!'

And they both laughed, insanely, like a couple of delusional maniacs. The nurse went away, Charlotte moved further into the wall. 'I stabbed my sister, you see,' confided Amira, as she reached for the catering-sized tin of instant coffee, 'she was really getting on my nerves, d'you know what I mean?' She saw Charlotte's expression. 'Oh, don't worry, I didn't kill her or anything! But she's got a nice big scar all down her arm now.' Amira said that as if this was a good thing, in fact she even sounded a bit jealous.

The kettle clicked off. 'I'll make it!' Amira ladled not one but two heaped spoonfuls of instant coffee into each mug. 'You'll need lots of sugar if you're new,' she said, dropping in three lumps. 'Keep your strength up, you see.'

She handed Charlotte her mug. It tasted like hot treacle. Revolting.

'Right then, shall we go?' Amira linked arms with Charlotte enthusiastically, the spilling coffee nearly melted her frilly nylon nightie. 'It's down in the basement, you're going to love this! It's better than anything you're ever going to see on the telly, Jerry Springer's rubbish compared to this lot . . .'

I can remember the panic that filled me as she led me down to the basement. I didn't want to go anywhere with this girl, she was clearly mad. But she wouldn't let go of me, she had a very firm grip. And the more she told me about what was going to happen down there, the more I wanted to run away. Sit in a circle of complete strangers? Listen to them droning on and on about their boring problems? And worse than that, worse than anything, talk about myself in front of them?! Absobloodylutely not.

'Daddy was a banker, Mummy was a lush.'
A middle-aged woman was talking to a small group of men and women, in what should have been a board-room, only it had been cunningly disguised as a therapy haven, complete with soundproof hessian panels on the walls. The patients were arranged in a circle, sitting in those industrial comfy chairs only ever seen in institutions. There was a coffee table in the middle of the circle, with a small artificial flower arrangement on it, and not one but two boxes of tissues.
Dr Lichtenstein had asked Marjorie to talk to

the group for about fifteen minutes, to tell them what had happened and why she was here.

'My mother drank morning, noon and night, which meant that Daddy spent a lot of time at work, largely on other women, whilst I was brought up by a succession of stupid and stupider nannies.'

Although she must have been in her late fifties, Marjorie spoke like a young girl. And she was doing her best to be mistaken for one too – her long, thinning hair, held back with a tortoiseshell headband, had once been a soft honey blonde, but had now turned nicotine yellow. She was dressed in an inappropriately diaphanous egg-stained negligée which revealed too much of her withered cleavage; this was topped by a pale-peach towelling robe with lace trim; fags and Cartier lighter in one pocket, large plastic bottle of water in the other. She'd applied lots of ruby-red lipstick sometime earlier, myopically, which gave her the tragi-comic mouth of a clown. Her pale-blue milky eyes were shrouded by black lids and cloggy lashes; she was obviously not the kind of woman who took her make-up off at night but the other kind, who tops it up in the morning. The whites of her eyes were yellow, as were her teeth, and yet she had the air of a woman who thinks herself a great beauty. Maybe she had been, once. Today, however, she looked like Bette Davis in *Whatever Happened to Baby Jane*.

'I am from a very good family, you know,' she

continued. 'We are one branch of an internationally renowned brewing dynasty. Do you want me to say which one?' she asked Dr Lichtenstein, big eyes batting.

'No, Marjorie, please don't,' he smiled, kindly, 'that's not why we're here.'

'Oh. OK.' She looked disappointed, she'd obviously spent a great deal of her life impressing people with her impeccable pedigree. Trading on it, even.

(The rest of the group spent the next few minutes trying to work out which family it was, of course, and so they didn't really hear the next bit.)

'I was brought up to believe that women had to look pretty, and men had to pay for everything. Daddy loved me to look beautiful, he used to say, "It's what you're for, darling."' She blushed at the memory, like a shy virgin. Ridiculous at her age. 'I remember being thrilled as a teenager when I realized that I wouldn't ever have to do boring things like go to the office, as I much preferred the idea of spending the whole day getting ready for parties! So much more fun, don't you think?!'

She looked up for confirmation from the group; she didn't get any. But she didn't really notice. Marjorie was evidently enjoying this opportunity to talk about herself. And the audience was not only captive, it was locked in.

'And so that's what I did. I spent my twenties having a ball, living life to the full, just so happy to be alive. Ah, it was a marvellous time,' she reminisced mistily. 'We thought nothing of jumping on an aeroplane to the South of France for dinner, or hightailing off in somebody's sports car to St Moritz for New Year. We used to have wild house parties at weekends, it was simply wonderful. I had lots of money, and lots of fun. I didn't know how lucky I was back then, I thought it would last for ever . . .'

Several people nodded at that.

'And then the 60s came along and ruined everything. I was completely waylaid by it all; I took all sorts of mind-blowing drugs, I drank everything I could find, I slept with everybody – you name it, I did it. Daddy used to pretend to get awfully cross with me in front of Mother, but secretly we both thought it was quite funny.' She sighed. 'I'd tell you all about it, but I can't remember much, the whole thing is just a haze now. All I know is that I woke up sometime in the 70s and everyone else had paired off and had children and settled down to married life, and I'd been left behind. Well, as you can imagine, I was furious! Those bloody boring girls had snapped up all the exciting men, there was nobody left for me. And anyone who was still available was quite frankly not up to much – they were either too poor, or not handsome enough, or not good socially. I had my attendants, of course,' she smoothed her frizzy hair with the palm of her hand, 'but I didn't like any of them. I hate it when they're all needy and desperate for you, don't you?' She giggled, girlishly. 'I only liked the ones who didn't like me.'

A couple of the women looked up, this sounded familiar.

'Anyway, I realized quite quickly that hanging around waiting for them to get divorced wasn't going to get me anywhere. But I needed a man PDQ ('pretty damn quick' stage-whispered a very thin girl to a very fat one) – Daddy wouldn't even entertain the possibility of my getting a job, he just wanted me to marry a rich and powerful man as soon as possible. So I was forced into it, really. I had no other option – I had to steal somebody else's husband!'

Her old parched face morphed into a wicked schemer.

'I enjoyed that part, it was fun. Honestly, when I think of what I did with who and where . . .' Her face lit up with excitement, not shame. She knew to defend herself though. 'And anyway, their wives were always complaining about them – I thought I'd be doing everyone a favour.'

She sank back into her chair.

'Only it didn't quite work out like that. D'you know, I think most of those men were just using me, they only wanted sex. I mean they bought me jewellery and suchlike, one even took me to Monte Carlo for the summer, but they didn't seem to understand what I needed from them.' She sighed. 'Then I fell pregnant. Completely by mistake, of course, it was a total accident. Honestly.' As they watched her unscrew the lid of the water bottle and take a big swig, the rest of the group couldn't quite manage to believe her.

'Now in those days, within our social set anyway, if one was expecting a baby one immediately got married. There was none of this running around planting your seed in any girl who'll have you and leaving her to cope with the baby on her own, oh no. The man would take care of everything, it was his duty.'

The emotion rose in her face, her neck reddened. 'But the father of my child was a peer of the realm, and also an MP. I was very much in love with him,' she waited a moment, it was clear from her soft watery expression that this wasn't a lie, 'and he promised to support me financially, but the deal was that I had to keep it a secret – the scandal would have been too much, apparently.' The ensuing years of bitterness and hatred had made their mark, and Marjorie's face revealed that hardness known only to the chronically disappointed.

'I could have had an abortion, yes, I could,' her chin jutted forwards in defiance, 'but I decided not to. I was determined to do things my way. Actually, I thought he'd come round to the idea once the baby was born. But he didn't, and the papers wouldn't print the scandal. They were either on his side, or Daddy's – this was in the days when the Old Boy Network meant something. I wouldn't have done it, but the father refused to pay up, and by now Daddy was seriously ill, and my mother was drinking herself to death, and so I needed the money.'

'And, of course, I wanted a little baby.' But it was definitely an afterthought. 'What woman doesn't?'

The group was sympathetic now, but not for Marjorie, for her child.

'Daddy died just after my daughter was born. My mother, in her drunken wisdom, decided that this would be a good time to disown me. She claimed she was horrified at my predicament, appalled at my behaviour. (She'd always been a frightful social climber, my grandmother used to refer to her as The Showgirl.) But I knew it was because she was jealous of Daddy's love for me, she always had been. Bitch!' She spat the word out. Deeply unattractive.

'Anyway. After a long legal battle, which used up all the money Daddy had left me, she was forced to buy me a tiny flat in Kensington but she never spoke to me again. She's dead now, thank god, and good riddance.

'So now, I am all alone in the world. I have a brother who gives me money when he feels like it, but I have to beg him first. In fact, my brother's paying for me to be here; big of him, considering he's living off what should be my inheritance. Personally, I think it's because his ghastly wife refused to have me for Christmas, after last year's debacle.'

She burst into tears. 'It's been hard, you know. Really damn hard. I've had to bring up my daughter on my own, whilst doing my best to find a father figure for her. The ungrateful girl didn't understand that, of course, she thought I was just out having a good time. She's one of those career women now, hard as nails, not a sympathetic bone in her body.

'It's her selfishness that upsets me. D'you know, I haven't had a moment's happiness since the day she was born. It's been a terrible struggle to keep everything going, and this isn't the first breakdown I've had. It's all right for her, she's left home now, she's abandoned me – she's got a very well-paid job and, well –' this was obviously too much for Marjorie, 'she's just met a lovely man who seems to be in love with her!' She snorted disdainfully. 'Although how long that will last is anybody's guess.'

Self-pity, envy, greed, all very nasty on a woman's face. In front of the group, Marjorie had become an ugly woman.

Dr Lichtenstein handed her a tissue. As she dabbed at her eyes, she asked the rest of the group, 'What will become of me? Will anybody ever be in love with me? I live on my own now in the same shabby flat, the central heating's broken down, I can't get a job as I'm trained for nothing, I have no friends, my daughter won't speak to me, I drink myself to sleep every night, I've tried all sorts of clinics and treatment centres

135

and alternative therapies and dating agencies, but nothing seems to work. I'm still upset about what happened to me, and I'm terrified of what's going to happen next.' She might as well have had the word 'VICTIM' tattooed on her forehead. 'All I need is someone to look after me, and then I'll be all right.'

It was a sad story, but nobody felt anything like as sorry for Marjorie as she did for herself. One member of the group, however, had been hanging on to every word as if her life depended on it.

Now I knew how Scrooge felt when he had been visited by the Ghost of Christmas Yet to Come. My past wasn't exactly the same as Marjorie's, but she'd certainly helped me to see my future.

I didn't want to end up all alone, resenting Amber and drowning in a sea of self-pity. I didn't want to be a victim of my own delusion. In fact, I didn't want my life any more.

Neither did I want to be in a clinic with a load of nutters basket-weaving my way back to sanity. But I was here now, and so I might as well hear what they had to say.

Something had to change, and it had to change now.

# CHAPTER 6

'And as freakish as these people may be, it's not exactly like I can't relate to what they're saying. It's more like I can sort of relate. Sort of completely.'

Augusten Burroughs, *Dry*

The first person I told my story to was Amira.

It was one o'clock in the morning, and we were sitting in the Smoking Room in the dark, having pre-arranged to meet there for a fag. It was completely illegal, of course, to leave your bed after Lights Out, but hey, we were rebels.

It took a while – for some reason I felt she had to know absolutely everything – but I got it all out.

'Gosh,' said a wide-eyed Amira, when I'd finished, 'how awful for you. Fancy being dumped like that, by the father of your baby. You must have been a right monster!'

'Me?! I didn't do anything, it was him who ran off!'

'Ssh! Keep your voice down.' Amira puffed on her fag. 'We'll get caught.' She blew her smoke on to the ceiling. 'So did you ever see him again?'

'No,' I said, 'I don't know where he went. I've had the odd cryptic postcard from around the world every now and then, but I don't really think about him any more.'

She looked at me.

'OK, OK – I think about him all the time.'

'Obsessively?' she asked.

I nodded.

She smiled, in an it-takes-one-to-know-one way. 'And what d'you tell your little girl, when she asks about her dad?'

'We haven't ever talked about it,' I said.

'What, never?!'

'No. It's as if he never existed.'

'Weird,' said Amira, stubbing her fag out on the sole of her slipper. 'I'm sorry, but that's like really weird. Oh shit!' She began to hop around the room, 'It's gone right through! Ouch, help, it's burning!'

It was the first time I'd laughed in ages. Dr Lichtenstein said being able to laugh again was the first sign of getting better.

Quite soon after I arrived at the clinic, I began to experience something I'd never felt before.

It would start in the morning, before I woke up. I'd know even before I'd opened my eyes that it was sitting on the end of my bed, like a great big eagle, flapping its enormous wings, ready to savage me with its beak.

It would be flapping in front of my face when anybody looked at me, when I had to speak, when I had to tell the truth. It would be screeching in my ears when I needed to hear what was being said. It would be digging its claws into my shoulders, physically trying to pull me away from anything I wanted to do.

But most of the time it flapped around in the cage of my body, desperately trying to scratch its way out.

Other patients talked about it a lot, having lived with it for most of their lives. I'd never allowed myself this far in before. Eventually, I got to put a name to it. Fear.

'Good morning everyone! My name's Debbie, and I'm your designated Alternative Therapist, just for today. Just my little joke!' She had one of those tinkling beautician's laughs.

She also had a really, really annoying sibilant 's'. (Despite learning about peace and love and all that shit in there, I hadn't become tolerant and accepting overnight, you understand.) I tried to catch Amira's eye, but she was too busy watching a foodie dispose of her breakfast, emptying out her pockets into the bin in the corner.

'And that's going to be the theme of this morning's session – Just For Today. That's right, everyone, we're going to look at living life just one day at a time. Now has anyone got anything to say about that?'

'Not today, no,' said a hardcore Geordie gambler who had lost everything except the tracksuit he stood up in, 'but can I come back to you tomorrow?' His sycophants giggled, Amira and I exchanged a look.

Our days were run to a strict timetable. We were woken up with a cup of tea in bed – the first and last nice thing that was going to happen that day. Then it was morning prayers and meditation at 8.30, if you fancied it, which I didn't, followed by an intoxicating combination of group therapy or one-to-one counselling with Dr L or if you were unlucky, both. Sometimes we were treated to a talk by an ex-patient, which was always interesting as they'd usually been through much worse than us and lived to tell the tale. No one missed these sessions, we were grateful for the contact with the outside world, even though without exception they were shiny, happy people. This was sometimes encouraging and sometimes infuriating, it depended on how I was feeling that day.

Lunch was only slightly nicer than school food, but we were supposed to eat as much as possible as many of us had been neglecting our health recently, to put it mildly. After lunch we had an hour's free time, during which most people had a nap – our journey to the clinic had usually been as physically exhausting as it was mentally draining, we were still very tired. I used to play solitaire, I couldn't switch my brain off enough to sleep.

Most afternoons, we were at the mercy of Debbie and her 'team' (Amira and I called them the Debettes) who were relentless in their determination to cheer us up. Personally, I hated this, although others found it beneficial. We were subjected to Art Therapy, or Yoga, or Drama Therapy (during which you were encouraged to act out your inner child, I hid behind the sofa during *Dr Who* because it was all I could think of) or my least favourite: Free Movement. This involved running around the room in your bare feet to floaty New Age music pan-piping out from Debbie's ghetto blaster. Just awful. Something called 'Dance Therapy' had been crossed off the timetable – I was grateful for that.

After supper, we had written homework to do. This could be anything from an essay on 'What I can control and what I can't', which was a horrifying revelation, to '50 Great Things About Me', which was much more difficult than you might imagine. I was stuck after number 7.

Once I started talking about myself, I couldn't stop. Don't get me wrong, I'd always seen psychiatry and the 'talking therapies' (I mean, *really*) as self-indulgent

141

nonsense, better suited to Woody Allen than the likes of me. The fact that I'd bought every self-help book ever published and they were still on my book-shelves, unread, tells you everything. I knew there was something wrong, but I didn't want to do anything about it. Didn't need to, actually. That was how I was; I knew best, better than you, better than the experts. It turns out that I was – well, incorrect. (I still have trouble with the 'wr' word.)

It was such a relief to get all that stuff out of my head and into the open air.

It wasn't easy though – in fact, it was the hardest thing I've ever done, but also the most worthwhile, I suppose. I cried, and cried, and cried. It was as if I was slowly defrosting all those years of frozen feelings. It was horrible, but it was good.

I also laughed a lot, and I screamed a bit, and I certainly wasn't one of those who had trouble expressing their anger. I was on an emotional roller-coaster from the minute I woke up until my brain gave in at night and I was finally allowed to go to sleep.

Funnily enough, I felt quite at home there. It was a bit like being at boarding school again. Only instead of not being allowed to feel the feelings, that's all you were allowed to do. And there was no Geography.

'Do you believe in God, Charlotte?'

'No.'

'You seem very sure about that.' Dr Lichtenstein picked up a leaf which had somehow survived the turbulence of the changing seasons. Today's one-to-one session was taking place in Hyde Park; Dr L said it would do me good to get out in the fresh air, see what the rest of the world was up to. As far as I could see, the rest of the world was in Hyde Park – it was packed, I'd yet to hear an English accent, they were all tourists.

'Have you ever had any spiritual beliefs?' the good doctor asked me.

So I told him.

When I was still too young to keep quiet in church, my parents gave me a book to read called 'Where is God?' It had nice pictures of a little girl in a blue dress turning over flowerpots and looking under cushions for him, crawling around under the bed and peering into the pillarbox, constantly asking the same question: 'Where is God?'

I used to really stare at each page, taking in the artist's detail, dreading getting to the last time she asked 'Where is God?' because the answer given by her mummy, and indeed the climax of the book, was 'God is everywhere'. This used to make me cross, really cross, because it made no sense. I was glad to be carted off to Sunday school in the church hall just before the vicar's sermon, grateful for the opportunity to colour in more pictures of camels and lambs and why couldn't Jesus have a pink frock?

Before I was sent away to school, from the age of six to eight, I attended a local convent run by terrifying nuns who were all called Sister Mary something-or-other. They were full of dark tales of religious terror, such as what happened to people who didn't say their prayers before they died. I used to lie awake at night, worrying about being pushed off a cliff and not having the presence of mind (or indeed the time) to get out a quick Hail Mary before I was cruelly dashed against the rocks below, which meant I would surely go to hell and be roasted on a spit for all eternity.

We were also shown a yellowing aerial photograph of a range of mountains. If you could see Jesus' face in it, then you were a True Believer. If you couldn't – well, it didn't matter because everyone could.

We had to pray for the poor handicapped children who would end up in Limbo (or

Polio as I mistakenly called it for many years). We quickly forgot childish dreams of getting married, or even more ambitious ones of running our own corporations – we all wanted to be Saint Bernadette when we grew up.

Religion played a big part at both my boarding schools. A very popular pastime at prep school was Kneeler Teas, which took place on a Saturday afternoon. It was entirely voluntary, and us nice do-gooding girls willingly gave up our free time to embroider covers for the hassocks for the school chapel. The fact that we were also given cream cakes and chocolate biscuits and hot-buttered crumpets to eat was just a small benefit from carrying out God's work, and not at all the only reason we had volunteered our services.

At the next school, it was a rule that the visiting clergy's sermon on a Sunday had to be at least twenty-five minutes long. This was too long for us to bear (mind you, five minutes would have been pushing it) and so we used to play the Sermon Game, devised many years ago by previous pupils who can only have been as bored as we were.

The idea was that you listened keenly for a word beginning with 'a', then 'b', and so on, all the way through to 'z', when you dropped your prayer book as a sign that you'd completed the game.

We were so poorly educated that we really believed this was possible (what religious word begins with 'x'?) and used to sit in our pews, hanging on his every word, realizing that time was running out and we were still stuck on 'k'. I usually started to make a mental list of 'Things I Would Rather Be Doing' at that point.

Imagine our surprise, therefore, when a Canon, no less, started his sermon with '**A**fter, or was it **B**efore, **C**hrist's **D**escent to **E**arth . . .' and within just a couple of minutes was finishing with '. . . and that's **W**hy Christmas, or "**X**mas" as it's sometimes called (we could hardly believe our ears), is approached by **Y**oung Christians all over the globe (the tension was unbearable) with such (yes, yes?) **Z**eal!'

Once the sound of nearly 400 prayer books thudding to the Abbey floor had finished echoing around the cloisters, he carried on. 'Good! Now that the Sermon Game is over and I have your full attention, I shall continue.' We felt cheated; it turned out that his wife was an ex-pupil of the school.

After that, I didn't bother with religion any more, because I didn't have to. It was the late 1970s, when the Church of

146

England was going through its happy-clappy phase, which meant young men and women in thick glasses and sensible shoes strummed guitars and banged tambourines with great gusto, as they sang songs with modern titles, like 'God is such a smashing bloke'.

Over in America, they were busy being born again, throwing themselves backwards into lakes of baptism and giving all their money to TV evangelists, but smiling all the way because, hey, Jesus loves me. PR-wise, the 70s was a very bad look for western religion.

Since then the only time I'd ever been to church was for weddings and funerals. But I was only going for the party afterwards.

'I'm not talking about organized religion, Charlotte,' said Dr Lichtenstein, as he studied the patterns on the back of the leaf more closely. 'I'm talking about God.'

'What, that old bearded man in a long white dress who sits up there on a cloud deciding who's going to live and who's going to die and getting it wrong most of the time, that God? No, I most certainly do not believe in him!' I didn't like the way this conversation was going. Maybe I'd joined a cult, maybe the clinic was just a front for the Moonies. 'And I hope a man of science like yourself hasn't fallen for all that rubbish either!'

He smiled, we walked on. 'So who's in charge of the universe, eh, Charlotte?'

I knew he expected me to say that I was, and so I didn't.

'Who d'you think is running this place? Who designed this leaf, who told it when to fall off the tree, who gets to decide what happens to you next, who stopped you from killing yourself?'

'What?' This line of questioning was beginning to annoy me, I'd always left the dinner party when it got to this stage. Pissed Pissopholy, I'd called it. 'Look, I don't want to talk about this any more, OK?' I stopped walking, I wanted to turn round and go back to the safety of the clinic.

'All right then, don't talk, just listen.' I had no choice, I had to walk on with him. 'I really like you, Charlotte, and I want you to get better. Normally I wait until my patients are open-minded or desperate enough to hear what I'm saying, but I think you're ready to understand this right now. And you're intelligent enough to get it straight away, if only you'd take the cotton wool out of your ears and put it in your mouth.'

I ignored his rudeness; no one had ever said I was intelligent before. I hoped this wasn't going to take too long; it was freezing, and Amira's tiny designer coat didn't quite fit me around the middle.

Dr L continued. 'An old friend of mine says that religion is for those who don't want to go to hell, and spirituality is for those who've already been there.'

Very clever. We dodged a small boy wobbling on a pair of rollerblades, obviously a much longed-for Christmas present. I stopped to pet an adorable pug puppy, hoping that might distract Dr L from his sermon. It didn't.

'Like you, I used to think that even the idea of handing over control of my life to someone else was just unbearable – especially someone or something I couldn't see. For me, being asked to believe in God was like being asked to believe in magic. I just couldn't do it.'

We passed some Japanese tourists taking a group photograph; I made an amusing face in the background, which they'd only appreciate once they got home.

'You see, I used to think it was my job to run the whole world, and for a while, that's what I did. But it began to get difficult, as I found I couldn't control it 100 per cent. People kept doing things I didn't want them to do. Things happened at random. It was pretty scary, so I tried harder. And the harder I tried, the more uncontrollable the world became. Eventually, I became so exhausted that I couldn't even deal with my own life properly. Which by now was tiny, as it was the only way I could keep it even remotely manageable.'

A deafeningly loud bell was ringing in my head. I decided to ignore it and smiled at a sweet little boy on a very new tricycle instead.

'But that nasty feeling of being out of control

kept coming back.' He hushed his voice and looked round, as if there was a possibility we were being followed by the Secret Service. 'Not everybody knows this, but I drank too much, I took too many drugs, I chased women, I spent money I didn't have, I ate too much, I ate nothing. I did just about anything to run away from my feelings about what had happened, what was happening now, what could happen in the future.'

I tried to imagine Dr L pissed at a party, injecting himself with heroin in the bathroom whilst shagging a blonde, working his way through the entire buffet and then sicking it up again, but I couldn't.

'Eventually, like you, I ran into a brick wall and was forced to look at myself closely. It turned out that I was the last person who should be in charge of anything. The more I found out, the less I knew.'

And the more he talked, the less I liked him. He was clearly some sort of born-again nutter. Pity, I'd thought him rather sensible up until now.

'But I had to find someone or something to take over from me, to look after the world, now that I knew I couldn't. Eventually, after a long search, someone who had suffered from similar problems suggested that I just let it go, and trust that whoever or whatever had been looking out for me so far would carry on doing just that. A big step, don't you think?'

'You're telling me; I've never trusted anyone in my life. People are, generally, completely untrustworthy.' So can we change the subject, please?

'Quite. Well, the good news for a control freak like me was that I would get to choose who or what it was – although he used the word "God", it didn't have to be the man with the beard from your childhood, and it didn't have to be the "God" from mine either. It just had to be a power I believed to be bigger than myself, that's all.'

'But that's mad, you can't –'

'I know.' He stopped walking, and turned to me. 'I gave him at least twenty reasons why this wasn't possible, and he sat and listened patiently to all of them. Then he gently asked me how being in charge of everyone and everything had been working for me so far, was I happy with the way my life was going?'

He smiled. 'That's when I thought I might as well give this new-fangled idea a go. Just for a bit, mind you – if it didn't work, I'd go back to my old strategy of full-on control, 24/7.' He started walking again, back the way we'd come.

'And?'

'It changed my life. I've never had to be in charge again.'

I wouldn't say he was boring, but Dr Lichtenstein banged on and on about the God thing all the way back to the park gates, even during the journey back to the clinic. The taxi driver probably joined a monastery after he dropped us off.

In fact, he was still going on about it as we walked up the steps into Reception.

'Mummy!'

Amber flew off the visitors' sofa and into my arms. I hadn't realized how much I'd missed her, she smelled of us. I hugged her tight; too tight, she pulled away. 'Are you all right?' She looked very serious for someone so small.

'Yes, I'm fine . . .' My father loomed into view. I stood up. 'What are you doing here? What's going on?'

'Time to come home, Charlotte. Mother's waiting in the car outside.' He looked embarrassed, shifty even. 'Best get a move on!'

I realized he probably hadn't been in a psychiatric hospital before. Mind you, nor had Amber. 'Why on earth did you bring her here?' I hissed.

'I told him to,' Dr Lichtenstein admitted. 'Amber needed to know where you were. You were ill, and so you had to come to hospital –'

'– and now you're better!' Amber was jumping up and down with excitement. 'I met Minnie Mouse, Mum! I've actually got a photo of me with her, an actual photo, in a frame and everything! And I saw Ariel, and Don Duck!' I smiled, this has been our joke since she'd first got it wrong when she was a tiddler.

'But I can't go home yet, I'm not ready –'

'Need a hand packing?' asked Dad.

'I'll help you,' said Dr L, and he led me off to the lift as my father gave Amber some more coins to put in the parking meter.

I didn't have anything to pack, of course, just

the carrier bag with the nightie and dressing gown that Sister Ellen said I could keep. Whoopee.

Dr Lichtenstein sat on the bed. 'Time to get on with your life, Charlotte. Your father rang me yesterday, and I couldn't give him a good reason for keeping you here any longer.'

'But the truth is that I don't want to go home!' I cried. 'I like it here, I feel safe. I'm not ready to deal with Out There.'

'You're fine. And besides, it's not cheap, this place.'

'Can't I get a scholarship?'

He laughed. 'No.'

'But I can't face it, I'm . . .'

'Yes?'

'. . . scared.'

'Bravo, Charlotte!'

As we said goodbye, he told me to be grateful that my family wanted to look after me, especially if I felt I wasn't able to take care of myself properly yet. 'Just let go and let God,' he whispered, as he peeled a sobbing Amira off me.

Yes, well, all that worshippy stuff may work for him, but there was no doubt in my mind that it wasn't going to work for me.

# CHAPTER 7

'Dependence on the creator within is really freedom from all other dependencies. Paradoxically, it is also the only route to real intimacy with other human beings. Freed from our terrible fears of abandonment, we are able to live with more spontaneity. Freed from our constant demands for more and more reassurance, our fellows are able to love us back without feeling so burdened.'

Julia Cameron, *The Artists Way*

I'd assumed they were taking me to their house. I was horrified when I realized we were driving towards Fulham. 'Um,' I ventured from the back seat, 'I don't think my house is – well, the best place for us to go. I think I left it a bit untidy . . .'

'Nonsense!' replied my father. He explained carefully, as if to a five-year-old, that once they'd got home from America, and Amber had gone back to school, he and Mum had 'redecorated' the house as a surprise for me. 'Which is why your poor mother's so tired.' (She was so excited to see me that she'd fallen asleep in the front seat.)

'Mum, I flew home all by myself! I was an unencumpered miner, just like the seven dwarves,' exclaimed the newly Disney-obsessed Amber. She chirruped happily all the way home, as I began to dread what they'd done to my house. (I couldn't remember every detail of my domestic obliterations at that point, but I was still confident enough to think that the state I'd left it in would be better than anything they could do.)

We decided to leave my mother in the car as it was a shame to wake Sleeping Beauty (in this case a hundred years not being quite long enough) and Dad fumbled with his key in the lock, which I noticed had been changed. The Victorian stained-glass panel in the front door complete with bin-liner feature, which I'd stuck on the day McQueen got run over, had been replaced with a modern version of decorative glass, which was not the same thing at all. It was hideous. My heart sank at the thought of what was waiting for me on the other side.

Then I noticed that my scrawny (albeit unpruned) rosebushes had been uprooted from the tiny front garden, and been supplanted by some rather dull privet. Dad saw me looking with dismay at the freshly dug flowerbeds. 'Roses got crushed,' he offered by way of explanation, 'wouldn't have survived the winter.'

'Right.' I felt a raw mixture of shame and anger, I think. (At least I felt something; Dr L would have been proud of me.)

'Come on, Grandad, hurry up!' squealed Amber, 'I want Mum to see what you've done to my bedroom!' I seemed to remember doing quite a bit to it; did I really throw her prized collection of dolls out of the window? I had a sudden flash-back of the big pink plastic beach buggy so enjoyed by Barbie and Ken sitting on top of a large pile of rubble out in the back garden.

Amber ran past us, straight up the stairs. There was no hall carpet, just floorboards, which some-body had evidently sanded and varnished.

The sitting room was the first room I saw; it bore no resemblance to the tatty one I'd left behind, it was warm and comfortable and full of beautifully co-ordinated furniture and a very luxu-rious creamy rug. 'This must have cost you a fortune!' I exclaimed, horrified. How was I ever going to pay them back?

Dad smiled. 'Stuff belongs to Matt, put the whole lot into storage when he left for the States. Said you could look after it for him, till you get back on your feet.'

'But I can't possibly accept this,' I spluttered – I hated being beholden to my brother in any way – 'what if I spill something on it?'

'Yes. Thought you'd be cross,' grinned Dad, annoyingly, 'my job to tell you you're saving him a small fortune in storage fees. Bloody daylight robbery, by all accounts! Both doing each other a favour, works out rather well.'

My brother's dining-room table looked just right in my dining room, and my mother had clearly scrubbed the kitchen to within an inch of its life, some of the paintwork had rubbed off completely. I didn't recognize a glass or a bowl or even the pattern on the plates perched on Matt's dresser, it was like being in somebody else's house.

I dreaded going upstairs, as I now had a very clear memory of the bathroom fiasco. 'Whole thing was rotten anyway,' said Dad, by way of explanation, 'had to go. Nice chap came, apparently did some work for you before but you'd forgotten to pay him. All square now.' He patted my back, and guided me into Amber's room.

'Look at my new stuff, Mum! Everyone at school's really jelly of me!' Laid out around her was the contents of a large pink suitcase; pens and stickers and new Barbies and matching outfits and make-up and groovy vest-and-pants sets and a fluffy handbag and some jazzy tights and in short everything a little girl could ever want. 'January sales,' said Dad under his breath as we left the room, 'your mother did very well.'

Surprisingly, the box room was full of boxes, arranged in an orderly way around the walls, their contents labelled in mother's unmistakable hand. 'Anything we could salvage,' explained my father. The window had been replaced and painted, the curtains were bold red-and-white gingham, the walls were a fresh sky blue. The single whitewood bed had crisp white sheets on it, and the duvet and pillows were puffed up, just waiting for a weary head. The look was Mediterranean guesthouse, with a Swedish twist. I thought I recognized the handiwork of –

'– Surprise!'

Yes, I was right. Arthur was waiting for me in the master bedroom, which was an absolute triumph. He'd really pulled out all the stops, it looked like a glossy double-page spread from *Homes and Gardens*. My brother's beautiful mahogany bed was covered in a faux fur throw, the drapes were swathed and swung, the bedside lamps were huge, giving the room what those design tossers call A Certain Importance. There was no trace of me left – or Joe, for that matter.

'Honestly,' Arthur said as he handed my dad a glass of champagne which had been cooling on top of a sort of pedestal thing in the corner, 'it's been like *Changing Rooms* around here, hasn't it. Bob? We've been up and down those stairs I don't know how many times – I must say, Charlotte, your brother's got excellent taste, I knew he would . . . oh, which reminds me, guess who's been Arthur's little helper?'

He walked over to the cupboard and knocked on it. The door opened and Jimmy made his entrance, draping himself around me with great drama, almost as if he didn't know I'd never liked him.

'Now you've seen everything, Bob,' said Arthur to my father as they sipped their bubbly, 'even a gay man coming out of the closet!'

My poor dad looked most uncomfortable, which only made us laugh more.

I was totally overwhelmed, I didn't know what to feel. I don't know if it was the sudden rush of their champagne to my empty head, or that my emotional defences were down, but to my horror I burst into tears.

'Thank you – sniff – oh god,' I sobbed, 'sorry. Sorry about crying, really sorry.'

'You should do it more,' said that nasty little Jimmy, 'it suits you.'

Arthur nudged him in the ribs and came over to put his arms round me. He smelt of sweat and white spirit and Givenchy aftershave, and usually hugging wasn't my thing; but this time I took what was on offer and hid in his embrace for as long as I could.

Which wasn't very long, and so I ran away, by taking another tour of the bedrooms and bath-room, marvelling at everyone's hard work. Half an hour later, Arthur and Jimmy left, satisfied that their efforts hadn't been in vain. I waved them off with a last 'thank you' and leant against the back of the front door. Suddenly I felt exhausted, drained, emotionally and physically wrung out. Downstairs, my father was playing Disney Trivial Pursuit with Amber on the dining-room table.

'I don't want to be rude or anything, Dad, but

are you going soon? I think I'll plug Amber into the telly, and have a nap in my new de luxe bedroom.'

My father cleared his throat. 'Thing is, Charlotte –'

'That's not your bedroom any more, Mum!' Amber looked like a mini-transvestite, she'd been trying out all her new make-up. 'You're going to sleep in the little room. Granny and Grandad live here now, isn't that cool?!'

It certainly made me go cold all over.

'Just till you get back on your feet again,' said my father, sheepishly; this obviously hadn't been his idea. 'Thought you could do with the help.'

'Help? Help?! Not from you!' I wanted to scream at him, but I didn't have the energy. Instead, somehow, I managed to say calmly, 'Thanks for the offer, Dad, but I think I can manage.'

'That's the point,' he replied, strangely bold. 'Don't think you can, not going to leave until everything's running smoothly. Left you on your own long enough,' he picked up the dice and shook it, 'cavalry's here now. Green, good!'

I knew it was pointless arguing – he was being driven by a force much stronger than both of us. But didn't they understand that this was *my* house, *my* bedroom, *my life*? I wanted to cry, but I didn't want Amber to see me upset.

Instead, I spun round and did a sort of march out into the hallway, just in time to see my mother letting herself in through the front door – with her own key. I ran up the stairs and threw myself on to my 'new' bed, hitting my head on the wall as I did so – there wasn't enough space in there for a proper tantrum.

I cried tears of pain and rage and disbelief – how had this happened? Why was I being held prisoner in my own home, which didn't even look like my home any more?

It would be fair to say that I wasn't quite as grateful for my parents' help as I could have been. I wanted my old stuff back, I wanted to lie on my own sofa. Once again, my bloody brother had come to the rescue. Once again, I hated him.

It was like I was frozen. Suspended in animation. I couldn't move from the sofa, I couldn't get up. It was the same sofa I'd spent the last part of my pregnancy on, lying there, waiting for Joe to bring me delicious food and gossip from the outside world. But now he wasn't here any more, and instead of being hopeful for the future I was fearful. Shit scared, actually, only at the time I didn't know that's what it was. So it came out as white-hot rage, I was furious with myself. This was definitely my fault, I knew that, I should have done something different. But what?

We lived on that sofa, Amber and I. Before the birth, it had been my favourite place, I'd been like a happily beached

161

whale. I think my reasoning was that if I stayed there, I might get some of that happiness back.

Now, it was my only place to be. We woke up on it, we only left it for short periods to forage for nappies and milk for her and fags and wine for me, we went to sleep on it.

It sounds silly, but I was too scared to go upstairs, especially at night. I was afraid of the memories, the painful shadows of a previous life. The bed was always going to be cold from now on, he wasn't in it. There was a pair of his boxer shorts on the bathroom floor exactly where he'd left them for weeks; I couldn't face touching them.

The worst part was that I still had no idea why he'd done it. Why had he gone? What had made him get up and go like that? How could he leave me, who he claimed to love so much? And Amber, who was his own flesh and blood, whom he had made? My mind was plagued with these questions, which went round and round and round, not leaving me alone for a minute. Why, why, why?

That was what was happening on the inside, anyway. On the outside, I pretended everything was normal. I didn't want my parents to know he'd left, because they'd have done the dance of I-told-you-so. Whenever anyone rang for Joe, I said he'd just popped out, or he was in the bath, or rehearsing. I'd left something under the grill, could I call them back? I tried to keep a list of who I'd told what, but I lost it. They stopped ringing in the end, he must have told his people. But I didn't tell mine, I didn't want anyone to know I'd been dumped. Abandoned.

I don't know how long I thought I'd get away with it, but in the end I didn't.

Tap tap! Tap-tap-tap!

I was asleep. What the fuck was that? Fuck off.

I tried to go back to my dream, which was all about killing Joe with an empty syringe, making an air bubble go round his bloodstream and into his heart. (This was my best thinking on how to kill him and get away with it – I'd have happily gone to prison for murdering him, but there was no one I trusted to look after Amber properly.) My plan was to stick it into his leg, just as he passed me in the street, casual as you like. No CCTV would pick that up. Nobody would know how he died, they'd never be able to detect such a tiny pinprick.

But how would I bump into him? I didn't even know where he was. I'd lost him. His sporadic postcards were from a different country each time, and they said less and less.

Somebody shouted my name, muffled, as if through glass.

I always went back to the knife behind the radiator in the hallway in the end. I'd never find him, but he might just turn up here on the doorstep one day. And I'd be ready and waiting for him, oh yes.

'Charlotte!' Actually somebody *was* shouting my name through glass, Matt had climbed over the wall at the front of the house and was pressed up against the sitting-room window, filling the gap between the curtains where they wouldn't close properly. Fully washable indeed!

The baby was asleep on my chest, I gently lifted her off and laid her down beside me, and wrapped her up in the warmth of the duvet.

Bloody hell, I thought, as I stumbled stiffly out to the hallway, what does he want? What time is it? My watch must have stopped, it said half past five. Was that in the morning or the afternoon I wondered, as I opened the door.

He was standing behind the biggest teddy bear I'd ever seen. It was wearing nearly as big a smile as he was, and had a shiny red ribbon round its neck. So common, so

164

unstylish. You wouldn't even steal it from Toys R Us.

'Where's my favourite niece then?' he grinned in his outdoorsy rumbustious way.

'Your only niece is asleep in the sitting room,' I said. 'Stop shouting, you'll wake her up.'

'Hangover?' he asked as he ducked through the doorway designed for tiny Victorians, not butch macho men.

'No, why?' I lied (I was permanently hungover), as I led the way through to the kitchen.

'You don't look that gre –' He'd walked straight in to the sitting room and stopped dead in his tracks. I went back to see what the problem was.

Some time later he referred to what he saw as my Tracy Emin installation – he reckoned she must have passed my house one day, looked in and rushed home with a great idea. My sofa was marooned in a sea of pizza boxes and silver takeaway cartons and nappies (clean, I might add) (well, OK, maybe there were a couple still there from the day before) and wine bottles and soda cans and chocolate wrappers and video rental boxes and dirty tissues and the odd shoe and leaflets on weaning and a tin of baked beans with the spoon still in it and tiny babygros, some still in their packets and others still covered in babysick. I'd intended not to smoke in the same room as Amber once she was born (despite having smoked like a chimney when she was in the womb – go figure) but hadn't quite managed to stick to that – there were cigarette butts on and in and under everything.

'What?' I said, defensively. 'What?'

I gave in eventually, and let him take over. He must have felt great, quite the big I-am, rescuing his older sister. At least he didn't tell Mum and Dad. The doctor said I had post-natal depression, so she prescribed anti-depressants. I suppose they worked, because the killing dream went away for a bit and I began to function again. They may call them happy pills, but they certainly didn't make my life any happier. I knew that I was never going to be happy again.

It was worse than I could have possibly imagined, living with my parents. Or rather them living with me. I was completely powerless, all my rights had been stripped away; I was supervised continually, watched like a hawk for signs of cracking up. Even though I hated them, I was very careful not to show it; at the first sign of any tension my parents would exchange a 'look' and I would know that I was one day further away from being left on my own. It was made very clear to me that if I wanted them to go, I had to prove that I was capable of looking after Amber, and myself.

For those first few weeks, I had no real responsibilities, it was like being a teenager all over again. I'd stay up late, watching old movies on TV or reading; then I'd wake up at about midday, have a long hot bath, get dressed and go downstairs for lunch which thankfully my mother hadn't cooked – it was always a powdered Cup-a-soup and a little something on an oblong strip of cardboard popularly known as Ryvita, followed by a watery low-fat nutra-sweet yoghurt which had once had a brief brush with a strawberry.

Then I'd read a magazine, or watch some mind-numbing quiz on telly until it was time to pick up Amber from school. We'd usually pop into Starbucks for hot chocolate and a sneaky snack on the way home so that we weren't entirely relying on my mother's revolting cooking for sustenance.

Not that we'd dream of telling my mother that – I didn't dare and Amber didn't want to. Whilst I was 'away' they'd bonded, really bonded. They'd always been friends, but now they exchanged secret looks which meant something to them, they stuck up for each other, they did lots together. I could see that Mum really loved her, and worse, Amber really loved her too. She just lapped up all the attention. To me, it felt like she was fraternizing with the enemy. I know it's not fair, and a nicer person would be happy that Amber had a solid female role model in her life blah blah blah; but I was hurt and jealous and determined to reclaim my daughter.

At first Amber treated me like an invalid, spoke to me very slowly and loudly as one would a deaf foreigner; but she soon realized that her mummy was in there somewhere. We got more creative with our happy hour; we joined the local library, we thought up names for imaginary pets, once we walked the whole way home from the bus stop backwards.

Strangely, I found myself really looking forward to this stolen time with her. What had once felt like a chore had somehow become the highlight of my day.

> Nobody tells you this. Once you announce you're pregnant, other parents smile and say things like 'it completely changed my life'. You're telling me.
>
> Here's the secret they don't want you to know: HAVING CHILDREN IS AWFUL. Sure, they're beautiful and fascinating and rewarding and you can't help but love them, even adore them sometimes, as they're just gorgeous and the whole thing's a miracle and wow, etc; but we know all that, it's the darker side they never talk about. It's a joy, of course it is, but it's also a fucking nightmare.

Firstly, it's the end of your personal freedom as you know it. Never again will you be able to 'pop' out to the cinema, let alone the shops, let alone a quick cup of coffee. For you, there will be no such thing as 'quick' any more. It goes without saying that you can't leave the child at home on its own – although I have to confess to discussing the idea of a big belt around the mattress at night with a similarly disenchanted new mother. Even though she was just kidding, I wasn't.

So you find yourself paying someone to sit on your sofa and watch your TV whilst simultaneously ruining your life; words like 'she wasn't very sleepy so I let her stay up for a bit' can strike the fear of God into a mother's heart, as a routine can take as long as a month to establish but just one evening to break. The only alternative is to take the little bugger with you.

This entails packing up the pram with bottles of juice and/or milk, rusks and/or carrot sticks, a couple of spare nappies, wipes and deodorizing bag for the disposal of the dirty ones, a special pram-sized blanket, a rain cover designed by the same people who design self-assembly flat pack furniture, Factor 60 waterproof sun cream, a parasol on a bendy stalk that won't stay up, a pram toy on a bungee string, a cardboard book with chewed corners not for reading but for teething, that very precious favourite toy from obscure aunt or obscure shop that causes you anxiety every time you leave the house as this could be the day it gets lost and you'll never find another one; and that cardigan which you bought in 'age 10' by mistake still in the bag with the receipt, which at this rate she'll be too big for by the time you get round to taking it back to the shop. And this is before you've even started to wrap her up in hundreds of different layers, just in case.

You can't even remember what you wear at times like this, in fact you can't really remember what you wear at any time, you've completely forgotten who you are and what you're for by now. So next time you're out in the High Street, spare a thought for the new mother pushing a buggy that resembles a small space station, and notice that she's wearing flip-flops even though it's mid-December, or a woolly hat in August. Hold the door open for her and the pram as you enter the shop by all means; smile at the baby to keep it occupied as she tries to remember what she came in for if you like; but don't, don't, whatever you do, ask her how she is or she might just burst into tears and tell you.

So you'd think I'd have enjoyed these new

responsibility-free days, having the time to indulge myself at last, wouldn't you? Oh no. You know me. I was too busy focussing on what was wrong with my life, rather than what was right.

'Why don't you just tell your mum and dad to fuck off?' asked Sabrina, as she replenished her wineglass. 'It's really simple.'

'I know, I know,' I held mine up for more too, 'but somehow I just can't. Whenever I try to Say Something, I'm railroaded into talking about something else. It's a nightmare, Sabrina, it's like being held captive in my own home. No, sorry, it's not *like* that, it *is* that! I can't even leave the house without filling out a form in triplicate first.'

'But you're out by yourself this evening, aren't you?' We were in our local wine bar, Mr Pickwicks, an old favourite haunt of ours. Sabrina and me were back to being friends now, she'd phoned when she'd heard of my demise; my mum had kept her talking for ages, apparently, and insisted on meeting her. Sabrina had had to come and pick me up this evening. There had been smiles all round from everyone, except me. I was still very ashamed about The Home Alone Incident.

This was our first face-to-face though, and it was still a little frosty. I think I was trying to recreate our closeness by telling her everything that had happened to me; I think she was a little shocked. Sabrina didn't really do breakdown.

171

'Well, yes, I suppose I am here by myself, and don't get me wrong, it's good to be out of the house at night. But they'll be waiting up for me when I get home. And I'll be asked twenty questions about where I went, who I saw, etc. Honestly, Sabrina, it's like living with the Gestapo.'

She laughed, but unsympathetically. 'Perhaps they're just interested in what you get up to! I'd have loved it if my mother had even noticed I'd gone out for the evening, she was always far too self-absorbed to take any notice of what I was doing.' She pushed the olives around in their little oily dish with a cocktail stick. 'Look on the bright side, at least you're not having to pay a babysitter.'

'I s'pose. But it's not just a passing interest, they're obsessed with my every move. They're just plain nosey.' I didn't like Sabrina sticking up for my parents, she obviously didn't understand. 'D'you know, they've even stopped me seeing all my other friends since I came home!'

'Which friends?'

'Oh, you know,' I couldn't think of anybody off-hand, 'just people – I can't face the Spanish Inquisition every time.'

'They seem to get on well with Arthur though, don't they?'

'God yes, they all became best friends when they were doing up the house – in fact they bonded a bit too well, he and Jimmy are coming for Sunday lunch next weekend.' I groaned at the thought.

'Well that's nice, isn't it?'

'I s'pose so; at least Arthur's cooking, thank god.'

Sabrina's phone tinnily trumpeted the arrival of a text message. 'So which other friends haven't you seen?' she asked, as she picked it up from the table.

'Well, there's –' I actually couldn't think of anyone off the top of my head, and anyway she was more interested in her phone than me, '– how's work?'

She smiled at the message, it was clearly something obscene. 'Great, thanks, going really well. I got the pay rise I asked for, in fact I've been promoted, I'm not –'

'Speaking of work, I don't suppose you've heard from your friend Piers, the glamorous film producer, have you? He still owes me that money, the little shit.' I drained my glass.

'No, nothing.' Sabrina sat up. 'I heard a rumour he'd gone to Amsterdam, but it's probably only gossip.' She drank. 'So – have you found another job yet?'

'Not yet, no. I'm so bored, it's really dull being unemployed, y'know. The days just go on and on and on, it's awful.'

'Have you been actively looking?'

'Who are you, my mother?' I snapped, without meaning to. She just raised her eyebrows. I sighed. 'Not yet, I'm waiting till I feel a bit better. I'm still so weak, you see.'

There was a pause. Sabrina went quiet, which meant she disapproved.

'I'm still sleeping a lot, I need a lot of rest, the clinic said so,' I continued. 'Sometimes I don't even wake up until lunchtime! It's really hard, I –'

Sabrina frowned. 'Who takes Amber to school then?'

'My dad. She loves it, they get on really well. I'm not surprised, he's much nicer to her than he ever was to me at that age.' I helped myself to one of Sabrina's cigarettes. 'Really spoils her.' I hoped the raging green-eyed monster within didn't show on my face as I lit the fag.

'He was probably out working every day when you were small, wasn't he?'

I opened my mouth and shut it again.

'So if you haven't got a job, what're you doing for money then?'

I exhaled, savouring the nicotine hit to my lungs. Needless to say, I wasn't allowed to smoke at home. My mother was apparently 'allergic' to cigarette smoke. 'Well, I don't really need any at the moment, Mum and Dad pay for stuff.'

She sat up. Oh god, here we go. One of Sabrina's Speeches was coming my way. 'Right. So let me get this straight: your parents have not only paid thousands of pounds for you to be treated in a private clinic, but they've also put your house back together again while you were in there. Added to which, they've put their own lives completely on hold in order to take care of you and your daughter in your own home, and now they've paying for everything until you can get

174

off your lazy arse for long enough to find a job, is that it?'

'Well, put like that –'

'From where I'm standing, Charlotte, it looks like you've got it pretty good. I can't believe you're so ungrateful.'

I was shocked. Shocked that she couldn't understand how awful it was for me. I decided to change the subject. 'Whatever happened to – oh, whatsisname, the one you went away with for Christmas, the American bloke?'

'Bill?'

'Yes, him, how did that work out in the end?'

'We're getting married soon, I'm moving to New York at the end of this month.'

'What?! Really?'

She nodded, and stubbed out her fag.

How could she leave the country at a time like this? What about me? She's supposed to be my best friend! 'But you never said . . .'

'Charlotte – you never asked.'

No, well, we just hadn't got on to her yet. I thought it better to change tack, so I tried to be nice about her news, even though it was awful. 'Wow, I can't believe it. You lucky thing, you've finally got the man of your dreams.' She gave a tight-lipped smile, I sucked on my cigarette. 'Honestly, why can't something like that happen to me? Why can't I have a lovely boyfriend?'

Sabrina picked up her mobile and slipped it into her handbag. 'I don't want to be rude, Charlotte, but you're not exactly a very good catch at the moment, are you?' She opened her purse and placed a £20 note on the table. 'This one-woman pity party you're having has just got to stop, the hard-done-by victim thing is such a bad look. What man in his right mind would want to be with a moaning Minnie like you?'

That hurt.

She got up from the table. 'Right, I've got to go. I'll ring you before I leave, if I get time.' She flashed one of her famous smiles, put her hand on my shoulder. 'Look, I'm sorry if I've been rude, but someone's got to tell you. You're completely obsessed with yourself; you should take your head out from up your own arse and have a good look around you. It's about time you got real, Charlotte.'

And she swept out of the wine bar, just like that, followed by the lascivious leers of all three regulars perched on stools at the bar, probably hoping to be mistaken for the cast of *Cheers*.

Somehow I managed to get myself out of there before the tears came. Bitch! It hurt, it really hurt – because even then, deep deep deep down, I knew it was true.

Once I'd got over the shock of Joe leaving us, and accepted that he wasn't coming back, I thought I'd meet a nice man who'd take pity on an abandoned woman and child. This man would not be my normal type, and I probably wouldn't fancy him, but he would be a good man and I'd slowly grow to love him. (He'd instantly fall in love with me, of course, despite my pushing him away again and again. He'd keep coming back until I gave in and let him love me, you see.)

I even knew what he'd look like; tall, but a little overweight, slightly red in the face with short hair that was on the retreat. He'd have a happy, open expression and clean fingernails. He'd be the type to wear a gold signet ring, he'd have to wear a suit during the week and he'd have a comfortable car, even though it was British and not German.

He'd have done well for himself, considering his father left the family when he was just a boy. He adored his mother, and had been let down very badly by a previous fiancée probably called Sue who'd dumped him a few weeks before the wedding. He was always being teased by his mates down the pub for being gay, as he hadn't been seen with a woman since.

I had it all worked out.

Every other Sunday, he'd have to take his mum over to his sister's for lunch and we'd probably row about this at first, but he'd made it clear that he wasn't going to stop doing that for anyone, and I would learn to treasure the time alone with Amber.

Eventually, we would go to visit his family too, and Amber would play happily with her step-cousins while I would bask in the love and acceptance I was receiving from this happy, well-balanced family.

Every Friday night, he'd bring flowers home for me and I would make him a delicious supper (having miraculously transformed into an excellent cook) and then I'd massage his poor aching shoulders and he'd carry me upstairs to the bedroom and we would have the most loving sex ever. Ever.

Of course I'd want to go out to work, but he wouldn't let me as he said I'd had enough hardship in my life and he was here now, there was no need to struggle any more, he would provide everything I needed. He'd be brilliant at DIY and gardening, and happily accept that it was his job to put the bins out and lock up at night and catch spiders. Amber would adore him, and after he'd officially adopted her, we'd get married and live happily ever after. Simple as that.

I haven't met him yet. I have a horrible feeling I never will.

'You heff no love, you heff no love!' That bloody au pair's voice was haunting me again. I turned my pillow over, that sometimes worked.

The window rattled, the wind was cold, it wanted to come in. I turned over, pulled the duvet tight around me.

'Victim thing . . . bad look' said Sabrina's voice, over and over, like a bad B-movie. And then my version: 'You're ugly, nobody's ever going to want you, you'll never get there, you're boring, I hate you, we all do . . .'

My feet were cold, so I put some socks on.

'Pity party, let's have a pity party!' said my insane brain. 'Only moaning Minnies invited . . .'

'Mum, can I come to your party if Minnie Mouse is coming?' Bloody hell, I was going mad again. My head was hurting me, I didn't want to hear it any more.

I sprang out of bed and put on the dressing gown the clinic had given me as a leaving present, which had been hanging by its hook on the back of my Swedish guestroom door. It looked like the Grim Reaper, waiting patiently for this time to come.

I tiptoed downstairs, avoiding the steps that squeaked in order not to wake the sleeping guards.

The kitchen clock – yes yes, Matt's kitchen clock – said that it was five minutes past two in the morning. I'd come in from the wine bar and gone straight up to bed, without saying goodnight to them. I'd taken the precaution of slamming my bedroom door instead. Then I'd had to wait until they came to bed before using the bathroom, in case we'd met on the landing. (It's quite hard work, this not talking to your parents thing, as any teenager will tell you.)

Camomile tea should do the trick. With a bit of honey, to stop it tasting like piss. No, forget that – this was most definitely a hot Ribena moment. And maybe a sandwich? My mother disapproved of sliced bread, said it was a waste of money when you could do it yourself; so I got out the bread and the board and the carving knife (now restored to its rightful place in the drawer) and cut the mouldy corners off some old cheddar being denied its natural right of going to waste in the fridge. I sat down at the kitchen table and sank my teeth into the doorstep I'd made, its crust being so crusty it scratched the roof of my mouth.

'Everything all right?' said a stage-whisper voice at the door.

I sighed. 'Hi, Dad,' I said, without bothering to look up.

'Room for two in there?' he asked.

'Whatever,' I said, hoping my tone of voice would put him off.

His slippers made the swishing sound of old people as he pottered around the kitchen, and I suddenly realized he was not making us a cup of tea as I'd thought, but gathering late-night contraband instead. There was a tiny tub of Ben and Jerry's hidden inside a large economy bag of frozen ready-cooked roast potatoes; a half-eaten bar of gourmet-dark chocolate slid down the side of his morning bran cereal box; and horror of horrors, a quarter bottle of Scotch wrapped in a muffling tea towel, right at the back of the drawer where the bin liners were kept.

'Dad!' I was aghast.

'Sssh!' He looked up at the ceiling. 'Don't want to wake your mother up. Want some?' He got two mugs, not glasses, out of the cupboard; to avoid detection I suppose, he'd clearly done this before. 'Cheers.'

We sipped in silence, feeling the fiery amber scorching a burning path down the back of our throats.

'Everything all right?' asked my father.

'Mmm,' I nodded. 'Fine. You?'

'Yup, all fine,' he nodded. 'You?'

'Haven't we done me?' I asked.

'Have we?' he asked. 'Oh.' All of a sudden, he looked very tired – old.

'You OK, Dad?' I asked. 'Really?'

'Course,' he said. 'What about you?'

'Yes, fine. You?'

'Fine. You?'

We smiled at our silliness, and then retreated into our individual worlds. I picked up the carving knife and absentmindedly started to smooth the breadcrumbs away into the little groove around the board.

Eventually my father got up. 'Want one of these?' he asked, reaching behind a plate in display mode on the dresser.

'Dad! How long have you been smoking?!' I

asked, horrified and yet excited at such rebellion. He'd noiselessly shut the kitchen door and was now lighting the gas on top of the cooker. 'I thought you gave up years ago!'

'So did I,' he said, puffing on the two cigarettes to get them going, 'turns out not to be true!' He shrugged his shoulders in mock surprise and handed me my cigarette. 'What's bothering you, eh?'

'Nothing, Dad, really.' I began to scratch the board with the carving knife. Nothing I can talk to you about, anyway.

'Late-night goblins getting to you, eh?'

I nodded.

We sat in silence, smoking and loving it.

Eventually, Dad got up.

'S'pose you should see this,' he said, as he shuffled over to the dresser and opened the middle drawer. I saw that it was full of envelopes – it hadn't even occurred to me that I hadn't had any mail since I came out of the clinic. Oh God, not another bloody postcard from Joe, please. No, it was a letter. 'Arrived while you were away.' He handed me an envelope. I recognized the writing immediately. I felt sick.

It was addressed to Amber, not me. 'Miss Amber Newman' he'd written, which wasn't her name. She was Amber Small, she was in my family, not his.

'It's been opened . . .' I looked up at him.

'Your mother thought it best, didn't want you getting any nasty shocks.'

I was too nastily shocked to get angry about that right now, so I filed it away for later. I couldn't believe what I was holding in my hand. 'What does it say?'

'You look.' He came and stood behind me, put his hand on my shoulder, as he puffed on his cigarette as if it were his last.

Inside was a Christmas card, a cheap tacky one. It had a scrawny robin with a glittery breast on the front. As I opened it, a banknote floated out. It was ten euros.

'About £6,' answered my dad, before I'd had to ask.

'To Amber' it said at the top, and then after the greeting, 'love from Daddy xxx'.

That was it. No 'sorry about fucking off and leaving you'. No 'I think about you all the time'. Not even 'I miss you'. Just one kiss. And no mention of me, of course.

The word 'Daddy' was scribbled, as if it was the kind of word he wrote all the time, like this was yet another card to his daughter, written as a matter of course, just one more Christmas card from 'Daddy'. Daddy! I was outraged. He hadn't earned the right to even call himself 'Daddy', let alone the casual by-the-wayness of scrawling it in signature. I still felt peculiar when I wrote the word 'Mum', as it always shocked me that I was actually somebody's mother – and I'd been with Amber for every single Christmas and birthday, year in and year out, thank you very much.

And as for 'love', what did he know about love?

I cried, I had to. It was all too much. My father gave me his last cigarette. I smoked it and cried some more. 'Silly really,' I sobbed and gulped, 'it's just a card. Doesn't even' – sniff – 'say anything.'

'Bugger must be somewhere in France,' said my father, 'French stamp, you see.'

I hadn't even noticed that. The postmark was smudged, of course it was; he'd probably hunted down a *bureau de poste* that specialized in illegible franking, there was no way of telling where it had come from.

'I don't know why it's upset me so much,' I cried into the proffered piece of kitchen roll, 'I'm sorry.'

For one horrible moment, Dad looked like he was going to cry too.

Fortunately, as if on cue, the door swung open, and there she stood, the Cold Cream Queen, resplendent in housecoat and curler, spluttering at the thick fog of smoke. In my panic to hide the evidence, I stubbed my fag out into the soft loaf of bread. (My mother never forgave me, and my father never owned up.)

I thought I'd go to sleep after that, but I didn't. I felt like a drowning woman, my whole life kept flashing in front of me. And the more I screwed my eyes tight shut, the more I could see.

Eventually, I got used to it. I didn't like being a single parent, but assumed that it

184

was only temporary, that something or someone would save me eventually.

If I said that I rose to the occasion and surprised all around me with my boundless optimism and organizational skills, would you believe me?

I hated it, every minute. The weekends used to stretch out in front of me, two long days and nights of giving everything to my child, and nothing to me. The school holidays were to be endured, the happy families to be avoided. I began to resent Amber, I couldn't help it. Occasionally I allowed myself to think about how different my life would be if I didn't have her.

I didn't have many friends, which was good, because I didn't want any. We didn't bother anyone, and so no one bothered us. It was a small life, but it was manageable. I preferred it that way. But I didn't like the feeling of being on my own, so I'd anaesthetize myself with drink and fags and TV and music and magazines and starting up projects and never finishing them. In short, I was uncomfortable in my own skin.

And I had discovered a modern-day equation: single + parent = lonely.

That night was one of the worst in my life so far. I hope I'll never forget it.

I'd never felt so lonely, alone and on my own. I

kept thinking about the card from Joe, and how poor Amber would never have a dad to sit with her downstairs in the kitchen late at night, and how I'd never get anyone to marry me and how I'd really, really fucked up. Here I was, a reasonably intelligent woman in her thirties, with both arms and legs in good working order; and yet I was penniless, friendless, unable even to provide a home for my daughter, relying on my parents for help. I was appalled at myself.

I kept thinking about Marjorie as I tossed and I turned in my bed that night, drowning in a sea of self-loathing, unable to get away from myself. I didn't want to end up like her, and yet I didn't seem able to change anything. It was like being in a mental hell; I was getting on my own nerves, it was unbearable. I felt wretched. I couldn't stop thinking for long enough to get to sleep. My head was shouting at me. I couldn't stop or start any thought, I was just going round and round, burrowing into my mind, getting nowhere.

I don't know what made me do it. Maybe it was the red wine I'd drunk with Sabrina, or maybe (as Dr Lichtenstein would say) it was the gift of desperation, but once I'd remembered it, I couldn't get it out of my head.

I got out of bed and I knelt on the floor. I put my hands together, like people do when they're praying, and I whispered, 'I don't know if there's anyone listening out there, but please, please, can you help me? I'm sorry to bother you, but I don't know what else to do. I give up. I'm stuck. I'll try anything right now, but I don't know where to start. I think I'm going mad. I can't bear my own head any more, I just want a bit of peace. I –' Then I realized what I was doing, and how ridiculous it would be if there was no one out there, and how ridiculous it would look if someone came in – I could hear my mother scrubbing the kitchen floor downstairs – and so I jumped back into bed again.

Strangely, I went to sleep almost immediately. But that was probably because I was tired.

Slowly, very slowly, I got used to the idea of being single.

I began to enjoy being in charge of my own remote control, eating biscuits in bed and growing my armpit hair to continental length in winter. I told myself that men were glorified sperm donors who couldn't do more than one thing at a time, just pointless very tall little boys. I liked nothing more than listening to other mothers at the school gate complaining about their husbands, it made me feel all warm and right inside.

When people asked if I wanted a partner, I'd answer vehemently 'God no! I'd much rather be on my own, thank you very much.'

What absolute nonsense. The truth was, I just couldn't quite get over Joe.

I yawned. Amira had taken up most of this first month's follow-up group session (After-Care was voluntary but vital, apparently) with some rambling nonsense about shopping but not buying anything for herself because she didn't feel she deserved it, and so she'd run up huge debts in just one day on Oxford Street, buying extravagant presents for her friends, and now resented having to pay off the credit cards. It was as if those bad people at Visa had forced her at gunpoint to go out and spend, spend, spend.

Dr Lichtenstein managed to cut her off before she told the story a third time by turning to me and asking 'And what about you, Charlotte? How've you been getting on?'

'Fine,' I said.

'Fucked-up, Insecure, Neurotic and Emotional,' piped up some titchy little anorexic with glee. I was tempted to knock her off her seat, but she probably would have shattered into tiny pieces and I wasn't sure I had the patience to glue her back together again.

'Fine, Charlotte? Really?' He didn't seem to buy it either.

'No, not really. But I don't want to talk about it.'

The group was silent.

So was I.

They were all staring at me.

'I just – well, I hate myself.'

Big Bonnie, an over-eating self-harmer with a

188

predilection for younger girls, nodded in recognition.

'Why's that, Charlotte?' asked Dr L.

The room was pin-drop silent. We all knew it was the first time I'd admitted to anything other than positive bullshit.

'Because – well, because I seem to have got myself into this terrible mess and now I can't get myself out of it. I'm stuck in the hell hole that is my life.'

'You can't do it alone, though, can you?' Dr Lichtenstein winked at me. I hadn't told him I'd started praying, if you could call it that. For some reason, I didn't want him to think I was doing what I was told.

'Can't your parents help?' asked Amira, whose parents were perhaps too helpful, she was utterly spoilt.

'My parents are doing all they can, and, anyway, I don't want any more help from them!' I snapped, without meaning to. 'It's not that – I just – well, there's something missing.'

'What d'you mean?' asked the tragic Marjorie, who was nursing a black eye from having bumped into the kitchen door whilst completely sober, allegedly.

I really didn't want to discuss this with the group, but – well, what the heck. None of them looked like they were capable of alerting the media at anything I was about to say.

'I can't do it. It's too big a job for me, I just

can't cope. There's not one area of my life that's going well, the whole thing's a disaster area.'

'You want a nice man,' declared Marjorie, 'that's what you need!'

I sighed and shook my head – how d'you tell someone they're stupid, superficial and spectacularly wrong about virtually everything without offending them?

'Love,' said the anorexic, who was really asking to be snapped in half, 'you need love.'

'Maybe Ginny's right,' agreed Doctor Lichtenstein, 'maybe that's what's missing from your life.'

We all thought about this, especially me. There it was again, that four-letter word. Wishy-washy nonsense, hearts and flowers, all right for other people but not for me. I'd tried that, and it hadn't worked.

'Wow,' said Amira. 'Love. Yeah.'

Marjorie started weeping, silently.

Ignoring her, I said, 'Yes, well that's all very well, but –' and here was a blinding revelation, at least to me, 'I don't even know what love is. How can I find something if I don't know what it looks like? Where do I start looking for it?'

Before Amira could come up with ten top tips on How To Get Your Man according to her guiding light, *Glamour* magazine, Dr Lichtenstein said, 'You find it inside yourself. We're talking about self-love here, Charlotte.'

This united the group, and we groaned as one.

'I mean it,' I carried on, 'where do I start? There's no such thing as Love College, as far as I'm aware. How can you study love? Has anyone ever got a degree in Narcissism? I'm not sure I even believe Love exists.'

Dr L told me off for using humour as a defence yet again, but fortunately the spotlight was moved away from me by the anorexic, who had another recovery joke for us: 'Denial isn't just a river in Egypt, you know.' My, how we laughed.

As we left the clinic, Amira asked me to go to lunch with her. I said no, because I couldn't face listening to her incessant chatter today. She had been phoning me far too much recently, wittering on about nothing for hours on end, I needed a break from her. And, besides, I was on a mission.

# CHAPTER 8

'When I loved myself enough, I gave up
the belief that life is hard.'

Kim McMillen, *When I Loved Myself
Enough*

'Oh hi, g'day!' grinned the cartoonish Oz,
who must have been lurking in the café
doorway waiting for customers, 'I was
hoping to see you again. Did you have a good
Chrissie?'

I looked round – no sign of Hugh Grant.
Damn. No sign of anyone. Actually, the place
was empty.

'How was the holiday?'

'What?'

'The one we booked together last time you were
here – Caribbean, wasn't it? You know, the vaca-
tion you refused to take me on!' He laughed,
snorted in fact, at his own 'joke'.

'Oh that,' I wasn't sure I could go through with
this after all, not without punching him anyway.

'I didn't go in the end. Could I have a decaff semi-skimmed latte, please?'

'No, really? You didn't go?' He looked genuinely disappointed as he ducked down through the gap in the counter, but was grinning again by the time he popped up on the other side. Did he not recognize bad news when he heard it? 'What happened?!'

'I er, well, I went somewhere else. Actually, make that a full-fat cappuccino. With caffeine. And lots of chocolate on the top.'

'Ah yeah?' He carefully selected a mug – this one said 'No Worries', and had a picture of a bloody koala on it, smiling. Jeez, the cheese. 'Where'd you go instead?'

To the loony bin. 'To a health farm,' I said instead, 'a really expensive one.'

'Yuk,' he said, as he fiddled around behind the counter, 'I hate those bloody places.'

How funny, I wanted to say, so do I. But I didn't.

'We were really busy here over Christmas,' he said, as if I might be interested, 'rushed off our feet.'

'Were you,' I said, flatly.

'No,' he replied, 'we weren't. I'd have shut up the shop completely, if it hadn't been for Keith.'

'Keith?' How long did it take one man to make a coffee?

'Yeah, y'know, the bloke who comes in every lunchtime, and I mean every single arvo.' I looked blank. 'Afternoon. He even got me to open up on

193

Christmas Day for him! I think he was sitting next to you the last time you were here . . .' He opened a carton of milk up, and smelled it.

'Oh, *Keith*!' Hugh Grant! 'Oh yes, him.' Keith? Keith?! What an ugly name for such a handsome man. 'Yes, of course, Keith! Er, how is he?' I asked casually, as Oz threw away that carton of milk and opened another.

'I dunno,' he wasn't paying enough attention to my question, he was trying to find a teaspoon instead, 'Keith's a quiet sort of bloke, keeps himself to himself. I don't like to bother the customers too much' – there was that inane grin again – 'unless they're beautiful, like you!' I ignored him. 'OK then, what are you going to do today, d'you need some help?' He handed me my coffee and led me over to a computer.

Could I remember even one thing he'd taught me last time? No. Did I (a) immediately confess to this and ask nicely for his assistance, not forgetting to add 'please' and a smile; or did I (b) get into an even worse electronic pickle than the time before, run to the loo for an implosion of frustration followed by a quick cry, only to discover on my return that he'd drawn up a chair beside mine and fixed it for me.

'OK, Charlotte,' he'd even remembered my name, 'she'll be right now.'

'Thanks.'

But he didn't go, he stayed there. I could feel myself beginning to panic again.

194

'Anything I can help you with?'

'Well, I'm here to find out about – it's just that – actually, it doesn't really matter any more, I . . .' To my horror, I couldn't get over myself enough to spit it out.

I took a deep breath.

'The thing is, I've got a question, which I think the super internet highway thing could answer.'

'Right-o.' He looked right into my eyes, making things much worse than they already were. I had to look away, his light was too bright. 'Are you OK today? You look a bit rough . . .'

'Thanks very much.'

'No, y'know – just a bit . . .' he was studying my face too closely so I studied the blank screen too closely, 'well, down, fed up, y'know. Are you crook?' Again, I looked blank. 'Sick?'

'No, I'm not, thanks, I'm fine,' I said, bottom lip a bit quivery, 'now then, can we get on?'

'You sure?' His voice softened. 'Are you sure you're OK?'

It was his fault, he asked me twice.

God, it was awful. I had a major emotional meltdown, right there in the internet café, spilling my guts to a virtual stranger. I felt helpless in the face of his kindness. Oh, the shame. If there had been a cliff nearby, I would have thrown myself off it.

In between bouts of uncontrollable sobbing, I told him the hideous truth about Christmas, and Sabrina dumping me, and the clinic, and my parents moving in, and just a little bit about Joe, and how it was his fault for sending Amber the card as I was nearly fine before that and the poor man just sat there, handing me paper napkins and nodding from time to time, expressing sympathy and anger and outrage and kindness at all the right moments. And of course the nicer he was, the worse I became.

Thankfully an actual customer came in, which gave me the chance to pull myself together. Having tended to her (an old lady looking for the butcher's) Oz arrived with another coffee and a more business-like air, and said, 'Right then, what's this question you have for the wonderful world wide web?' There was that big smile again. 'I love to surf,' he said. (That much was obvious, although I couldn't think why he needed to tell me that now.)

It seemed pointless to lie. I'd been planning on telling him that I was a famous author who was writing a book that I needed to research, but now I realized that if it was true he'd think it odd I didn't have my own computer. So I just came out with it.

'My question is,' I took a deep breath, which unfortunately turned into one of those great big shudders you get after you've been crying at school, 'well, I just want to see what happens, you know, if you ask the computer, um, something like "what is lve".' I swallowed the last word, hoping that he hadn't heard it.

But he had. 'Wow,' he looked at me, surprised but strangely impressed, 'Cool. Sounds like you need to Google!'

'Whatever,' I prepared myself for some sort of strange computery goings-on as I stared at the screen, quite keen to get started now, 'Shall we?' I blew my nose on a paper napkin as he typed in the question.

'Are you feeling lucky?' he asked, nudging me so hard I nearly fell off my chair.

'Certainly not!' I retorted with indignation, realizing too late what had prompted him to ask.

Almost immediately, lots of 'stuff' came up on the screen. Oz began to laugh. 'Crikey,' he said (disappointingly, as I'd always thought Australians said 'strewth') 'look at that. They've found 119,000,000 results in 0.25 seconds. Wow . . .' He gazed in awe at the screen. 'Don't you just adore the internet?' he asked, eyes wide with wonder, face lit up like a small boy in a sweetshop.

'Web definition' it said at the top: '***Love – a strong positive emotion of regard and affection.** "His love for his work"; "children need a lot of love".*' You're telling me. In fact, that reminded me, it was nearly time to pick. Amber up from school.

The irrepressible Oz was more excited about this project than I was. I was still covered in shame about bursting into tears in a public place, and as I left the café he was promising to have sorted all the information into a researchable order by tomorrow morning.

Yeah, right. Like I was ever going to go back there again.

★   ★   ★

197

'G'day, Charlotte!' chirped Oz. 'How are ya?'

It was somewhere around lunchtime the following day, I think, and Hugh Grant was in his usual seat.

'Wow, you look great!' said Oz, taking me in with his eyes, which made me feel even more uncomfortable than I was already feeling. 'Fantastic! Cool . . .' He was clearly impressed.

So was I. For the first time since leaving the clinic, I'd made an effort with my appearance. Well, I'd washed my hair, and put a bit of make-up on, and found some clean clothes. Not for any particular reason, you understand, I just felt like it, that's all.

'I'll sit here, shall I?' I asked, taking up what was going to be my usual seat from now on, next to the only other customer, oh gosh, Hugh Grant, who was glued to the screen. 'Hi,' I smiled my best. He didn't look up. He didn't have to – his profile was handsome enough. Oh wow.

'D'you want a coffee?' Oz called over, from behind the bar.

'I'll have a hazelnut mocha with a shot of vanilla, thanks!' I called back, hoping to sound as sophisticated as I wanted to be.

I took off my coat and hung it on the back of the chair. I couldn't quite see what Hugh Grant was doing on his computer, but it was clearly very absorbing. He didn't even look up when I brushed his arm with the sleeve of my coat, completely by accident.

Fortunately, I could remember how to start things up. But before I could, Oz was at my side clutching a sheaf of papers. 'I went through all that info,' he said, 'here's the results. It's 50p a print-out normally, but because it's you . . .'

Well. He must have been up all night – he'd printed out and sorted through about 300 of the 1,000 results, putting a line through the ones that were repeated or no good for one reason or another.

It turns out that lots of people had decided to call their websites 'I love so-and-so' – you can fill in the blank with 'cats' and 'dogs' (obviously), or 'the outdoors' and 'cheese' (fair enough), or 'calculus' and 'the Iraqi information minister' (bizarre). There was one for Oz, *www.ilovetheweb.com*, and one for me *www.ilovemymum.com*, and there should have been one for Hugh Grant *www.ilovenobodye-noughtonoticethem.com*.

But the most sites by far were dedicated to lonely hearts, and dating agencies, and romance – which probably explained the big grin on Oz's face. After nearly an hour of watching me surf the net (I had all the technical terms at my fingertips now, quite literally) he came over and said far too loudly, 'By the way, if it's a bloke you're looking for, I could probably help you there.' And he winked, horribly.

Fortunately Hugh Grant stood up at that point, gathered his things up, paid and left, which gave my blush enough time to die down to bright red.

'I am not a lonely heart!' I explained, as soon

as the café door had banged shut behind him. 'The last thing I want right now is a boyfriend.'

(This was one of those rare moments when you don't know what you mean until you're saying it, and then it makes perfect sense. A chance to impress yourself with your clear thinking, even if you had no idea you felt like that until you heard yourself saying it right then.)

'I want to find out about all sorts of different kinds of love and how to bring them into your whole life, you see, not just the romantic part. It's not just about finding a man, you know, in fact I suspect it's more about *not* finding a man.' Wow, that was brilliant.

'Wow, that's brilliant,' he said. 'Look, I don't mean to be kind of weird or freaky, but can I help you with this? It's just that – well, it's a really interesting idea and I feel kind of involved with it now, and I'm not exactly busy . . .'

'Er, well, um – yes, I suppose so.' Excellent! He could do all the boring bits for me. We agreed that I'd come in for an hour a day if I could spare the time (hilarious – like I had anything else to do) and he'd do any work required in between. Outwardly I was a bit reluctant at such commitment, but inwardly I was thrilled – this gave me a legitimate reason to see Hugh Grant every day, get to know him, marry him, have his babies, live happily ever after.

'But,' and I have no idea where I got the courage to say this from, it just sort of popped out, 'I have to tell you that we are never going to be an item, do you understand?'

'An item?' He looked confused.

'Together – you know, romantically linked. Partners, dating, that sort of thing.' I thought it best to spell it out. 'We are never going to be boyfriend and girlfriend, OK?'

'Aw yeah, right,' he looked confused as he picked up my empty coffee cup, which had a boomerang for a handle. 'Oh!' the realization was slow but sweet, 'did you think, when I said I could fix you up, that I meant me? Oh no!' he laughed, too much, 'I meant my mate Craig. I've already got a very beautiful lady of my own, thanks. Although,' a shadow glanced across his face, 'she gave me a right bucketing this morning. Still,' his face brightened up again, 'she'd better behave herself, eh? I know where to find a new girlfriend now, don't I? Plenty of the women gagging for it on the internet!' And clutching the sheaf of internet research close to his chest, he walked off towards the bar, chuckling to himself.

I left the café feeling good that we'd got that out in the open. I was relieved. And shocked. Oz was a total twat, what woman in her right mind would go out with him?

Why do we fancy the men who don't fancy us, and vice versa?

How often have you wished you could take it further with so-and-so, who has everything you're looking for with a partner, but you can't because you just don't fancy him?

Similarly, if you do manage to get hold of that sexxxy man, why is it so disappointing to discover as soon as you step one foot out of the bed that you've got nothing in common?

(Obviously, it's a good idea to wait until you meet someone who ticks both boxes, but how often do they come along in a girl's lifetime?)

To me, it is the ultimate romantic conundrum.

I heard somewhere that women grow to fancy the men they love, and men grow to love the women they fancy. I've never been in a relationship long enough to find out if that's true.

In this case, for example, Oz fancies me, but I fancy Hugh Grant. Chances are Oz will turn out to be a darling, and Hugh Grant will turn out to be an arse. So do I become friends with Oz on the offchance that one day I'll fancy him, or do I throw myself at Hugh Grant on the offchance that one day he'll fancy me? Or do I carry on waiting until someone comes along who ticks both boxes, like Joe?

I suppose the answer is wait and see.

Grr.

Arthur and Jimmy turned up at 7 o'clock in the morning to cook Sunday lunch.

(This was a Big Day in our house, my mother had talked of nothing else, she was so looking forward to 'having someone else cook, for a change'. Dad and I were actually capable of cooking – we just weren't allowed to, that's all.)

They reeked of booze and smoky nightclubs and sweaty dancing, and their eyes were like spinning saucers, the Ecstasy was still whooshing round their bodies. 'We're still out from the night before!' they declared as they swept past me and into the kitchen, carrying several stiff-looking carrier bags filled with posh delicacies from pricey deli-catessens in central London. The gay lifestyle had come west.

'What are you making?' I asked, as I bundled them into the kitchen and tried to shut the door as quietly as possible.

'Well!' said Arthur, who had flushed apple-pink cheeks, being in love suited him, 'we're having aubergine slices with pomegranate juice and mint to start . . .'

'. . . then for the main course it's ham with black treacle and pineapple glaze . . .' Jimmy provided.

'. . . and rhubarb, Muscat and mascarpone trifle for pudding!'

Oh dear. 'Lovely!' I said, trying to think how to put this. 'Um, my parents are quite plain eaters, you know.' And so was I now, it sounded disgusting.

'Ooh, we do know, yes,' said Arthur, who was wearing a 70s 'retro' (only we knew he'd had it all along) black velvet jacket with a thread of silver glitter running through it, giving him more than a hint of Liberace, 'we experienced your mum's cooking when we were doing the house up, didn't we, Jimmy?'

Jimmy mimed somebody dying a grisly death from food poisoning, which Arthur seemed to find very funny. 'We had to bring our own sandwiches in every day! We pretended we were on the Wilkins diet,' he laughed at Jimmy's antics, apparently helpless, 'which we told them was the gay version of the Atkins diet, can you imagine?!'

I could.

'And bless 'em, they believed us, didn't they, Jimmy?'

'Yes, Martha, they did,' simpered Jimmy, basking in the spotlight of his lover's gaze.

'D'you know, Charlotte,' Arthur continued, 'your parents are much nicer than I was expecting them to be. Honestly, you are naughty, you'd made them sound like a couple of monsters, and they're pussycats really. We thought they were fabulous, didn't we, Jimmy?'

'Loved them,' replied Jimmy, looking at me as if I got everything wrong all the time, 'really thought they were fabulous.'

'Especially your mother,' continued Arthur as he unpacked some very expensive-looking cheese, 'what an amazing woman. We had such a laugh with her, didn't we, and my god is she strong, a real *tour de force*, everything a woman should be. We loved her, didn't we, Jim?' We nodded. 'And she absolutely adores you, she was very worried, y'know, about –'

'Look, I'm going back to bed,' I said, 'is it OK if I leave you to it?'

'It most certainly is not!' retorted Arthur. 'We're still pissed, we're off our tits, love, we can't possibly do all this by ourselves.'

'We'll watch, if you like,' offered Jimmy, 'tell you what to do. Look, we brought the book with us specially!' He lumped out a big thick Nigella and slammed it down on the table.

In case you didn't know, the trouble with gay men is that they are control freaks, every single one of them. And better than you at everything. I had no idea until then that I am crap with an aubergine, worse with a pomegranate, and it seems I can't even cut up the humble mint leaf properly.

Eventually, after too much heckling and hiccupping from the audience, I slammed the knife down on the chopping board and burst into tears of frustration and rage and self-loathing. 'I can't! I just can't do this! I hate bloody cooking and I hate bloody Nigella and I hate bloody you two for making me do what you said you would do and then you come round here and you've got no intention of doing it and you're treating me like your slave and it's still the middle of the night as far as I'm concerned and you can all fuck off, the lot of you!'

There was silence after that, and Arthur and Jimmy exchanged a look and an 'oooOOOoooh!' in that 'she's having a queenie fit' handbags-at-dawn way. As one, they stood up and sat me down, barely able to conceal their delight – they'd been itching to take over since I began.

Jimmy threw away my feeble attempts and produced a spare pomegranate from a bag – it was as if they'd known this would happen – while Arthur made me a cup of tea and put one of my father's classical compilation CDs on, 'for purposes of soothe' he said. (Mother only liked Neil Sedaka.)

Things calmed down a bit after that, until Arthur settled himself beside me at the table and said 'so – found a job yet?'

'Don't you bloody start,' I muttered into my mug, 'I'm not well enough to work.'

'You should register for Disability Allowance then,' said Jimmy as he banged the outside half of the pomegranate with a wooden spoon, the blender beneath catching the little red 'rubies', as Nigella calls them. (Honestly, what a palaver, can't you buy it ready-juiced?)

'Listen, I know I don't feel very well but I'm hardly in a wheelchair!' I scoffed.

'He's got a point, you know,' said Arthur, whose common sense had clearly been taken away by the In-Love Fairy, 'you could at least sign on, Charlotte.'

'What d'you mean, sign on?!' I was outraged. 'Like an unemployed person, you mean? Take money for doing nothing? No thank you – I've never sponged off the state and I'm not going to start now.' (I'd always felt very strongly about this, not only because I thoroughly disapproved, but also because it would mean asking for help, which had always been a question too far for me.)

'But they'll give you some money, a fresh start . . .' said Arthur, gently. 'That's what they're there for, you should use them – why not?'

'Because I can handle this myself!' I spluttered, knowing as I said the words that it was obvious to everyone, including me, that I couldn't. 'I've always managed up till now . . .' I trailed off.

'Charlotte, darling – if you keep doing what you've been doing, then you'll only get the same results,' said Arthur, squeezing my hand sympathetically.

'That's the true definition of madness!' announced Jimmy, stirring. Who died and made him the Dalai bloody Lama?

'Look, why don't you just find out about it?' asked Arthur, the stale alcohol on his breath wafting across the kitchen table. He was trying to be sober, but he didn't fool me, I knew him too well.

'Look, why don't you just mind your own business?' I replied, in a similar tone.

He sat back in his seat and folded his arms, exasperatedly. 'Because your dad asked me to talk to you about it, that's why.'

I opened my mouth to protest, but he continued.

'No! Don't be angry, we're just trying to help you, Charlotte, that's all. I can't bear to see you like this, I want you back – where's my big powerful friend gone, the woman who refused to be beaten?'

'I don't know,' I whispered, not wanting Jimmy to hear me, 'I don't know.' As the classical music swelled to crescendo, I swallowed the big lump in my throat and mouthed, 'I'm scared.' My hand flew to my mouth; I couldn't believe I'd said it.

'I know,' he sympathized back. We squeezed each other's hand and had a little weep, a secret one, just between us.

Or so we thought. 'I've been on benefits, loads of times!' announced Jimmy, with all the delicacy of a lumberjack. 'It's really easy, piece of piss.' Nice. 'Well, it's what we pay our taxes for, isn't it?' Like he'd ever paid tax. Like I ever had either, come to think of it, I'd been strictly a cash-only employee.

'It's worth finding out about, Charlotte, surely?' yawned Arthur, the night's activities coming back now to haunt him, 'they might just be able to help you get back on your feet. And let's face it,' he drew nearer, hushed his tone, the breath was even worse close up, 'the sooner you get yourself the right way up again, the sooner your parents will bugger off!' He yawned again, and stood up to stretch. 'How much longer, Jimmy? I'm starving. And I can't wait to get you home to bed . . .' They lurched lasciviously towards each other, managing somehow to kiss during the bump.

In the end, I shut them up by agreeing to at least think about investigating the possibility of maybe going down there to pick up a few leaflets, perhaps.

Lunch was a triumph. My family didn't necessarily want to eat it at half past ten on a Sunday morning, but nobody said anything. Not even me.

I'd been there once before, when I was still foolish enough to think that the Child Support Agency would be able to get some money out of Joe.

It was awful, a big dark building known locally as The Lubyanka, with the obligatory drug addicts hanging about outside, begging for money, harassing people. I had to stand for over two hours in the queue to be seen, only to be told I was in the wrong line, so then I was sent to another part of the building, to sit on a really filthy sofa in a holding area with handwritten notices on the walls saying things like 'Please Leave Your Weapons At Reception'.

There were screaming kids everywhere, being slapped by scary mothers, the sort who give babies bottles of tea. And after all that, by the time I was at the head of the line, the woman I needed to see was at lunch. Everyone there looked so depressed, really demoralized, just – well, grey. I got so pissed off with it all, I just walked out in the end, and never went back. (I'd regretted it later, of course, as it meant my case was immediately closed, never to be renegotiated, but – well, that's what I was like then.)

As you know, all Good Intentions and diets start on a Monday, and so the next day I found myself standing outside that DHSS building once more, willing, but furious. 'Offices to Let' said the huge billboard outside, 'Security Patrolled Premises' said the boards over the windows, and some graffiti artist with a sense of humour had drawn a different disguise on to each of the Alsatian dogs depicted underneath.

There was a notice stuck on the front door, giving details of where they'd moved to, but as I wasn't familiar with this part of town I didn't have a clue where that was.

Well, at least I came here, I said to myself as I pulled my coat tightly around me and perched on the soggy bench right outside and lit a sneaky cigarette, at least I can tell them I tried.

'Ow bloody 'ell!' screeched a loud female voice as it arrived at the entrance. 'They've moved already, 'ave they?!' she asked me. I was shocked at the intrusion, I wasn't expecting to talk to anyone I didn't know today.

The woman in front of me was – well, a vision.

This was a fatter person who dressed like a thinner one. She was wearing fuchsia pink peep-toe strappy stilettos, in this weather, tired be-bunioned feet with metallic toenail polish bursting out through the spaces between the straps, which looked most uncomfortable; her obviously fake-tanned thick legs were being held together by a pair of too-tight Burberry print calf-length trousers; and she wasn't, like me, wrapped up warm against the winter chill, but dressed for spring instead in just a flimsy lemon velour hoodie with diamanté butterfly trim. She clearly thought her bosoms were her best asset as no attempt had been made to disguise their hugeness; a skimpy turquoise T-shirt was struggling to contain them, its flashy gold D&G logo stretched and badly distorted across her chest. It looked as if she had a couple of puppies stuck in her bra, and they were desperately struggling to get out.

Not only was her squashy belly-button pierced, but so were her ears, with lots of gold hoops up each side. She had enough make-up on for two nightclub singers and a stripper, and her greasy dyed blonde hair (with roots that would have put an eighties Madonna to shame) was scraped back into a high ponytail held back with a fake fur scrunchie, completely inappropriate for a woman of her age which, thinking about it, was probably the same as mine. She wasn't beautiful, and she wasn't pretty, but she'd 'made the most of herself', as my mother would say. It was a strong look, and a hideous one. She looked like a wannabe foot-baller's wife. On acid.

'They moved to the new place already, 'ave they?' she asked me, as if I was the world expert on the Relocation of Government Offices in the London Area.

'S'pose so,' I muttered, wishing she would go away, 'it's all on the door.'

She wheeled her buggy containing two dozing brown babies up to the door and studied the notice. 'Oh, that's OK,' she shouted over her shoulder at me, 'it's only round the corner. We can trek it, you comin'?'

It was assumed that I was, and once she'd gathered up a carrot-topped child (called Rev, for some reason, but he didn't look particularly religious to me) from the huge puddle he was jumping in and out of, we were all making our way round the corner to the new building.

'I'm Gloria Bean,' she said, over the clatter of the click-clacking her heels were making on the pavement. 'What's your name, love?'

'Charlotte,' I said, rather stiffly, assuming that my upper-middle-class British boarding school accent would show her the difference between us. 'My name is Charlotte Small.'

It did. 'What you going in 'ere for then? You don't seem the type.'

'I'm just gathering some information. I,' I drew myself up, 'am a single parent, actually.'

'Are ya? Join the club!' beamed Gloria, excited

at probably the only thing we had in common. She was really far too friendly. 'Fucked off, did they?'

'Who?'

'The fathers.'

I tried to stay nice. 'I only have one child, and she only has one father.'

'Oh right, sorry.' Her little boy said he was thirsty; without missing a step, Gloria scrabbled about in her Louis Vuitton bag (white background, multi-coloured logos, as sold by Africans on beaches) and gave him a box drink, which she had somehow strawed with only one hand. Clearly this woman was a professional – I still hadn't mastered that technique, and Amber was nearly nine. This was all the more amazing if you took her fingernails into account – they were long, very long, like curved talons, and painted in leopardskin. 'I've got six in all.'

'Six children?' I was aghast at the thought of giving birth six times.

'Yeah, thassit – my eldest is twenty-four and these two are six months. I can't stop avin' babies – I must be mad, eh, Rev?' She threw her head back and roared, it was one of those traffic-stopping full-blown m'hearty flirty pub laughs; a man in a white van bipped his horn at us, grinning as he passed.

She waved back in an all-are-welcome way. 'Cheeky bugger!' she said through her smile.

'Is that why you're going to the Benefit Office, then?' I ventured. 'To get money for the children?'

'Well, sort of. I'd explain it to ya but – well, this is your first time, innit?'

'Yes.' And last, if I had anything to do with it.

'It's a bit complicated, y'know. You've got to know what you're applying for, and whether that will affect what you've got already. Sometimes one benefit cancels out another, see? The trick is to learn how to play the system, and not let it play you.' She smiled at me. 'Don't you worry, s'easy when you know how!'

'Right.' It sounded awful. I tried not to sound patronizing, but she needed some guidance. 'What about getting a job?'

'Ooh no, not me!' Gloria laughed. 'Why would I want to do that? I've got kids to look after, innit!' She tutted. 'And don't tell me to get a childminder neither. I don't agree with this mums-going-to-work bollocks. They're my kids, and no one's going to bring 'em up right like me, see?'

I did see. We chatted a bit more along the way, and despite myself, I warmed to her. A bit.

Ah, the benefit of hindsight! I didn't know it then, but this woman was about to change my life. One of Dr L's favourite horribilisms was about HOW to change by being Honest, Open and Willing – Gloria Bean helped me to be all three.

She was one of those people you just wanted to be around; when you hung out

214

with Gloria, you knew everything was going to be OK. She was a safe place to be, a soft place to land. She had a huge heart as well as a huge arse – she'd been knocked off her feet many times, but she'd always stood up again straight away and carried right on, dealing with life on life's terms, seldom thinking any further ahead than one day at a time.

She wasn't just any old common-or-garden cockney-sparrer tart-with-a-heart, though, oh no. Gloria had some pretty funny rules, and God help you if you broke them. And she had a completely unique moral code. For example: Gloria was happy to provide plenty of false information to the state benefit system, but if one of her kids told even a little white lie, they would be punished for it straight away. It was fine for her to gossip about other people, but if you said something even slightly unfavourable about a friend of hers she'd yell at you for it. If money was tight, she would think nothing of stealing a large box of soap powder from the supermarket; but if one of the kids had helped themselves to a pound coin from her purse, she'd go mad at them. And yet she'd give herself freely – every Wednesday afternoon she did hair-dressing at the retirement home at the end of her street, but she never charged them a penny. And she didn't tell me that, someone else did.

It was pretty confusing at first, but once you'd worked out what was acceptable and what wasn't. The World of Gloria Bean made sense. It was a soup of do-as-you-would-be-done-by mixed with give-when-you-can-take-when-you-have-to, seasoned with a pinch of looking-after-me-and-mine. It's a different way of doing things, but it works. They should teach her in schools.

I didn't know all this when I was walking along the road with her that day, of course. But I felt as if I was being gently guided along a path by someone who had walked it before me. I liked that feeling.

'Well I never, this must be it! Posh, innit? Amazing what they can do with taxpayers' money, when they put their minds to it . . .' We were standing outside an imposing architect-designed glass building, quite the cutting edge of office blocks. Gloria was fiddling in her shoulder bag, a gaudy Gucci number, which I assumed to be fake (but later found out was real, Gloria was a big fan of designer handbags); I ventured a smile at Rev, who scowled back.

'Now then, what's your phone number? Write it down for me, love.' She handed me a pen and the back of an official-looking envelope. 'Here – you take my card,' she said, giving me one of those thin pastel-shaded business cards you can get printed cheaply in Safeways, 'you call me if you want any help, all right? And remember, don't agree to anyfink they offer you without talking to me first – oi, you! Come 'ere!' She caught Rev just as he was about to run out into the traffic. 'Say goodbye to Char then!' she commanded.

I winced. I just wasn't a 'Char', was I?

'Bye, Char,' said the little boy, shyly, head hanging down.

'There's a good little boy!' Gloria cuffed him playfully on the back of his head and grabbed the buggy. 'See ya!' she said, and disappeared through the newfangled revolving door, expertly inter-cepting little Rev before he managed to go round again.

I stood outside the building and lit a cigarette, while I thought about what to do next. I was a bit discombobulated, this wasn't what I'd been expecting. Instead of drug addicts hanging around outside begging, there were cheerful-looking people handing out leaflets for a free Valentines Dance taking place in the Town Hall the next weekend. The sun had come out to turn the day from a cold grey one into a crisp white one, and people were sitting on the benches outside sipping coffee, eating a sandwich, having a chat. This was an urban planner's dream come true; not what I'd been expecting at all.

I was free to leave, but I didn't. As I stood outside that building, I knew I had a choice. I could either go in, and get some money and/or a job, and do things differently, which meant being willing to ask for help and support, and even worse, receive it; or I could go home and continue with what I'd been doing, which meant relying on my parents for as long as I could whilst waiting for something to happen, which it no doubt would eventually, but what and when?

I'd already thought about this a thousand times but, what the hell, let's go down that path one more time.

I'd been hoping Joe's Christmas card to Amber was an indication that he was about to come back to us. In fact, I'd got another of his irritatingly cryptic postcards this morning – this one just had a question mark on it. And it was posted in London. But what would he find, if he were to turn up on the doorstep tomorrow? A broken woman, who couldn't even look after her own child. Not a good look, as Sabrina would say. He probably wouldn't want to stay.

And what if he never came for us, and I'd spent all this time just waiting, not getting on with my life? How foolish would I feel in the old people's home, saying, 'I was waiting for a man to rescue me, but he never turned up. I'm only here because both my parents have died now, and I don't seem to be able to look after myself.' The other residents would be sure to have lots of entertaining stories – what would I have to tell them about? Would I be sitting there sucking my rice pudding in silence, full of regret that I never did anything worth mentioning?

A couple of giggling girls walked past me; one of them was clutching a brochure with the word 'College' on it. Aha! New thought: I could always train for something. But what? An elderly Indian man got up from the bench beside me to greet his friend and they went into the building together. As I sat down in the space he'd left, a voice in my head said, *You're only halfway through your life, it's not over yet.*

I sat there, listening to my thinking, until I got a cold bum. By the time I got up, I knew that it was time to reinvent myself. By the time I was going through the revolving door, I'd decided that I was worth saving after all, that I'd give myself a chance to show Joe and the rest of the world what I was capable of. (As they say, the best revenge is living well.) Sod it, I decided to go for it, whatever 'it' is!

I remember that day very clearly. That was definitely a 'Biography Moment'.

It's a great feeling, Doing Something About It. Call it what you like, 'taking action', or 'getting with the programme' – boy, it feels good. I treated myself to going round in the revolving door twice, and sprang out of that place, positively skipping down the street. I felt as if I had been relieved of my burden of 'should's and 'must's and internal wagging fingers, and was now someone who was joining in with life, who had a chance at last.

Ridiculous really – all I'd done was pick up lots of brightly coloured leaflets and booklets and brochures, and I'd printed off loads of possible jobs from a touchscreen computer. And I'd even shown the two ladies next to me how to use it, they'd been very grateful. It really couldn't have been any easier, there were even free telephones plugged into the wall if you wanted to call about a job right now, but I thought I'd have a look at everything once I'd got home. Yes, this felt good, Charlotte Small was back in the driving seat.

'Hi, Mum!' Amber came out of school clutching a great big folder full of artwork, and something made out of clay which had been painted many colours. 'We get to bring this home today, isn't it great?!'

Normally I'd have muttered something about having to lug it around and why they couldn't just keep it at school I didn't know, but today I somehow managed to keep my mouth shut and pretended instead to be interested in what she'd done. 'This is great,' I said, referring to the thing of clay as we waited at the bus stop, 'it's really – great, Amber, well done.'

She smiled proudly. 'I know.'

I was feeling so full of the milk of human kindness, I even managed a nod and a half smile to another mother in the bus queue. She didn't return my good wishes, I'd obviously pissed her off in the past. Oh well.

'D'you really like it, Mum?'

For God's sake. 'Yes! I really love – the colours, Amber, good choice.'

'Thanks.' Her eyes narrowed at me. 'Are you sure?'

'Yes, Amber, it's great, really great.' Why on earth was my approval so important to her?

Our bus arrived.

'Really really?'

'Amber! Stop it.'

We sat on the top deck, as usual. (We liked looking into the flats above the shops, as at this time of day the lights were on but they hadn't drawn the curtains yet. Amber and I were nosey people.)

'I made it for you,' she said.

'Did you? Thanks. I'll put it with the others.' In a box under my bed, 'for safe keeping' I'd told her. Well, they were too hideous to put on display. I mean you just couldn't –

'You don't like it, do you?'

No, of course I don't. 'Yes, of course I do!' Get off my case!

'What is it then?'

Ah.

'You don't know what it is, do you?'

'Of course I do, it's obvious!'

'So what is it then, Mum?'

Torn between telling the truth and not hurting her feelings, I said, 'Let's get off here – I want you to meet a friend of mine.'

Oz was glued to a computer, it looked like he'd been there all night. 'This is just such a cool project, I've turned up all sorts of stuff – oh, hi there!' He turned his full beam on to Amber. 'I didn't know you had a beautiful sister, Charlotte!'

She giggled, I didn't. 'Why are you wearing shorts when it's winter?' she asked. I hadn't even noticed, but he was sporting a large pair of baggy Bermudas, with big blue and white flowers, and those awful plastic sandals with embroidered Velcro bars across the foot, fortunately without socks. 'Aren't you freezing?'

'No, I'm not freezing,' he replied, 'but I am cool . . .'

Amber giggled, I could tell she liked him. 'But why are you wearing them now?'

'I dunno – I always do. It's part of the café's look, I suppose – and I don't like wearing strides if I can possibly help it.'

'Strides? What are they?' she asked.

'Strides? See, that's ocker for trousers.'

'What's ocker?'

'Ocker? Don't tell me you don't know what an ocker is? That's incredible, you'd think a sticky beak like you would know something like that, wouldn't ya, Mum?' He winked at me.

'What's a sticky beak?'

'I just can't believe you don't know what a sticky beak is, you being the daughter of a whingeing pom an' all . . .' He led her over to the bar and perched her up on a stool. 'Fancy some tucker? I could throw a couple of snags on the barbie if you like, we could shoot a couple of tinnies maybe, once you've been to the dunny of course . . .' As he laid on the comedy Down Underisms with a trowel, and Amber became more and more entranced, I leafed through Oz's printouts of his research.

He'd fed the word 'love' into various 'search engines' (no need to applaud, thanks), which had come up with all sorts of nonsense. There were hundreds of 'are you in love?' questionnaires to be filled in, and thousands of love poems to be sighed at, and millions of lonely hearts to be married off.

He'd done lots more undoubtedly fascinating research too, but, to be honest, I just wasn't that interested. I was only here to stop Amber from asking me awkward questions and to stop Oz from thinking I only ever came in at lunchtime, when Hugh Grant was there.

'Hey, Oz,' I called over, 'this is great, well done! Fascinating, all of it. Really, really interesting. Any chance of you just telling me what you've found out, as we're a bit pushed for time?'

But Oz was totally absorbed. He was going through Amber's art folder, genuinely and appreciatively, complete with appropriate 'ooh's and 'ah's and 'bonzer's. How did he do that? I wondered; whenever I tried it just sounded sarcastic. I wasn't very good at faking sincerity.

I suppose the difference was that he really meant it. He really did seem to think her artwork was just that, works of art. He even asked if he could put a couple of her paintings up on the wall of the Down Undernet Café.

Now a nice person would be pleased that Amber and Oz were forging a friendship, especially as her dad was out of the picture. But not me. I was immediately jealous of his instant rapport with her, and so I went to the Ladies to have a word with myself. And whoever was listening Up There. A small part of me just didn't want him stealing her from right under my nose, like I felt my mother had – I wanted her to myself. She was mine. But a larger part knew that this was the healthier option for Amber, she shouldn't be relying on me for everything. But there again . . . ooh, I was really getting on my own nerves. I stood up and flushed the loo and told myself to shut up and get on with it. By the time I came back, Amber was beaming from ear to ear.

'Here,' she said, handing Oz the piece of prize pottery, 'what d'you think of this?' She looked at me, to check my reaction. I managed to keep my face in neutral.

He studied it closely, held it right up to his eyes. Scrutinized it. Shook his head, completely foxed. 'What the hell is it?' he asked. How rude! I wanted to kill him.

'It's a habstract,' she announced, proudly. 'It's how I feel, you see.'

She might as well have been showing him Michelangelo's David. 'That's amazing,' said Oz, gravely. 'Amazing. You are a very special little larrikin.'

Having promised Oz I'd be back tomorrow, I dunno, probably around lunchtime, at a guess, we left shortly after that. Amber asked me if we could pop in on Oz after school again. 'I don't see why not,' I said, unaware that I was committing myself to doing this virtually every day from now on. 'Why've you brought all this art stuff home today, anyway?' I asked, as we turned into our road.

'Oh, Mum, don't be silly,' she smiled, 'you know we always bring stuff home at Half Term!'

Half Term?! Was it mid February already? Gosh, doesn't time fly when you're enjoying yourself . . .

My dad had bought Amber the video of *Monsters Inc* as yet another special treat (I didn't mind her being spoilt as long as it wasn't me who was doing it) and so once she was drugged up with that, I went upstairs to my bedroom. I told them I was going to plough through all my leaflets and job opportunities, but really it was to have a nap before supper. It had been a long day, I was exhausted.

My mother had put my phone messages on my

bed, as usual. (They were all written on the backs of old envelopes, which she saved in a big bulldog clip, under the heading of Waste Not Want Not – buying a pad of paper would have been a crime of spendthrifticity.)

There was a record-breaking number from Amira, six or seven I think, none of which I planned to return as it would involve her usual non-stop chatter and I just wasn't in the mood today, and one from 'someone who says her name is Gloria Bean'.

If you had told me yesterday that a common slapper with dodgy designer gear and six children from seven different fathers (more about that later) was going to ring me, I'd have shuddered at the thought. But when I read that she had, my heart did a little skip. I even thought about returning her call, but of course I didn't. She must be so busy, why would she want to speak to me?

And besides, I was very busy too.

Doing nothing.
So far, I'd been very busy achieving nothing. I'd been hoping someone else would achieve it for me. Which was why I had nothing to be busy about.
And yet, if you'd asked me to do something for you, I'd have been far too busy.
Doing nothing.

'Did you get my message, Char?'

'Er, yes.'

'You up for it then?'

'Up for what?'

'The Valentines whatsit, down the Town Hall, Friday night.'

'Er, I don't think so.' The very idea made me nauseous. The thought of dancing in public made my body go into spasms of the wrong kind. 'No thanks, I can't.'

'Why not?'

You can go off people very quickly, can't you? 'Well, because I'm busy.'

'Doing what?'

I'm normally quite good at lying my way out of tricky situations, but for some reason I couldn't think of anything except the truth: 'I've got to fill in all these benefit forms, apply for jobs, update my CV, that sort of thing.' There, that got her.

'Great! You can come round early, I can tell you what's worth getting and what's not, and then we can go out and boogie the night away!'

I had never boogied anything away, and I wasn't going to start now. Just to make that absolutely clear, I said, 'And I've got Amber, of course. I think my parents are out that night . . .' which was true, actually. They still celebrated Valentines, tragically. In fact, I think it was their wedding anniversary.

'Then bring your Amber wiv ya! She's the same age as my Chanel, in't she?' She was. 'Yeah, go on, they'll have a laugh together. And I'll ask old Mrs O'Nions next door to babysit, it'll be cheaper then, we can go halves!'

'Mrs O'Nions?'

'Yeah. Her real name's Onions, but she used to work as a dinner lady so she got teased something chronic about it. So she got a job at another school – thought if she said it differently nobody'd notice. And, can you credit it, they didn't neither – they're all so bloody thick at that Southfields, I wouldn't let my kids near the place . . .'

'Look, Gloria, I really don't think –'

'Oh come on, Char, don't be so bleedin' boring – I'll see you Friday night, about six, OK? The address is on my card, see ya darlin', byeeeee!'

Over the next few days I thought up every possible reason for not going, and every possible excuse to give Gloria when I rang her up to get out of it, but I never quite managed to do that. It turned out that posh and bossy Charlotte Small wasn't brave enough to say 'no' to rough and ready Gloria Bean.

Which is why, that Friday evening, I found myself waiting for a bus to her house. I'd had to bribe Amber to come too, with the promise of a visit to the big Disney Store in central London next weekend. It's quite something to be relying on an eight-year-old for moral support, but as Arthur had whisked Jimmy off to Marrakesh for the weekend, I had no one else to ask.

I had no intention of going to the dance, mind

you, and so I took the precaution of wearing my least disco outfit – tracksuit bottoms, newly shrunk in my mother's boil wash, and what was probably one of the first fleeces ever made. Further inspection of her card revealed that Gloria called herself a beautician! Looking like that! I thought this was hilarious, and was still chuckling about it as I looked for her street.

I'm ashamed to say that I'd assumed someone like Gloria would live on a high-rise tower-block run-down council estate, but she didn't. It was a normal terraced house, very like mine, identical in fact. Only bigger. ('Housing Trust,' she explained later, 'very helpful people. They even paid for the loft conversion – mind you, I had to fight for it.')

But I was most shocked by the woman who answered the door. She had dark poker-straight hair, cut into a Cleopatra style; an over-all tan that shimmered under a very chic simple black dress with a neckline which had stopped plunging at exactly the right moment; a small diamond glinted around her neck and equally subtle earrings showed off a perfectly polished face with just enough make-up to be flattering, but not obtrusive. In short, standing in front of me was what Joe would have called a 'classy bird'.

Who then ruined it by screeching, 'Wotcha, Char! And you must be little Amber, my darlin', your mum's told me all about you!'

'G-Gloria?' I stammered. It couldn't be, could it?

'Yeah?!' She looked at me as if she knew I was

mad. 'Oh, sorry!' she ushered us in, 'I forgot you've only seen me with crap hair – I only do that when I've got to look like White Trash, when I'm going down the social. I grew me roots out specially this time, took me ages.' She smoothed down her glossy hair. 'Good this, innit? It's a wig, in actual fact. I call it me Posh Totty look.' She led us through to the kitchen, at the back of the house. 'I like to dress up, see – I don't like doing the same all the time, that's boring, innit, Amber?' I began to undo my coat, which was difficult as Amber was holding on to my arm with the vice-like grip of the shy child.

'Oh, Char,' said Gloria, spotting my home-leisure outfit, 'you comin' like that?'

I took a deep breath, and said out loud the sentence I'd been practising all day. 'I'm sorry, Gloria, but I'm not going to the dance with you tonight.' There, it was out.

Instead of being cross with me, she seemed to be disappointed. I began to feel like a complete heel, and then I remembered the second sentence. 'But I'm happy to babysit for you instead, for free.'

She brightened up instantly. (Gloria never refused an act of kindness, especially if it wasn't going to cost her anything.) 'Oh, OK then, if you don't mind – Chanel, run next door and tell Mrs O'Nions we don't need her after all, will ya? And take little Amber wiv ya, darlin'.'

Little Amber was terrified of these larger-than-life people. She had to be peeled off my leg – she was clamped to it limpet-style – and only agreed to go once I'd whispered the words 'Cinderella nightie' into her little ear. Chanel, who was beautiful, olive-skinned and inappropriately dressed head-to-toe in up-to-the-minute sex-bomb fashion, beamed a toothy grin and sweetly took Amber's hand as she led her out into the hallway, her little high heels clacking on the wooden flooring as they went.

'You sure you'll be OK here on your own, Char?' asked Gloria, as she flicked the kettle on. It was one of those see-through ones, you could actually see the water boiling. I'd always wanted one but assumed they were too expensive.

I looked around me – the walls were virtually wallpapered with kids' paintings and drawings and school photographs and timetables. Her cupboards had been kicked at and her table had been picked at but there was still an air of spotlessness about the place. A couple of dozing cats were curled up in each other on top of the basket of washing, which was waiting for the previous load to finish. Next door to it the tumble drier was humming with clean heat and fresh laundry. There was tea and toast in the air, it was everything a kitchen should be – the heart of the home.

'Oh yes, I'll be fine, really!' I reassured her, and myself. But I don't think either of us was entirely convinced.

'Well, look, Mrs O'Nions is just next door if you

231

need her. C'mon, I'll show you where everyfink is, while we're waiting for the tea,' said Gloria.

It wasn't the most beautiful home I've ever seen, or indeed the most tasteful, but it was clean and cosy and comfy. It was suspiciously well-furnished, if you like that sort of thing. I assumed (wrongly, as it turned out) that Gloria had a relation who worked at a furniture discount store.

'Oi – get your dirty feet off that settee, now!' Gloria ordered Rev, who was in the 'front room', ensconced on the tan leather sofa, playing some sort of computer game. Without taking his eyes off the screen, he did what he was told, first time. 'I love that computer,' said Gloria, as we left him to it, 'best babysitter I've ever 'ad. He's bloody good at it, an' all. Well, the school says he is – I wouldn't know, I'm not the computer type myself, are you?'

'Well, I never used to be,' I replied, with a shudder, 'but I'm getting better at it now. It's not as hard as it looks. And it can be quite fun. I could show you if you like –'

'Ooh no, not me, thanks!' She laughed. 'Makes me go hot and cold all over, that sorta thing. Ooh no, no.' There was a loud squeal, which came from upstairs. Gloria took off, in hot pursuit. 'Now what's going on up here, what's all this racket about, eh?'

The twins were in the bath. Well, what was left of it – they were playing a very giggly splashing game, and the floor was awash with soapy water and plastic bath toys.

232

'Ah, in't that cute?' Apparently unbothered by the state of the bathroom – I was still a little sensitive about baths and water and floors and ceilings – Gloria gazed lovingly from the doorway at their chubby cheeks and cherub curls. They were classic brown babies, the sort missionaries would want to rescue and keep as their own.

'Can I go out now or what?' said a disembodied voice. We moved further into the room – behind the door sitting in the laundry basket reading *Sugar* magazine was an overweight, spotty teenage girl, one of those poor imitations of J-Lo, the kind you see in shopping malls. She didn't bother to look up.

Gloria's tone changed from doting mother to irritated single parent. 'No, Lori, you can't go out; not until they're in bed. And you're supposed to be watching them, making sure they don't drown, not bloody readin'!' She snatched the magazine away from the teenage girl, who was as shocked as I was at the force with which this was done. Then Gloria dropped it from a great height into the bath – we were aghast.

'Mu-um!' wailed the girl. 'You can't do that, that's not bloody fair! Just because you can't –'

'I think I just did do that, Lori! And you'll watch your mouth, my girl, there's visitors present.' She spoke through gritted teeth, her eyes flashing. 'Now get out of there, before your fat arse breaks it and start looking after them proper or I'm not paying you a penny, OK?'

The girl didn't say anything, but maintained her sulky outlook whilst trying to get out of the basket by flailing her arms and legs around, unsuccessfully.

'You're stuck, intcha?' Gloria did her best to keep a straight face. 'Come on, I'll give ya a hand.'

I watched in silence as they wrestled with each other, both trying desperately not to laugh, and then both cracking up. The twins stopped clapping the bubbles to make it snow, and clambered out of the bath on to the slippy floor to grab hold of their mother's legs, one each. Needless to say, everyone ended up in a heap on the floor, all roaring with laughter, all thinking it was very funny. I'd never seen anything like it. And the look on my face seemed to make them laugh all the more.

'Oh bloody 'ell, I'm going to have to change now!' moaned Gloria, whose dress was soaking wet. 'Right then, Lori, I'm leaving you in charge. C'mon Char!' She led me away from the chaos and up some stairs to the next landing.

'Lori's a nice name,' I said, just for something to say.

'Yeah,' said Gloria, 'I've named all my kids after cosmetics, in actual fact. I thought it would be nice, what with me used to be a beautician, y'know.'

Oh dear. 'So what are they all called, then?' I kind of wanted to know, but didn't, if you know what I mean.

'Well.' We were in Gloria's bedroom now, which was the very opposite of what I'd expected. It was – well, plain and basic. But very modern. The walls were white, the floorboards had been painted white, it was a shrine to minimalism.

Or rather, it should have been.

Despite her best efforts to create a still point in a turning world, Gloria's larger-than-life personality was bursting out of every orifice. Brightly coloured clothing had been unsuccessfully jammed into the chest of drawers which couldn't quite shut; the cupboard door was open just enough to reveal a mountain of excitable shoes, and on top of the cupboard were a series of polystyrene heads, each with a different wig. Gloria sat down at the dressing table, which was covered in make-up and brushes and hairspray and tongs and lots of other unidentifiable gadgets – in short, all the accoutrements of a woman who takes a great interest in her appearance. The opposite of me.

Noticing my roving eye, she asked if I liked her bedroom. Oddly, I could tell she wanted my approval.

'It's lovely, Gloria,' I said, and meant it. It was simple and uncomplicated, but still had plenty of personality. Like her.

She stood up and opened one of the bulging cupboard doors to reveal its contents, which were positively ablaze with colour. How different from my own wardrobe, which consisted mainly of black, dark grey and a bit more black, with some navy blue and two white-ish T-shirts thrown in for a bit of light relief. She chose a similar dress but in red ('I call this my "Danger Woman at Work" outfit, Char – I got it in the sale down Versarchys!') and I averted my gaze as she took off her clothes and told me about her kids.

'Chris – that's Christian, as in Dior, but he prefers to be called just Chris – well, he's twenty-four now. He lives on and off with his girlfriend Lazy Linda, who's a right bloody cow. We don't really see eye to eye; she can't cook, won't clean, nothing like that – makes him do all the work. She won't even get a job! Anyway, don't get me started on 'er, she does my head in, she does. 'Ere, Char, do us up would ya?'

I zipped up the back of the dress, but not without noticing that Gloria had only a g-string on underneath, a sparkly one, a tiny sequinned butterfly straining to hold the string bits together. I'd always wondered what sort of woman wore these cheesewires; now I knew.

She sat down at the dressing table and looked at herself in the mirror, admiringly, unashamedly. She clearly liked what she saw. (I hated looking at my reflection, I've always wanted to look like someone else. Anyone else.) I sat on the bed and watched as she began to repair her - make-up.

'Then there's Lori, you just met her. She's – oh gawd, hang on – yeah, fifteen at the moment, and a right bloody handful. Still at school, just; thinks she should have the lifestyle of a twenty-five-year-old, even though she behaves like she's six. I'm expecting trouble from her when she's older, I can tell ya. When she leaves school she's going to work at the Virgin Megastore, she reckons; not if I have anything to do with it she's not. She's a clever girl, you see, really good at reading and writing an' that lot. I want her to train as a nursery nurse, be one of them really well-paid nannies. I mean, they don't have to like kids, not really, do they?'

'Lori?' I was racking my brains. 'Is there a make-up company called Lori something?'

'Yeah,' Gloria turned to look at me, as if I was a bit thick, 'L'Oréal!'

'Oh yes,' I somehow managed to keep it together, 'of course.'

'Then there's Chanel, who's eight.' She stopped applying mascara to look at me. 'You have heard of Chanel, have you?'

'Oh yes, yes. Wow,' I was in full admiration, 'you look great.'

Gloria had finished her make-up and put her own hair (shoulder-length, dark orange colour, just for today) up in a chignon – she looked really good. Then she ruined it by pulling bits of hair out, making it look like she hadn't finished after all. A final application of something which made her lips wet-look, and she was ready.

I was torn – a part of me was glad I was staying behind, I didn't want to have to stand next to her, as I'd look so awful in comparison. But a bigger part was wishing that I was going with her, I'd forgotten how much I liked her. It's hard to describe, but I sort of forgot myself when I was with Gloria Bean, nothing that mattered seemed to matter that much. I found her totally absorbing.

She stood up. 'Now then, which shoes d'you think, Char?'

I didn't bother to answer, I could tell she was one of those people who knew which pair she was going to wear anyway.

'Then there's little Rev, bless 'im,' she said, taking one gold strappy out of the cupboard, and getting down on her hands and knees to look for the other.

'As in Lon?' I asked. Couldn't be, could it? 'Rev-lon?'

'You got it!' she confirmed, from the depths of the cupboard.

'And your beautiful baby twins, what are they called?' I asked, almost unable to wait for the answer.

'Max and May,' she replied, reversing out of the wardrobe. 'Found it!'

I was frowning.

'Factor and Belline,' she explained, as she wobbled around on one leg.

Of course.

'Listen, Char, if you ever want a make-up lesson or a new look or anything, you will say, won't you?'

'That's very kind, Gloria, but –'

'I wouldn't mind, honest. In fact, I love doing makeovers, they're my favourite. I don't do it as a job no more, just every now and then, for friends. It's great to watch someone be completely changed. You just tell me when you're ready, darlin'.' She swapped her previous earrings for long dangly glittery ones that looked like shooting stars. 'Anyway, it's the least I can do innit, what with you babysitting for nothing tonight, and everything.'

'Thanks, Gloria,' I said as I got off the bed, 'I'll bear that in mind.' That was the nicest I could be; my mind was saying things like 'over my dead body' and 'I'd rather have pins in my eyes than let you anywhere near me', but she needn't know that.

'S'OK!' she said brightly, as she smoothed down the duvet. 'Any time.'

I reckon we both knew back then that it was going to take a little more than a makeover to get me up and running, but Gloria's offer made me feel warm and nuggy inside. I think that's what it was, anyway.

'Right then, wish me luck, Char.' She did a twirl in front of the full-length mirror on the wall, her unrestrained bosoms were on full display. 'Gloria Bean is on the pull tonight, what'ya think?!'

'I think you're mad, that's what I think!' I laughed, to cover my horror. 'You've got six kids already, in case you've forgotten. Surely you're not . . . you are, aren't you!'

She smiled. 'Let's just say, one's too many, six isn't enough, shall we?'

Mad.

It was really bugging me. Why did Gloria's house feel like a home, and mine didn't? Even before Matt's furniture had moved in, my house just hadn't felt right. But Gloria's did. Why? Even though it was a sea of swirly carpets and nasty nets, and there wasn't a book or an educational toy or even a vegetable to be seen, this house felt like a home.

After she'd left, I walked round the house, looking into each room. Yes, all the beds had been made, and it was as tidy as it could be considering its inhabitants; but there was this extra ingredient everywhere, which I just couldn't identify.

It took me a while, but I got it in the end.

Love. This house was full of it, you could touch it, see it, hear it, smell it, know it. And even though I didn't think I knew what it was, I could tell it was there.

I was getting closer. At least I could spot it now.

I found out that night that Gloria's kids were only well-behaved for her, and nobody else. It took me hours to get the little buggers settled, they were far too busy taking the piss to go to sleep. They must have really enjoyed sending me up and down the stairs for drinks and packets of crisps and allegedly legal sweeties and utterly confused me with what lights to leave on and which ones to turn off. Eventually exhaustion took over, theirs and mine, and we all gave up.

And despite her assurances and my requests, Amber had been no help at all. She'd barricaded herself in Chanel's bedroom and refused to come out until I said the password, which of course I didn't know. Having tried 'Harry Potter' and 'Avril Levigne' and various characters from the Simpsons in succession – each of which produced more giggles than the last – I gave up trying to get her and Chanel to keep the karaoke rap down to a minimum and went downstairs.

It was 10.38 p.m., according to the digital clock on Gloria's gleaming chrome cooker. It was a Saturday night, and here I was sitting at someone else's kitchen table, having worn myself out on someone else's kids, about to start ploughing through a mountain of job descriptions and applications and benefit forms. Wow, I really knew how to live, didn't I?

Gloria had been almost childishly excited about this dance before she'd left, and I'd secretly thought her rather pathetic for it. But who was out there right now, living life, enjoying herself? And who was indoors right now, alone, with no life, finally getting round to doing something she'd been putting off for nearly a week, feeling like crap? To be honest, I felt a bit silly; I was probably missing a really good night out, just because – well, I don't know why I didn't go. Fear of the unknown, I suppose.

I did what I had to do, though. And actually, I enjoyed it. I made myself a cup of normal tea (no Earl Grey here, of course) and pinched a few biscuits from the tin, and – well, made a few decisions about how The Rest Of My Life was going to be.

I decided to find a job first, as I felt I needed to get back out there amongst people. I also knew that once I was financially more independent, my parents would no longer have any reason to stay. I even had a Plan B, which was to apply for all the benefits Gloria recommended, if I couldn't get a job within the next six weeks.

Impressive, huh? OK, maybe it doesn't sound like much, but it was a huge step for me – I'd never taken charge of my own life, I'd always just reacted to what or who had turned up. But this felt good.

Gloria came home at about midnight. Alone, thankfully.

'No luck?' I asked.

'Nah,' she flumped into the sofa, and took her dancing shoes off. 'Usual crowd, I already knew most of 'em.' She saw my face. 'From school, actually, not from sleepin' with them. You could do with being a bit less judgemental, Char, d'you know what I mean?'

I felt myself blush, to the roots of my hair. I was mortified, she'd read my mind.

'I'm not a tart, you know. As it happens, I'm very fussy about who fathers my kids.' Gloria kicked her legs up, stretched out. 'Ooh, put the kettle on, would ya, love? I'm gaggin' for a cuppa tea.'

I welcomed the opportunity to take my burning face into the kitchen. I was hurt, not by being caught out, but by her sharp words. I actually wanted to cry. But only for a split second, as righteous indignation soon took over. I mean really, what was the woman playing at? Six kids, by different fathers – she was a moral disgrace. And all paid for by the state, thank you very much! She was bone idle, too, hadn't worked for years, as far as I could tell. By the time the kettle had boiled, I had decided to Say Something. Nobody got to call me judgemental and get away with it.

Needless to say it all went horribly wrong. I won't go into it now, but I ended up in tears, apologizing profusely for turning into my mother, ready to throw myself under the next night bus that came along.

While I wiped my eyes with a scented tissue from the box on the coffee table, Gloria told me her story. It was extraordinary, mad, but very Gloria.

When she was four, and her sister was only two, her mother had popped out for a packet of cigarettes and never came back. Her jobless father did his best to carry on, but he couldn't really manage, and gave up quite quickly. The little girls had been placed in various foster homes, but Gloria's sister had become a bit of a handful, and so they were soon put in care, permanently.

'Look, I don't want to go on about this, OK? It's been and gone now, it's just the past, that's all. I'm just telling you because – well, because I like you, I s'pose.'

Gloria had felt responsible for all the kids in the home, and spent most of her time looking after them, because she was good at it and the adults weren't. She'd always felt that she was born to love, and was in her element with these abandoned children. She was especially protective towards her sister, Marie.

'Gosh, it's great that you were allowed to stay together, isn't it?'

But as soon as the sisters were old enough, they left the children's home and went their separate ways. The last Gloria heard, Marie was on the game in Birmingham. She had no idea where any of her family was these days, and didn't care neither. Sorry. Either.

Gloria, however, got a job in the local beauty salon, and stuck with it for a year or so. But she was sacked for being caught red-handed stealing a sterilizer – one of her teenagers from the home had just had a baby, and couldn't afford any equipment.

'Tight-fisted bastards, they were only using it for tweezers an' that.'

However. The fear of poverty never too far away, Gloria had taken the precaution of having an affair with the salon owner's husband, and was soon pregnant. A large sum of hush money was handed over, followed by a monthly allowance which was supposed to continue until Chris(tian) was sixteen.

'And did it?'

Lori's father was a drug dealer, so he had plenty of cash.

'He ended up in jail though, still in there s'far as I know.'

So Chanel's dad had had to be chosen very carefully. By now, Gloria had had to give up being a home beautician, as she was too busy with her babies. And she was very happy being a mum, it was all she ever wanted for herself. Oh, that and money. She wasn't about to bring up any more children on the pittance offered by the welfare state, it just couldn't be done.

'What about the Child Support Agency, couldn't they help you?'

Try as she might, Gloria just couldn't find a man rich enough.

'So I slept with two black guys in one month.'

Neither knew about the other, but both paid for their daughter's upkeep in full. One saw her, one didn't.

'Were you ever in love with any of these men?'

Rev's dad was Gloria's childhood sweetheart. He'd been begging her to marry him since they were thirteen, but she'd turned him down because she didn't want ginger kids. And he was as poor as she was. But ten years ago, he'd emigrated to America, become something big in IT, become a mega-millionaire, married an heiress, and then one day after the annual visit back to London to see his dear old mum on her birthday, he'd made the mistake of popping in to see Gloria as well.

'It'd be OK, if he just gave me the money and shut up about it, but he wants me and Rev to go and live over there, so's he can pop in when he wants. Bloody nerve! He's only still paying because I've threatened to tell the wife. His mum's all right though, she loves having little Rev over here, all to herself.'

Gloria was not about to abandon all her other children, as she knew only too well how that felt, and so just to prove her point she had decided to have another baby. The twins' dad was a Nigerian minicab driver called Keko (or 'Cakehole' as Gloria called him), who had originally paid to father them for immigration purposes; now he had fallen hopelessly in love with them all, and worked all the hours God sent to pay for anything Gloria wanted. He wanted them to live together as one big happy family, but Gloria was having none of it. 'Why would I want some bloke hanging around the house, bossing us all around? No thanks, mate!' But she did let him stay the night every now and then, when it was, in her words 'the wrong time' – the next man to get her pregnant had to be richer than God.

It was an insane story but, of course, it all made perfect sense. Gloria had raised herself, Gloria had made her own rules. Money was security, security was love. The fathers and the government were paying for Gloria to give these kids every-thing she didn't have – a happy, stable home and plenty for all. She was a career mother, and bloody good at it.

Now all good female friendships involve an exchange of information, and so I told Gloria all about Joe and my current obsessive crush on Hugh Grant, and how Oz's attentions brought me out in a rash, etc.

'D'you know what, Char,' she said, as she drained her third mug of tea, 'I think you're expecting too much from a man. They're just for fun, y'know; men are just for fun. Remember that, and you won't get disappointed.'

'Fun'? I thought. What the hell is that?

It says in the dictionary that 'fun' is a source of enjoyment, amusement, diversion, etc.

Up until then, the only time I laughed was at other people's misfortune. I wouldn't have known 'fun' if it had popped out of a Christmas cracker with a label on it. I looked it up in the dictionary: '**fun** (fʌn) *n.* a source of enjoyment, amusement, diver-sion, etc.'

So I decided to make a list of all the things I enjoyed, found amusing and/or diverting. It took me ages, it's harder than you think.

It turns out that I enjoy: a hotel room paid for by someone else; a good book with lots of pain and tragedy and an uplifting end; a long walk along a deserted beach on the Isle of Wight on New Year's Day; problem-solving for other people; playing the piano – but only when no one can hear me; doing word puzzles and brainteasers instead of the washing-up; dunking chocolate biscuits in tea and going to the cinema by myself, in the afternoon.

I am amused by stand-up comedy, radio panel games, penguins and meerkats and anthropomorphism generally, weathermen, soap operas, Brighton pier and little children who take themselves far too seriously.

And I find TV documentaries, clearing out cupboards, ironing, decorating, and listening in to other people on their mobile phones utterly diverting.

And going on holiday's a fantastic thing to do, even if it's just for a weekend.

Making the list was quite fun too.


I left Amber asleep in Chanel's bedroom, and on the way home in the cab, I promised myself that the next time Gloria was going out I would force myself to go with her. Who knows, I might even enjoy it.

It had been a long day, but I still managed to get down on my knees before getting into bed that night. I just wanted to say thank you to whoever had been listening to my prayers, and so I did. (But not without taking the precaution of putting my slippers under my bed first, so that I could say I was looking for them, in case my mother came in.)

I didn't go to sleep immediately – it took me a while to work out what the feeling of butterflies and nervousness and smilishness inside me was. It was good old-fashioned excitement. I realized that I wasn't so scared of the future any more. In fact, I was more curious than afraid. Things were definitely looking up.

# CHAPTER 9

'If it's love you want more of, cause someone who has less than you to have more love. If it's compassion you think is missing from your life, find someone who has even less compassion and be the source of compassion for them. Whatever it is we would seek to have more of, find someone who has less and be the source of it.

Be the source of what you would choose for yourself in the life of another, and you will experience that you have always had it. It's always been there. And the more that you give away, the more that comes back to you. In fact, it doesn't even come back to you. The more you give it away, the more you realize you've always had.'

Neale Donald Walsch, author of
*Conversations with God*

I spent the next few weeks job hunting. It wasn't quite as easy as I had thought.

I'd printed off all the vacancies I could, without any of my usual 'no way' or 'you're kidding' or 'I'd rather have pins in my eyes' discrimination. Most of the jobs on offer were for cleaners of Indian restaurants – 'Bengali speaker preferred'. I thought 'Mobile Merchandising Operative' sounded interesting, until I realized it was just a fancy way of saying 'travelling salesman'. My father wouldn't let me apply to be a bus driver, it was a man's job, apparently; my mother said I'd be a useless sandwich maker, I didn't wash my hands enough. Gloria wanted me to be a motorcycle technician as it would be a great way of meeting men; Amber wanted me to work as an irrigation fitter because she wanted to know what that was. I didn't. (Arthur said I'd make a great dominatrix in an S&M nightclub, further investigation showed that this was Jimmy's idea. How helpful.)

I did go for several interviews, however. It was soul-destroying. Even though nobody said anything to my face, I wasn't quite as employable as I'd thought.

I wasn't glam enough to be bar staff in the local pub. I was too unfit-looking to work on the Reception of a gym. I wasn't good enough at maths to work in a central London casino. I wasn't brave enough to be a dental assistant. I tried canvassing on the streets for a while, but couldn't be nice enough for long enough to earn any money at it.

Finally, finally, the good people at Starbucks took me under their wing and trained me up to be a barista.

I felt like crying on my first day. It was like being the new girl at school, only I was too old and it wasn't cute any more. And everyone else seemed to be more exotic and interesting than me, they were called names like Jarmila and Frederico, they had cute little mobile phones and lots of friends to text and text back, they were studying subjects like Humanities at college, with loving parents who'd paid their fees and this job was to pay for living expenses. They were all really, really, really Nice. They made me shudder. There was a lot of smiling too, far too much. I didn't think I'd last the day, but Gloria said I had to give it a month. She came in every day, just to check up on me.

And the work was so hard! Who'd have thought there was so much involved in making a cup of coffee? God, they take it so seriously – it took me at least three days to learn how to make a simple cappuccino. And another three to be able to do it in less than half an hour. It's a nightmare! Never again would I stand tutting impatiently on the customer side of the counter, huffing and puffing at the delay.

I was exhausted by the end of each day. My feet hurt, my back hurt, my hands were aching and so was my jaw from all that bloody smiling. But d'you know what? I loved it. It felt good to be part of the human race again, I felt connected, exhilarated, exhausted. And I was grateful to have a job.

I spent some of my first pay packet on taking my parents and Amber out to Sunday brunch. No, I hadn't gone soft – my mother's cooking was still awful.

That shift started just like any other. It was Friday, only an hour to go until I finished work, and it was moderately busy. I was enjoying myself – our shift supervisor Minh hadn't turned up for work, and so I had put myself in charge. Well, not only was I the longest-standing employee there, having almost two months under my belt now, but I was also the one with the most English.

'I'll have a grande skimmed cappuccino, please, your ladyship!' Who the – it was Jimmy, smirking at the sight of me behind a bar. 'So it's true, they really have let you make coffee for people! I'm sorry, I just had to come and see for myself.' I smiled back through gritted teeth, and shouted out to Gabor the other barista, loud and proud as Barry our trainer would say, 'Grande skimmed cappuccino to go, please!'

'No,' said Jimmy, 'it's to drink here. I'm meeting a friend.'

'Arthur? Isn't he working today?'

Jimmy handed me a £20 note. 'Yes, of course, he's always bloody working, it's so boring.'

'Well someone has to pay for your lifestyle, don't they, Jimmy?' I handed him back the change. 'Sorry, we haven't got many notes in the till, so I'll have to give you seventeen pound coins I'm afraid.' Pathetic form of revenge but anyway. 'So who are you meeting?'

'That, my dear, is none of your business.' And he tapped the edge of his nose with his finger just to make sure I knew exactly what he meant. Irritating little shit.

'Yes, can I help you?' I turned to the next customer and ignored him, but made it my business to find out who was Jimmy's mystery friend. I noticed that he didn't choose a table tucked away in the corner, but one right in front of the espresso bar. Hmm.

During the next lull, I tried to call Minh again, to find out what was happening. No reply. Gabor said she'd been fine yesterday.

''Allo, Char, how's tricks? A'right, Gabby?' Gloria, dressed in full military combat gear, complete with camouflage peaked cap with 'G.I.' in large silver letters on the front. The twins were dozing in their double buggy, bottles of far too strong blackcurrant juice hanging out of their mouths, rather sweetly holding hands as they slept. There were an inordinate number of carrier bags hanging off the buggy handles – if one of them moved the whole lot would have tipped over.

'Gawd, I'm knackered!' she would have announced to the whole queue, if there had been one. 'I've just done all the weekend's food shopping, and I've only got half an hour till I pick up Rev and Chanel, so I thought I'd treat myself to a hot chocolate.'

'Hot chocolate to have here – with plenty of whipped cream!' I shouted to Gabor, who was standing right beside me. He jumped to it, but I had to ask him to start again as he put his fingers inside the mug, which is a big Starbucks no-no.

'You're getting really good at this, intcha?' said Gloria, with admiration. 'I think it suits you, working.'

'Don't tell anyone, Gloria,' we both leaned forward, 'but I love it! I really love my job – bet you never thought you'd hear me say that, did you?'

'No, but you do keep saying it. Mind you, it shows – you look really happy, Chas!'

'Chas!' I laughed. 'No, no, no! Char is one thing, Gloria, but Chas is just too much. How would you like it if I called you Glos? Or Glozzer?'

She laughed. 'Yeah, fair enough. Listen,' she leaned in to the counter, 'if old Cakehole comes in here looking for me, you ain't seen me, OK?'

'OK, but why?' I felt sorry for Keko, she led him a merry dance.

'He's driving me bloody nuts. Just cos I let him

255

'ave a bit last night, he keeps followin' me round with holiday brochures, wanting us to go to Timbuctoo with 'im for a couple of weeks. I've told him we're going nowhere, but he don't seem to be taking no for an answer.'

Another customer came in through the door, Gloria got her purse out. 'How much is that, please?' she asked, artificially loudly.

'It's OK, Minh's not here. It's on the house,' I hissed. (When Minh was there, Gloria usually gave me the money, and then I rang it up on the till and pretended to fiddle around, and gave it straight back. Don't ask me why, it just felt right, that's all. I always paid for it with my own money at the end of the shift, so it wasn't really stealing.) 'Now why wouldn't you want a holiday? I think that's a great idea. When was the last time you had one?'

'Well – er, never, in actual fact. Unless you count a day out to Bournemouth with the London taxi drivers' charity club when I was a kid. Bloody freezing it was.'

'What! That's the only holiday you've ever had?'

'Yeah, well, what would I want to leave home for? I've got everything I need here in London, inn-I?'

Gabor butted in to agree with her at this point; we both smiled and agreed with whatever he was trying to say until he went away again.

'Right, madam,' I said, rather authoritatively I thought, 'that's it. We're going on a holiday together, you and me.'

'But –'

'No, Gloria, I've decided.'

She smiled. 'Yeah, and we all know how stubborn you can be. But I ain't goin' abroad,' she declared, stubbornly.

'Oh don't be silly. Why on earth not?'

'Don't like flying.'

'Well how d'you know, if you've never done it?' I couldn't bear Gloria's fear of the unknown, it saddened me that she had no idea what was out there in the big wide world. I had an idea. 'Ever been to Edinburgh?'

'No thanks – I hate them bloody bagpipes, and that haggis.'

'Have you ever actually eaten haggis, Gloria?' I smiled, she knew I was teasing her now. This was a woman who only ate vegetables on Christmas Day.

There was actually somebody waiting to be served, who cleared her throat. We looked up.

'Ooh, wow, look at you! Oh – my – God . . .' Gloria's voice contained a respect I had seldom heard from her. 'You look gorgeous, love, just gorgeous!'

The girl in front of us was what I can only describe as a punk peacock. That is, she was wearing the traditional punk costume of bike boots and leather jacket and mini-kilt and even had the requisite mohican, but she'd added her own feathers and beads and sparkles and dangly bits and pieces to the outfit and her make-up was extraordinary, but beautiful. Gloria was right, she looked fantastic. A walking work of art.

'Thanks,' she said, shyly. 'Um, can I have –'

'Amazin',' continued Gloria, still in awe, 'now where d'you get all this from?'

'Oh I made most of it, I'm at art school, doing a fashion degree. Glad you like it,' she said. She was a sweet little thing, very young. Oddly reticent for someone who was making such a bold statement.

'What would you like?' I asked.

'Um, I'll have a tall peppermint tea, if that's OK.'

As I shouted it out to Gabor, the penny dropped. This was who Jimmy was meeting! This was the girl he'd left Arthur for last time! Why on earth was he meeting up with her now? And why here, right under my nose?

'You all right, Char?' asked Gloria. 'Oh look, there's Lola!' She waved, whilst whispering to me, 'School mum, lovely girl, gets a discount on Jimmy Choos.' She saw my puzzled face. 'Posh shoes. God, Char, get with the prog, will ya?' She carried on waving. 'And little Frankie and little Mary! Oi, Lola! I'm comin' over!' And she bundled the buggy through the tables and chairs, leaving me to face The Enemy alone.

Fortunately, the phone rang. 'Hi, Charlotte, it's Minh, listen –' The line went dead.

I just couldn't think of anything to say to the Punk Peacock. I was very aware of Jimmy watching me like a hawk. Fortunately another customer arrived, a little Irish lady wanting a 'normal cup of tea'.

Do I tell Arthur or not?

A pannini and a smoothie.

A skinny muffin and a latte.

The phone rang, poor Minh only got a few words out before being cut off again.

Would I want to know?

Dry latte.

'When did you last grind your decaff, please?' asked a voice that I thought I recognized, but I couldn't see anyone.

I looked at the timer on the counter. 'About forty-five minutes ago, it's got a quarter of an hour to go.'

'Good,' said a voice from behind the cookie jars.

It was Wendy, in her wheelchair. You know, black Wendy the one-armed probably-lesbian, from the TV station, who I used to answer the phones with, that Wendy.

'Wendy!' I was actually quite pleased to see her, I have no idea why.

'Charlotte!'

'Hi! How've you been?' Strangely, I almost wanted to know.

She eyed me suspiciously. 'Do you actually work here?'

I was wearing a green apron with the Starbucks logo on it, I was standing behind the counter, and she must have seen me operating the till. In the old days I'd have pointed that out to her, but somehow I managed just a simple 'yes!' (Dr L had told me to cut the sarcasm – sometimes I remembered.)

'Gosh,' she said.

And anyway, I always felt a little bit bad about being mean to her. She was in a wheelchair, after all, which couldn't be easy. 'Now then, what can I get you?'

'I'll have a decaffeinated semi-skimmed white chocolate mocha syrup dry macchiato with a quadruple shot, please.'

Then I remembered that she was also not a very nice person. You probably don't have to work at Starbucks to know that this is a very complicated drink indeed. I, however, was determined to remain unfazed by her ridiculous order. 'What size would that be?'

'Venti,' she replied.

'To go, Wendy?' I asked.

'Yes, please, Charlotte,' she replied.

I didn't bother to shout it out, I wrote it on the cup for Gabor instead. Needless to say, he'd never heard of such a thing and had to look it up in the manual. I decided to keep Wendy chatting so that she didn't notice, I didn't want her thinking I was running a shoddy show here.

'So – how are you?' we both said at the same time.

Wendy's Christmas in Jamaica had been wonderful, most fulfilling, everyone had been thrilled to see her blah blah blah. She was so busy talking about how great she was that it took her a while to ask how my Christmas had been. I said I'd been ill; there was no need to tell her the full story, now, was there?

Her eyes widened when I told her. 'Oh how awful, you poor thing. Are you sure you're fit to work?'

'Yes, thanks, Wendy,' you bloody cheeky cow, 'I'm much better now.'

'Look, I tell you what, Charlotte, why don't I buy you a coffee?'

'No thanks, Wendy, there's a £5,000 fine if we're caught drinking behind the bar. Thanks for the offer though.' Hurry up, Gabor, let's get this patronizing cow's drink to her as soon as possible. 'So, Wendy, what have you been doing since we were made redundant? Did you manage to find yourself another job?'

'Um, well yes.' For some reason, she looked a bit shifty.

'Good for you – what is it?'

'I'm a – well, I can't really tell you.'

'Oh come on, Wendy, it's only me.' What on earth could she be doing that was so secret? Was she undercover Drugs Squad? Her disguises must be rather limited . . .

'No, I'm sorry Charlotte, but I'm not allowed to give you that information.'

Now, of course, I had to find out.

'Doesn't matter actually, Wendy, I know already.'

She looked relieved. 'Yes, I thought you did. I knew you wouldn't normally have turned down my offer to buy you a drink.' She smiled, pleased with herself for having known something that I knew that I didn't really know at all.

I smiled at her. 'You got me, Wendy.' This was fun.

'Yes, there's no way you'd be so nice to me otherwise. Don't forget, I know what you're really like!' And she tapped the side of her nose with her finger, which was the second time somebody had done that to me today, and the second time I'd been irritated by it.

'So how long have you been doing this job?' I asked, as Jimmy and the Punk Peacock got up to leave. Damn, I'd forgotten to keep an eye on them, had they been looking as if they were having an affair?

'Since January actually, Charlotte.'

'Right, Wendy.' Oh no, they were hand in hand. And Jimmy was waving goodbye at me with the other one, so he knew I'd seen. 'So what d'you think is the best thing about it? Which part do you enjoy most?'

'Well the best thing about being a secret shopper, especially a disabled one,' (yesss!!!) 'is that if I see staff in the stores I work for treating the customers badly, then I immediately file a report, and the offending person is sacked straightaway. So you see, I feel as if I am doing the community a great service. It's a wonderful job, I really love it.'

'Oh I bet you do, Wendy,' I said, 'and I would imagine you're very good at it too.'

'So this is where you've been hiding, is it?' Good God, Amira! Whatever next? 'Any chance of a fag in the loo and a good old gossip?'

'Certainly not, Amira, I can't think what you're talking about.' I glared at her, but Amira had never been one for subtle signals.

'But you said I could pop by any afternoon and –'

'What would you like to drink, Amira?' I asked, firmly. Fortunately Wendy was busy casting her professional eye over the rest of the café, checking that the tables were clean and that all the crockery had been bussed, etc. Although how she could see properly from down there I don't know.

'Well OK then, I'll have a chai tea latte.'

'Chai tea latte!' I shrieked at Gabor, who muttered something back in Hungarian. 'That'll be £1.70, please.'

'But you said I wouldn't have to –'

I coughed as loudly as I could, but Wendy still raised an eyebrow.

'Sorry, Wendy, do go on. I think you were just about to get to the interesting part . . .'

'We're off now, Char – see ya later, OK?' Gloria and Lola and their various kids nearly ran Wendy over as they pushed their double buggies out of the door.

'Anyway,' Amira continued, 'look out of the

263

window, Charlotte – look what my parents bought me as a present for passing my driving test!'

'If this drink takes any longer to make, I will have to mention it in my report . . .'

'Took me ages to get here though, I didn't realize how far away you are from North London. And I kept getting lost.'

The phone rang.

'One venti decaff semi-skimmed white choco-late mocha syrup dry macchiato with a quadruple shot to go!' announced Gabor, very red in the face, but very proud of himself.

'Thank God!' said Wendy and I, together.

'Charlotte? It's Minh.'

'It's not very hot . . .'

'I'll have a tall Americano please, and I don't mean the drink!' Oh no, Arthur!

'Isn't it gorgeous! It's a brand new convertible mini, my parents bought it for me for passing my driving test. Fancy a spin, Charlotte?'

'Listen, I'm at the airport – my father's very ill, I'm trying to get a flight home.'

'Did you rock and roll the jug? This foam is hardly creamy dreamy . . .'

'You haven't by any chance seen Jimmy, have you?'

''Ere, Char, did I leave my cap behind?'

'So can you take over for a bit? It's only for another hour or so, Franc comes on at 4.30.'

'And that steam wand doesn't look like it's been bled and cleaned for some time either . . .'

'I'm probably being stupid, but well – I think he might be seeing someone else. I know it's wrong, but I went through his text messages last night, and . . .'

God, please help me. Actually no, help them. They need you more than I do.

'Amira! Put that cigarette out right now, Starbucks is a smoke-free zone, coffee absorbs aromas. Gloria, your hat is under the chair where you left it. Gabor, please make Wendy's drink again, only add "extra hot" into that list will you? Now then, is there any chance you could pick Amber up from school for me, Amira? Arthur knows where it is, you can take him on to the tube station and send him back to work where he belongs. And then if you bring Amber back here, I will personally make you that chai tea latte. Yes, Minh,' I said into the phone, 'I can stand in for you. I hope you get a flight soon. Good luck.'

Wendy was very impressed.

Mind you, so was I.

Amira crashed the car on the way back to Starbucks.

I know.

Fortunately, thank god, thank you thank you thank you, Amber was OK. She was very shaky, but she wasn't hurt. I had never hugged her so hard or so long. The police-woman was very nice, she helped me to keep calm. As Amber and I walked home, holding hands, we agreed that it was best not to tell my parents. I held on to her little hand extra tightly, I wasn't going to let her go so easily again.

Amira, on the other hand, broke her nose on the steering wheel. Turned out she'd been stoned. She'd had to have a joint, apparently, to calm her nerves before driving her new car on her own.

She rang me the day after. I thought it was to say sorry, but no. I listened patiently as she complained about her spoiled face, her damaged car, the police's bad attitude. Only then did she ask about Amber.

I didn't say anything. I just put the phone down. I don't need a crazy-maker in my life. We never spoke again.

'Mum, Mum, please can I stay the night at Chanel's? Please? Pleasepleasepleasepleaseplease?'

It was Amber's ninth birthday party, and I was exhausted. Gloria and I had managed to blag the upstairs room of her local pub for free, and we'd been up most of last night. Gloria always made a big deal of any public holidays or anniversaries. She loved celebrations and parties. I didn't.

I'd been ordered to make the 'Happy Birthday' banner, which involved sticking hundreds of m&ms on to the cut-out letter, a very fiddly job indeed. Meanwhile, Gloria had copied and coloured Disney pictures on to the other side of an old roll of unspeakable wallpaper that she'd been hoarding in the cupboard under her stairs. By midnight, even though I only had two letters to go, I was ready to pack it in and go to bed, but she'd made me stay up until it was finished.

She was right, of course; it was all worth it when I saw Amber's little face when my Dad dropped her off at the party the next day. (They'd taken her out to lunch, and now he had to go and help my mother pack. They were having a new carpet fitted at their house the next day; they thought this would be a good time to see how I did on my own for a few days. 'Can always come back,' Dad had said. I had tried not to look too excited about their departure.) It wasn't so much gratitude that lit up Amber's face, but something more like hysteria – our homemade decorations looked really terrible, we all had a good laugh.

It was a family affair: Lori had brought her ghetto-blaster for musical bumps. We used Amber's new Disney All-Time Classics double CD, which her beloved Uncle-bloody-perfect-Matt had sent over for her birthday.

Gloria's eldest, Chris(tian), had somehow borrowed (or possibly stolen) a moth-eaten Balloo outfit and had been scaring all the children out of their wits by jumping around the room ROARING at inappropriate moments. Throughout the party, his girlfriend Lazy Linda had been standing by the window with her arm hanging out of it, fag in hand, smoking as if her life depended on it, eyes permanently skywards.

Little Rev had eaten so much additive-ridden orange food that he was running round and round the room on his own, not unlike a dog trying to chase its own tail, in a demented circle of hyper-activity.

And the twins were sitting under the table, pushing the candles from the Dumbo birthday cake up each other's noses.

Amber had really enjoyed herself, despite Chanel's protestations that Disney was too babyish for them now, and half-way through the party she'd actually come over specially to give me a big hug and a kiss by way of a thank you. I'd thought my heart was going to burst with pride and love for her, and only Gloria saw me quickly wipe away that tear. Keko, who'd been sitting quietly grinning in the corner with a bottle of Coke, winked at me.

It was nearly the end of the party now, and some parents had already arrived to pick up their children. I had been dreading this moment, as I had no money for party bags, which all her other friends handed out to children as they left. I'd told Amber that a balloon each was just going to have to do – that had gone down like the proverbial lead one. Gloria was busy wrapping small portions of cake up in Barbie napkins (I know, I know, it was my mother's contribution, she didn't know what was Disney and what wasn't, apparently) and handing them out to the departing kids as if they were wild truffles which had been expensively hunted and snorted out of the ground by specially trained pigs in Bavarian forests. (Not that anyone in that room except me knew what that was all about, and now that I thought about it, neither did I. Anyway.)

'And where's my birthday girl?!' boomed a familiar voice.

'Oz!' Amber ran towards him, and gave him the sort of hug normally reserved for me. He'd brought her a present; cuddly toys of Kanga and Roo, naturally.

As she was saying thank you to him, and smiling prettily, Chanel rushed over and Amber went bright red. They both looked up at him with big, adoring eyes. I suddenly realized that a certain amount of discussion had taken place between them on the subject of Oz – in fact, it looked as if Amber had a bit of a Father Thing for him.

He, however, had turned his attentions to Gloria (who was in Disney fancy dress, as Ariel, the Big Mermaid in this case), flirting back outrageously, flicking back her long red wig, saying things like, 'Do you say this to all your girlfriends?' and 'Me? Oh no, I'm just a housewife!'

Now Amber was getting pissed off because he wasn't giving her enough attention, and actually I was quite grumpy too. Well, I didn't want poor Oz to become Father No. 7 (8 actually), although it was probably none of my business. I could feel myself getting ratty, I must have been tired.

'Mum!' My daughter's impatience caught my attention. 'Can I sleep at Chanel's house tonight or not?'

'Not!' I replied sharply. Before she could launch into the full whine, I told her that her grandparents were waiting for us to come home, to say goodbye. 'Family is family, Amber, I'm sure Gloria would agree.'

She would have done, had Oz not been bombarding her with invitations to a free introduction to the internet, anytime she wanted, no worries. The more she said no, the harder he tried.

Dear Keko offered us a free lift home in his minicab, as we had so many presents to carry. We left without saying goodbye to Gloria and Oz. Well, we didn't want to interrupt anything.

Amber and I grizzled at each other all the way home, right up until we stepped out of Keko's car and saw one of those shiny gift-wrap silver hologram carrier bags, winking at us from our doorstep, as if it had every right to be there.

I knew immediately who it was from. Too late, she'd already seen it. I snatched it up before she could.

The blasted key wouldn't go into the lock properly at first. I wanted to push her into the house as quickly as I could, just in case he was hiding somewhere and could see us. I was terrified, I felt panicky and exposed. Once we were safely in, I leaned back against the door, my heart was banging inside my chest. I felt sick in my stomach, my chest, my throat. My eyes hurt. Bastard! How dare he play these games?

There was a pile of vintage 1950s luggage standing in the hall. 'Good, you're back,' said Dad, as he came out of the sitting room, folding up his newspaper. 'Got to go, old stick. Mother's in the car, waiting.'

Really? How long had she been there? Would she have seen Joe leave the bag on the doorstep? I opened the front door and looked at their car, parked outside – there she was, sitting in the front seat, head back, mouth open, probably snoring. She wouldn't have seen a thing.

'Wanted to get off quickly,' Dad said, by way of explanation. 'Matt rang from America; sent something over for us, waiting at home.' Oh right, so that was it. The prodigal son had clicked his fingers, I had to be pushed aside. Charming.

(I was about to go down that old familiar Route to Resentment, but then I remembered that I actually wanted them to leave, didn't I? So this was a good thing. I cancelled the sulk.)

'Wouldn't leave till I'd said goodbye though. Sure you'll be all right?' Dad looked so concerned, his watery eyes gave me a lump in my throat.

But I was also my mother's daughter. 'Don't be silly, we'll be fine! Won't we, Amber? Amber?'

Amber had shot out of the front door to the car and was hugging my mother, who had somehow forced herself to wake up enough to hug her back.

'Off you go, Dad, you know how you hate driving

271

in the dark.' I helped him carry the luggage out to the car, and after many more goodbyes and safe-journeys and take-cares and promises to phone, they left.

The last time I'd waved them off like this, I'd been rigid with fear. This time, I was still a little frightened, but in a good way – most of it was excitement. We went back into the house. My house.

'Right then, Amber,' I rubbed my hands together, 'it's you and me, kid!'

'And this,' she said, holding up the wretched glittery bag.

'Go on then.' I sighed. It had to be done sometime, might as well be now.

'It's a teddy!' declared Amber, holding up something you wouldn't want to win at the fair. 'And some stickers!' Random.

'Lovely, darling,' I said, as neutrally as I could. She began to open the envelope of the card, I counted to ten and then eleven and then remembered whoever was in charge Upstairs and asked for this to be OK. Please.

It came with a badge. 'Nine today, Dear Daughter,' she said out loud, proudly. 'To Amber, my best little girl.' She struggled through the excruciatingly sentimental poem, and then read, 'With all my love, Daddy. Kiss, kiss, kiss . . .' Her little voice trailed off, as she studied my face. Neither of us knew what to say. He'd never been mentioned before, and now he was right here, in the house with us.

'Are you OK, Mum?' My heart was thumping so loudly she could probably hear it.

'Er, yes, I'm fine.' Her little worried face worried me. 'Um, right then, let's see – what shall we do now?'

I did what any British person would do in a crisis; I walked into the kitchen and put the kettle on. As I filled it up, I noticed I was shaking. I could feel the eagle beginning to flap and scratch inside again, The Fear was here.

'Mum?' Amber was standing in the doorway, clutching her new teddy, not sure what to do with herself. She looked so tiny, so babyish, so adorable. I couldn't bear what was going to happen next. But I knew I had to.

'Come and sit down,' I said, as kindly as I could. 'Juice?'

'No thanks.'

'Milkshake?'

She shook her head as she climbed into the chair.

'Smoothie? Toast? Ice cream?'

'Mum . . .'

'Fry-up? Eggy bread?'

'No.'

'No what?'

'No thank you!' She was calmer than me, she was smiling. 'I'm not hungry. Mum, I've just had my birthday party.'

'Oh yes,' I must be going mad, shit, 'I forgot.' I poured the boiling water into the mug. 'Well, d'you want money then? A gold medal?'

She was laughing now.

'A damehood, perhaps?' I squeezed the tea bag. 'It would look very cool on next year's party invitation: 'Dame Amber Small invites you to . . .' My voice faded away. Maybe, after the conversation we were about to have, she'd prefer to be Dame Amber Newman. She was about to have that choice. I added the milk, I squeezed out the tea bag, I threw it away, I noticed the bin was rather full, I took out the bin bag and put it in the dustbin outside, I fitted a new bin liner, there was nothing else to be done. It was time to sit down now, and do the right thing.

'Amber —' I began.

'Is this about my dad?' she asked.

'Yes, darling,' I replied through the lump in my throat, 'it is.'

'Oh goodee!' she said, excitedly. Well, she had been waiting nine years for this.

Taking a deep breath, I sent another request Upstairs to ask for the right words to come out of my mouth in the right order.

They came, and somehow I managed to tell my little girl without drama or incident all about her father; how he didn't leave because he didn't want her, but because he still had a few more things to do before he could be a good daddy. (I made that up, sounds good, doesn't it?)

It turned out that my mother had already dropped a few hints about Joe, but nothing specific, of course. My father had rebuffed all her enquiries, changing the subject immediately. She hadn't asked me about it because she had been too scared – she said she didn't want to make me angry.

Strangely, this upset me more than anything else. My own daughter, afraid of me. But she certainly wasn't afraid of me now; she climbed on to my lap and curled her arm around my neck, like she used to do when she was a toddler. I rested my head lightly on hers, my silent tears running into her hair. I had hated talking about him, and yet now that it was over, I felt an overwhelming sense of relief.

And – well, love. Although I had always loved Amber, I hadn't always been able to *give* her love. You know, I'd never started it off. I'd always had love for her inside, but now I seemed more able to get it out. And I could give it freely, I didn't always have to see it coming back. Was this what they call unconditional love? I didn't care what it was called, it felt really good.

We both sat quietly for a bit, thinking, and then Amber said, 'What does he look like?'

'I don't know what he looks like these days,' I replied. 'He used to have spiky hair, and he wore very tight trousers.'

'Have you got a photo of him?' she asked.

'No, darling,' I replied, 'I'm afraid they all got thrown away.' Bit of an understatement perhaps, but true.

Needless to say, getting Amber to sleep that night

was difficult. The questions came thick and fast:
'Does he have brown hair and blue eyes, or blond
hair and brown eyes, or brown hair and brown
eyes or blond hair and blue eyes, or does he have
green eyes?'

'Have I got any other brothers and sisters now?'

'He's probably been to Disneyland already,
hasn't he?'

'Is he kind to animals?'

'Come on, Amber, snuggle down. I'll stay with
you until you go to sleep.'

'So is he going to come back now?'

'I don't know, sweetheart,' I mumbled into her
head, 'I don't know.'

'Hope not,' said one part of me. 'Hope so,' said
another.

There's an ancient Chinese proverb that
says, 'Be careful what you wish for.'
Wow, they knew a thing or two, those
ancient Chinese, didn't they?

So. This was the moment I had been waiting for,
praying for, longing for. But now that it was here,
I didn't want it. Not now, anyway. Not right now.
Couldn't Mum and Dad have gone tomorrow?

Over the last few months, I'd learned to enjoy
my own company a little more than before, but it
felt weird to be on my own tonight. There was a
roaring silence in the house. I missed my father
rustling the newspaper during the rude bits on

TV, and the relentless click-clacking of my mother's knitting needles, as she made little matinée jackets for abandoned charity babies she'd never meet.

I went into the kitchen, just to check they really weren't there. They weren't. But the fridge was stocked with at least enough food for the week, and there was more in the freezer. The food cupboards were a testament to my mother's conviction that we could all be snowed in at any minute.

I was suddenly overwhelmed by my family's kindness. Horribly, I suspected it had always been there, I had just mistaken it for interference.

For the first time in my ungrateful life, I rang my parents just to say thank you. It was a quick call, they weren't entirely sure I was better after all, was I feeling all right? Was I sure?

As soon as I had put the phone down, it rang. What if it was Joe? What would I say? I decided to screen the call, and went out to the hallway table to listen to the answer machine. As I stared at it, I noticed that there had already been one call – I had a vague recollection of the phone ringing when I was telling Amber all about her father, but I'd ignored it.

'Hi, Charlotte, it's me, are you there?' I hate it when people say that, don't you? 'It's Arthur.' Yes, I do know your voice, thank you. 'Pick up if you can hear me.'

Pause.

'How odd, I just tried to call and the line was busy – oh well, maybe someone else was leaving a message. Anyway, we haven't had a good old natter for ages, I'd love to speak to you – doesn't matter what time of the day or night, I'm bound to be awake.' He sounded a bit strangled, I knew exactly what was coming next. 'Um – I've had a terrible row with Jimmy, our biggest ever – yet. We've been arguing for a few weeks now, I just think there's something going on, Charlotte, things aren't right between us and – oh,' his voice dropped to a whisper, 'he's just walked back in!' Now he was shouting. 'So YES, if you could GET BACK TO ME with those FIGURES AS SOON as possible, I'd be very GRATEFUL. Thank you very much and GOODBYE!' End of message. Wow, he must be upset. He didn't even ask me to kiss the photo of Matt for him.

Poor Arthur. How terrible to be so dependent on someone else for your happiness. Wonder if that other message is from Joe?

'Hi, Charlotte, it's only me.' (Amira.) 'Please call me back, please? I just want to talk to you –' Sighing, I did what I had done each time she'd called since the accident, which was most days – I deleted the message without even bothering to listen to it.

Then I wandered around aimlessly, from room to room. All the bills for running the house were neatly organized in a cardboard folder laid out on Matt's dining-room table. Paperclipped to the front was a cheque to cover the next couple of months' running costs. 'Just to keep you ticking over,' as the post-it note said in Dad's neat and tiny writing.

Now what? I'd already thanked my parents, but I hadn't phoned Matt for months. (In fact, I couldn't remember when I last called him at all – now I thought about it, I realized he always rang me.) I hadn't even said thank you for lending me his furniture yet, and he did that months ago. I'd meant to, of course, I just hadn't got round to it.

And there was no way I was going to gush all over him, he'd just love that.

And yet, he'd done me the most enormous favour. If it had been anyone else, I'd have thanked them and bought them flowers immediately, wouldn't I?

I know, I'll call him on his mobile, sorry, 'cell'. With any luck, he'd be in a meeting, I could just leave a message. I couldn't remember what the time difference between here and LA was, but surely he'd have turned it off if he was asleep. It took me ages to find the number, and when I did it didn't work. I had to ring Dad for it in the end, and by that time I didn't really want to speak to Matt at all, but I forced myself to dial the number anyway.

It didn't switch straight to his message, but rang one long ring several times instead. Just as I was debating whether or not to hang up, an American male voice answered, 'Hi, this is the Hunk Hotline, how may I help you?'

Eh? 'Sorry,' I said, 'I think I have the wrong number.'

'No, ma'am, I don't think you do. Now don't be shy, give it a try.'

At least I think that's what he said; the Hunk Hotline was being conducted from a very crowded place, I could hardly hear him.

The man continued in his mock-camp tone. 'OK – which one of our young male studs would you like to make a reservation for? Let me tell you who we have available today: my name is Stu, I have ten inches, I would be glad to help you out, or we have young Frankie here, he's blond and very, very hot . . . Zack is fully-booked, as ever . . .' I thought I could hear laughing in the background, '. . . or we have a special offer on Mighty Matthew, the well-endowed Englishman, he's doing two for the price of –'

'Hello?' This was Matt's voice.

'Matt?' How peculiar all this was. 'It's Charlotte.'

'Charlotte! Hi! Charlotte, wow! Um, could you hold the line a moment . . .' He covered the mouthpiece up, but I could still hear a muffled, 'For fuck's sake, Stu, it's my sister!' or something like that. 'Sorry, I'm in a restaurant having lunch with some friends, let me go outside,' he was obviously weaving through tables, 'what a wonderful surprise to hear from you. Sorry about Stu answering the phone, I was in the bathroom and came back to find him chatting to you. He didn't say anything, y'know, weird, did he?'

'No, not really, he was quite funny actually. I wasn't aware you were working for the Hunk Hotline . . .'

'Oh, that old one, OK. That's typical Stu, sorry.'

'What if I had been someone from work?'

'Impossible, this is my F&F number.'

'F&F?'

'Family and Friends.' He was outside now, I could just hear the odd American car horn and obligatory sirens in the background. 'So, how're things?'

'Really good, Matt, really good. I was just ringing to say –'

'Is Mum all right? She's not ill, is she?'

I'm sorry, but the level of concern in his voice really got up my nose. 'No, she's fine,' I said, curtly, 'she's tough as old boots, that one.'

'I think she's more fragile than you think, actually,' Matt said.

'Yes, well, whatever.' I was aware that this call was probably costing me a fortune and didn't want to spend that kind of money talking about my mother. 'I rang to say thank you.'

'For what?'

'For lending me your furniture,' I said. 'For everything,' I found myself saying, 'for being a really good brother. Thank you. Anyway, how are you?' I asked, before he could think that I was overly grateful. Not that I really wanted to know, his life was always just perfect.

'I'm good, thanks.' He sounded surprised that

I'd asked. 'Working hard, playing hard, just having lunch with friends, y'know.' He sounded so cool, so American, so lifestyle. And so damned happy. 'I've just bought a new house, we just got a puppy, in fact –'

'Look, I don't want to keep you away from your friends for too long –'

'Please do, with any luck they'll pay the bill!' He laughed. I could hear that perfect smile from here. And I hated it when rich people pretend they've got no money. Time to go before I say something I'll regret.

'Anyway, that's it. Just wanted to say thank you, that's all.'

'OK, that's cool. How's Amber?'

'Really good, sends her love. Got to go, left something under your grill. Bye!'

'Oh, OK! Really great to hear from you, Charlotte, thanks for ringing. Really means something, y'know.'

'Yes, all right, Matt, bye.'

And then I put down the phone and burst into tears.

I hate the word 'lonely'.

But that's how I was feeling. There's a huge difference between being on your own, and being lonely. I could be in a crowd of people sometimes, and still feel lonely.

But there's a cure for loneliness. You just

have to take a deep breath, ask God for courage, and pick up the phone.

'Gloria,' I said, 'I'm feeling a bit wobbly.'

'Yeah well, so'm I – it's not easy clearing up someone else's party in high heels and a mermaid tail, y'know. My feet are killing me.'

'Oh God, sorry, I forgot all about that.' How selfish of me, I couldn't believe I'd gone without helping to tidy up. 'We had to rush off to catch my parents before they left.'

'Don't matter,' she replied, 'I got Lazy Linda to give me a hand. Eventually. How are you, anyway?' she asked. 'You rushed off before I could say goodbye properly.'

'I'm fine,' I said, more out of habit than anything else. How ridiculous. 'That's a lie,' I said instead, 'I feel horrible.'

'Yeah, I'm not surprised. I always feel like shit on my kids' birthdays.'

'Do you?'

'Yeah – it's one of the few times when I really want their dads to be around, dunno why. Part of the happy families dream, I s'pose. Bloody awful sometimes, this single parenting lark, innit?'

It sure was. Gloria always knew how to get straight to the heart of me. I had a little cry for myself as I told her about Joe's presents and my parents' absence.

'You sound like you're about to drown in your own shit, my darlin'.' Nice imagery. 'Feeling sorry for yourself is a killer, innit? Well, Char, I'm afraid I can't let you do that any longer.' She brightened. 'You're coming out with us tonight, and I won't take "no" for an answer!'

Oh no. 'Who's us?'

'Me and the girls – Carmel, Vicky, Maureen, Patsy, um, who else?, oh yeah, Rita and Kathleen, y'know, that lot. We always go out in a gang, first Saturday of every month.'

I'd heard about these women of course, but never met any of them. I wasn't sure I wanted to, either. I could just about deal with Gloria, but her friends sounded mad and scary. And despite my determined promise to myself that I would go out next time Gloria asked me, I hadn't. I'd always managed to find an excuse.

'Yes, but what about Amber?'

I didn't want to go, but she was right, as usual. Let's face it, my only plan for this evening was to wallow in self-pity. Eventually it was agreed that Mrs O'Nions would babysit hers, and Chris and Lazy Linda would do mine – 'Do 'em good to shag on someone else's sofa for a change,' said Gloria. 'I'll bring 'em with me, Cakehole's coming to pick us up in half an hour, so be ready, OK?'

Her 'girls' were indeed scary women, but in a good way. There were no victims here, that's for sure. I had never met such a collection of big, passionate personalities. They were all 'living life large', as Gloria would say.

And they weren't like Sabrina's friends, who had

had to know the status of my career, car, house and husband before deciding if it was worth the effort of getting to know me. These were friendly people, and any mate of Gloria's was instantly a mate of theirs. And they laughed at all my jokes, which made me like them even more. I was surprised that they didn't get hopelessly drunk, but then neither did I – for some reason, I didn't really want to. We had a good night – it was fun. By the end of the evening, I had lots of numbers to call next time I needed to chat to someone, and they all had mine.

'Well? Did you enjoy yourself?' asked Gloria, as we left the club to a series of wolf whistles from the bouncers on the door. 'I wish you'd 'ave a dance, Char, it's such a laugh!'

(She'd come as a sexy cowgirl tonight, complete with Dolly Parton wig, big white Stetson and tiny rhinestone-studded waistcoat with matching fringed denim skirt, and white cowboy boots. I was appalled when I'd seen her, I thought we were going line-dancing. And she'd made me swap some of my clothes with Lazy Linda too – 'Well, it's not like she's going to be wearin' 'em for long, is it? And let's face it, Char, you need to brighten yourself up a bit.' I knew better than to argue, and actually I didn't look that bad in the end. Lazy Linda looked awful, though, very dreary.)

'Yes, I did enjoy myself, I really did,' I said, still exhilarated from all that warmth and laughter. 'It was fun and your friends were great, very kind to me. Thank you, Gloria.'

'They weren't being kind, Char, they liked you! Honestly, I wish you could see what we can see,' she said, looking at me. 'You've really changed since I've known you, Char.'

'I know, and it's thanks to you.' I turned to face her. 'Why d'you do it?'

'What?'

'You know, scoop people up and look after them, like you did with me.'

'Oh, don't be silly,' she took off her hat, she looked a little less like a porn star now, 'I don't do anything, I –'

'Why? What's in it for you?'

'I dunno, I just like – loving them better, I suppose. Makes me feel good. Now, where's that bleedin' Cakehole got to? He said he'd wait out here for us, but I can't see him nowhere, can you?'

We agreed to give him five more minutes, and huddled together in a doorway while we waited.

'I suppose I'm an old hippie at heart,' she continued. 'I just want everyone to be happy, that's all.'

'So what's your theory on love, Gloria?' I asked. 'What d'you think it is?'

'Now don't you go trying to trip me up with your clever ways, Lady Charlotte,' she warned. 'I'm not very good at all this deep stuff, as well you know.'

'Please?'

She jiggled her legs, to keep warm. 'Well I reckon that if you want something, you've got to give whatever it is to someone who's got less than you.'

I said it for her. 'Someone like me, you mean?'

She smiled at me. 'Well, yeah, I s'pose. And then once you feel you've got it, you give it back, and I pass it on to someone else, and so do you, and we all pass it round to each other, you see? And then there's enough for everyone, we all get what we need. Speaking of which, have you got any milk in your house? I'm gaggin' for a nice cup of tea. Oh look, here he is – where the bloody 'ell 'ave you been? We've been freezing our arses off out here!'

I liked Gloria's idea of how to get love in your life. And the part about giving it away to keep it. It was a great theory, but was it true?

# CHAPTER 10

'Until one is committed, there is hesitancy;
the chance to draw back, always ineffective-
ness. Concerning all acts of initiative (and
creation), there is one elementary truth the
ignorance of which kills countless ideas and
splendid plans: that moment one definitely
commits oneself, Providence moves too.

All sorts of things occur to help one that
would never otherwise have occurred. A
whole stream of events issues from the deci-
sion, raising in one's favour all manner of
unforeseen incidents and meetings and
material assistance, which no man could
have dreamed would have come his way.

Whatever you can do, or dream you can,
begin it. Boldness has genius, power and
magic in it.

Begin it now.'

Goethe

'I think you should tell him to fuck off!' said the anorexic. 'I mean, he can't just come swanning back into your lives without any explanation, can he?'

For once, I agreed with her. I might bring her in a biscuit next month.

'Oh give the guy a break,' moaned, guess what, a guy. 'He's coming back, isn't he, to take responsibility for his kid? What more d'you want?'

I was beginning to wish I'd never mentioned Joe in the first place. But it was really bothering me, and Dr Lichtenstein said we must use the group for ourselves, that's what it was for. I'd arrived a bit late, and they'd all looked even more miserable than usual. I'd thought it might cheer them up to listen to someone else's problem for a change. So I'd 'put it out there', as they say in the therapy world.

But my plan to help them had backfired on me. Even though I hadn't actually asked for their opinions, they'd all decided to tell me what I should do, whether I wanted to listen or not. (I have to admit, before this, I'd have done exactly the same. But now that I was on the receiving end of unsolicited advice, I didn't like it very much.)

'I'd lure him into the house with a nice cool glass of champagne, and then have my wicked way with him!' announced Marjorie. 'You don't want to lose him again, do you? This could be your last chance to get a man, you're not getting any younger, you know.' Cheers.

As the suggestions became more and more bizarre ('Why don't you tie him up and leave him there for nine years, same as he did to you?' from a very ugly little man who insisted he was a sex addict), I decided it was time to stop all this, before it got too silly. 'The thing is,' I said loudly, to quieten them, 'the thing is that he hasn't even contacted me yet. The Incident of the Birthday Present On The Doorstep was three weeks ago now, and I haven't heard a dickie bird since.'

That shut them up.

But not for long.

'He might be waiting for you to get in touch with him.'

'Maybe it wasn't him who put it there in the first place, maybe someone else did it for him.'

'Yeah, maybe he's dead and this was in his will or something.'

I was getting annoyed now. 'Or maybe he's been kidnapped by aliens, who knows!' I snapped. 'Anyway, all I can do is pray about it, and let God sort it out, while I get on with the rest of my life.'

Now that really did shut them up. Every pair of eyes in the group was staring at me now, as if I was some sort of Jesus-bothering socks'n'sandals-wearing ankh-encrusted freak.

'It's not a religious thing, it's a spiritual thing . . .' I began to splutter. I could feel myself going bright red, right down to the roots of my hair. I appealed to Dr Lichtenstein to help me out, which thank God (or whoever) he did.

'Charlotte has a point,' he smoothed. 'Projection is a terrible waste of time, especially when we don't have all the facts. We can imagine all sorts of scenarios, if we choose to. We can actually hurt ourselves with them, feel real pain sometimes, even if they're only real in our imagination. Much better to stick to what is, rather than what may be. Thank you, Charlotte, for demonstrating that to the group.'

He really knew his stuff, Dr L. Recently, I'd started to listen to what he was saying – well, sometimes, anyway – and he was usually right on the money. In fact, the only reason I'd come back here every month was to catch a few more of his nuggets of wisdom. I looked round at everyone else; those of us who had followed his suggestions seemed to be doing really well. Many from the original group had disappeared; we hadn't seen them since leaving the clinic, they were probably back out there doing their worst, not ready to get better yet. But there were even fewer of us here today than last time . . .

'Where's Amira?' I suddenly asked.

Ginny, the anorexic immediately burst into tears. Bonnie, the overeater fished inside her industrial strength bra, and produced a hankie for the poor girl. The rest of the group became very shifty, shook their heads, looked down at the floor, someone whispered, 'I thought they were friends . . .'

'Amira's dead, Charlotte,' said Dr Lichtenstein, gently. 'I'm sorry, I assumed you knew.'

'Dead?' My blood froze. I hadn't expected him to say that, I'd expected him to say she was in Dubai or Harrods or something. Dead? 'Dead? Are you sure? But she's been calling me continually. Yes, that's right, she rang three times the other day . . .' I didn't tell them that I hadn't answered any of her calls, or explain why not; the group needn't know how stupid and selfish she'd been.

'She committed suicide, about ten days ago. Hanged herself.'

Little Ginny's crying worsened. Big Bonnie put her arm round the girl, who sobbed into her ample bosom.

'But –' I was stunned. 'Why?'

'She didn't leave a note,' he explained. 'We have no idea. Her family's mystified. Apparently, she was her usual chirpy self the day before. There's no official explanation for it, it's very sad.' He sighed, shook his head. I was touched by the depth of his feelings, he must lose patients all the time, and yet his compassion was almost tangible.

I couldn't believe it. 'And the unofficial explanation?' I asked Dr Lichtenstein, still wanting an answer. 'What's your theory?'

He turned to look at me. 'I have no idea, Charlotte. I have no facts to go on. Could have been anything – fear, low self-esteem, isolation; all of those are killers. We'll never know the truth, we can't project, you see? We just have to accept it.'

But I couldn't. All those times I had refused to

speak to her were racing through my mind. What if she had been ringing to ask for help? I felt terrible about being so cruel, not giving her a second chance, just cutting her off like that. Oh God.

She'd hanged herself. What a grisly way to go. And a dramatic one. How awful for her family, to have found her. How shocking. How typically Amira. How selfish.

I decided to tell them what had happened. 'Could I have saved her,' I asked Dr Lichtenstein, 'if I'd returned her phone calls? Was I too harsh?'

'Charlotte,' he said, kindly but firmly, 'this isn't about you. This was her choice. We'll never know what was going on in that poor girl's head that day. But it's important that we learn from Amira's passing, or she becomes just another wasted life.'

A discussion about emotional boundaries followed, but I didn't take any of it in. She had been so kind to me when I'd first arrived at the clinic, and I'd been so quick to stop the friendship, after she'd made just one mistake.

Yes, but what a mistake. She could have killed my daughter.

I'll never know if I contributed to her death or not. Sometimes I think I should have discussed it with her once I'd recovered from the shock, see if we couldn't have salvaged some of the friendship. That's what I'd do now.

At other times I think she was on a crazy journey anyway, and that our situation was just one of many torments that drove her to kill herself.

Then again, perhaps Dr L was right, and it wasn't anything to do with me.

Poor, poor Amira. I knew how bad it had to get, in order to want to take your own life. On the bus home, I had a chat with Upstairs and asked that I never go to as dark a place as that again. I'm pleased to report that I never have. Yet.

To my surprise, I hadn't felt suicidal since Christmas. I had clearly decided I was worth saving now, that life was worth living after all. I cleaned up my act a bit after Amira's death; I stopped drinking, I stopped smoking, I stopped eating junk food. (I didn't stop taking no exercise though, there is a limit.)

I also stopped going to group therapy. I still spoke to Dr Lichtenstein every now and then, when I needed to, but I didn't go back to the clinic. Not because I was ashamed of being the last to find out about Amira, but because I was eager to get on with it. I'd heard enough wisdom, I'd heard enough theories, I'd heard enough. I wanted to actually do that big scary thing, Real Life.

And anyway, if I got out of line, I'm sure Gloria would be the first to tell me.

Can you believe it, I was promoted to Shift Supervisor! Me! Apparently, Wendy had filed such a glowing report that the Starbuckians had decided I was worth encouraging up another rung of their ladder. I just couldn't believe it! As soon as they told me, I phoned my parents and Gloria, who were almost as excited as me. Honestly, I was so chuffed, I strutted around with a puffed-out chest for the rest of the shift.

Outside, it was a crisp, sunny day (strangely, I had begun to notice the weather now), and I was in a brilliant mood. At last, the world was beginning to feel like a good place to be, things were definitely looking up. I decided to pop in on Oz, tell him my good news. Mistake. Inside the Down Undernet Café it was all doom and gloom.

She was wearing a crisp white blouse with black embroidery detail on collar and cuffs, topped by city suit with big wide shoulder pads and tight executive miniskirt to just above the knee; really sheer shiny tights specially chosen to show off perfectly waxed legs, high heels of the type that make men melt and women wince. Top all that with a pinhead of blonde hair that had not been just stuck but glued down to her bony skull, add dark eyes with red lips and you have a perfect picture of Oz's girlfriend. An eighties version of Jean Harlow's *Bombshell*. Scary.

'This place is a dump!' (She had the same accent as him; they must have been childhood sweethearts whose relationship had changed once they came over here, when she got a proper job and he started to work on his dream. Just guessing.) 'I mean the whole café is filthy, it looks really daggy, Shane! Doesn't it?' Louder. 'Doesn't it?!'

Shane? Oz's real name is Shane? How Bondi Beach is that!

She was strutting around as if she owned the place, which it turned out she did. 'This so-called "business" [and she did the fingers to go with that] of yours is a total and utter failure. It's costing me a fortune, Shane, it's a bottomless pit! I had no idea things had gone this far down the line. Jeez, the place is a bloody dive.'

'Aw, fair suck of the sav, Rosheen,' protested Oz, shooting me a quick sideways glance to say hello, 'it's not that bad, is it?' He winced, he already knew the answer.

'Yis, Shane, it is!' she spat. 'No wonder you don't get any customers! This looks like a seedy beach bum's bar, not the buzzing metropolis of hi-tech global computerized infotainment you told me it was going to be.'

I couldn't help it, I sniggered.

'And who are you?' She swivelled round on her stiletto; if we'd been standing on turf she'd have got her foot stuck.

'Oh, I'm just a customer,' I said, airily, 'who really loves this place.'

Both Oz and I were surprised to hear me say that – we didn't realize until then that I did.

'Well, I wish there were a few hundred more of you,' said Rosheen, tetchily.

'There's Hugh Grant,' I volunteered. 'Keith, rather. He comes every day!'

'Oh wow, hold the front page!' said Rosheen, with more than a hint of sarcasm. (She was rather good at it; she would have put the old me to shame.)

'Look, let's just give it a few more weeks, eh, Rosh? Come on, love, we're only minutes away from it being a runaway success . . .' Oz tried to ooze up to her, but it was pathetic and she was having none of it.

'Oh no, don't you come the raw prawn with me! You know perfectly well that this café is going nowhere, and never has been. Well, I've got news for you, Shane Dobson; I am not prepared to finance this shithole any longer.' She was nearly crying with frustration. 'Y'know, I've kept my side of the bargain, and you haven't! This just isn't fair, Shane!'

'Oh, come on, Rosh, don't work yourself up.' Oz stood up and walked towards her, I sat down on a chair by the door. (They didn't seem to mind me being there, which was great, this was like watching an episode of *Home and Away*.) 'It'll work out, honest – I just need a bit more time . . .'

'*NO!*' Rosa Klebb screamed at him, 'I've run out of time, I've run out of money, and I've run out of patience too! This place is a total gutser, and you know it.' She was right, of course, the Down Undernet Café was never really going to be a big money-spinner. It was a cosy, friendly place; a one-off, not part of an anonymous chain. That's probably why I liked it so much.

'C'mon, love, give us a hug . . .' Oz moved towards her, she sprang back.

'No, Shane, no! No more, this is it!'

But she didn't look him in the eye when she said that, she looked away.

Oz said what I was thinking. 'Rosh, is there somebody else?'

'No!' She was appalled at his suggestion, she was shocked, she was clearly lying.

Oz slumped into a chair. 'Who is it?' he asked in a much quieter voice.

Rosheen sighed and shook her head. She was probably deciding whether to own up or not.

I began to feel that I shouldn't really be there after all, and crept towards the door.

'There's no need to go, I've nearly finished,' she said, with fatigue. 'And besides, he's going to need all the customers he can get from now on.'

'Rosh –'

'Yis, Shane, this is the end of the road for me, for you, for us.' She picked up her briefcase and one of those beige macs that only office workers wear. 'I've had enough. For once in your life you can sort your own mess out. Like I said, you've got until the end of the month to either make a go of it or I'm pulling the plug.'

'But you can't do that!' protested Oz.

'Can't I?' she replied. 'Watch me.'

And with that she left.

Oz stared at me.

I stared back.

'Wow, what a woman . . .' he said, as we both looked out at Rosheen on the street. She hailed a taxi and jumped in.

'Yes,' I said. 'She's not what I expected . . .'

'No?' he asked, as he picked up Rosheen's lipstick-stained coffee cup from a nearby table.

'No! You're chalk and cheese,' I said. 'She's really together, efficient, smart, no-nonsense, organized, very intelligent, obviously extremely capable, and you're . . . not.'

'Don't I know, that's the trouble!' He took the cup over to the bar area, grinning inanely at his own hopelessness.

'Doesn't it bother you?' I asked, following him.

'What?' he asked, turning on the tap, 'Doesn't what bother me?' He really was the most infuriating man I'd ever met.

'That she's left you!'

'Nah, she's always saying that.' He grinned. 'She'll be back! She's just joshing.'

(She wasn't. He discovered that the next day, when she came back with two burly men and a van to pick up her stuff from their flat above the shop. Turned out she'd been having an affair with her boss, hence the fast-track career and the long hours, the disinterest in Oz's business until it was too late. Oz was devastated. But only for a couple of days – we'd abandoned the love project long ago, but he'd kept all his research, and still had all those online-dating website addresses. So he very quickly returned to his usual laid-back self after that. Amazing.)

'Well, what about the fact that you're going to lose this place at the end of the month?' I continued.

'Oh yeah, no, you're right.' He looked crestfallen. 'Oh. Yeah, that's what she said, isn't it?'

'Can she do that?'

'Well, yeah. Everything's in her name. She's got better credit rating than me, see.'

It turned out that they'd been childhood sweethearts whose relationship had changed once they came over here, when she got a proper job and he started to work on his dream.

'Really?' I said. 'Who'd have thought?'

'Yeah,' he looked really downhearted. 'We'd not been getting on too well back home. The deal was, right, that we would come over here for a fresh start. She was going to work her way up the corporate ladder and I was going to be an entrepreneur.'

I tried to keep a straight face at the thought of Oz starting a business empire of any sort.

'Trouble is, she's done that and I haven't. It takes time to get things going, y'know, Charlotte –'

'How long have you been in London?'

'Just over a year. She's been paying all the bills for a while now, my money ran out pretty quick. Pisses me off, that, y'know, I don't feel like a man with his own business any more.'

I managed not to say he didn't look like one either. His hair was more untamed than ever, it seemed to be growing out instead of down; his T-shirt was spotted with unidentifiable blobs of stuff, but there weren't enough of them to mask the fact that it was advertising a Rolling Stones World Tour of '97; the shorts were fading and about to disappear completely on the sitting-down part, and he was wearing flip-flops, in this weather. Oz looked more like he ran a surfboard than a business.

'I don't know what to do nixt, Charlotte,' he was saying. 'Rosheen is not joking, she'll do what she says, I know she will.'

'But she can't!' I didn't realize I was so passionate about the place. 'That would be awful!'

For the first time since I'd known him, Oz looked really upset. 'I know, but Rosheen doesn't really do "fair". I'm doing everything I can to keep her sweet at home, if you know what I mean,' – I did, unfortunately – 'but it's not enough. When it comes to business, she's ruthless. I've done my best, but I guess I'm just not cut out for this.' I felt badly for him, and I hated her.

The café door opened, letting in a blast of crisp air – it was Hugh Grant! Oh my god, oh my GOD. I shook my hair so that instead of looking like it hadn't been brushed this morning, it hopefully looked more like I'd just stepped out of an under-wear catalogue.

'You OK?' asked Oz. 'Has something flown into your ear?'

'Coffee?' I offered Hugh Grant, breezily, as if I worked there. In fact, I found myself walking

301

behind the bar and putting on the Sydney Opera House apron that had been hanging there untouched since the beginning of time.

Hugh Grant shot a confused glance at Oz, who shook his head and shrugged his shoulders back. None of us knew what was going on.

'Tea,' he said.

It was the first time he'd spoken to me, and admittedly it was only one word, but my little heart sang whilst I went about the business of making him the finest cup of cha he'd ever had. To my horror, I saw that Oz only had one kind of tea, PG Tips, and not the wide choice that would have necessitated me questioning Hugh Grant further, which meant that he would have had to talk to me again. In fact, I could see now that this whole bar area was disgracefully ill-equipped, disgracefully dirty and – well, just plain disgraceful. No wonder Rosheen had called the café a dump. It was.

'I might have a coffee, now that I'm here,' I called over to Oz. I tried to turn the espresso bar on but it was as dead as a dodo.

'Doesn't work,' he said, scratching his head, as recent events began to sink in and he wondered what to do next. 'Never has.'

'But –'

'Just for the show.'

No wonder every cup of coffee I'd ever had in there was disgusting. Now that I thought about it, I'd never seen him using the big chrome machine. It turned out that he'd hidden a huge catering-size tin of instant coffee under the sink, and the next-door cupboard housed a battered electric kettle and one of those silly tiny battery-operated whisks, for 'the cappuccino effect'. And there were things in the fridge that looked like they were visiting from another planet.

I took the most lovingly (and I really had gone to some lengths, overcoming many personal hygiene standards) prepared cup of tea ever made over to Hugh Grant's usual computer.

'Thanks,' he said.

That was two words now. And he must know I exist, otherwise where did the tea come from? Ooh, I'd sleep happy tonight.

Meanwhile, Oz had picked up the accounting records from where Rosheen had left them, on the floor. He might as well have been reading them upside down for all the sense they were making to him.

'I don't want to do this, Charlotte, I feel like a nong,' he said to me, with a wobbling chin, 'but I think I'm going to have to throw in the towel.'

That was when I said to him 'Oz, I've had an idea.'

It's amazing how once you've committed to doing something, everything sort of falls into place, isn't it?

I think it's God's way of saying that this is a good idea, that it's the right thing to do.

What other explanation can there be for it?

Once I decided to go into partnership with Oz, everything began to slot in amazingly well. It was difficult, but I handed in my notice at Starbucks; they were sad to see me go, but they understood. They even gave me one of their old manual espresso bars, as they were replacing them with the quicker automatic version, that actual week. (Clearly they didn't think we were going to be much competition . . .)

And I received the most extraordinary letter from Piers, Sabrina's friend the film producer, who I used to work for:

*Hi Charlotte,*

*Listen, I'm really sorry for landing you in the shit last Christmas. Thing is, I'd been taking too many drugs and had to do a runner for various reasons. Anyway, in the end I went to rehab and now that I'm clean and sober I can see that my behaviour was atrocious.*

*I would like to apologize for any trouble I may have caused you, and quite understand if you never want to see me again, but perhaps it would be nice to meet up for a coffee sometime?*

*With love,*
*Piers*

Inside the letter was a cheque for exactly the amount he owed me. Which was exactly enough to cover the cost of giving the Down Undernet Café a smart new look, and there was exactly enough left over for next month's rent, which went straight to Rosheen.

With careful planning on my part, and happy-go-luckiness on Oz's, we managed to get most of it done in one weekend. We made a good team, when it came to getting things organized – I made them happen, and he kept them happy.

There was still lots of paint left over from the redecoration of my house, and Arthur and Jimmy were more than willing to come and show us how to do it. They bossed Dad about relentlessly, but he took it like a man. (Mum stayed at home, she sent a pot plant instead.)

There was a sticky moment when the Punk Peacock turned up unannounced, keen to help, but Arthur somehow managed to get over himself long enough to delegate the decoration of the Ladies and Gents to her.

Even Hugh Grant volunteered his services as a fixer and fitter. Unfortunately, I didn't really get a chance to impress him with my wit and repartee, as I was too busy barking orders to the workers and ticking things off on a list as long as two of your arms. He arrived with a huge toolbox, and was brilliant at DIY; Gloria and I nearly wet our pants with excitement.

Team Gloria excelled themselves. Chris(tian)

produced two hundred white mugs from I dread to think where, although it took him and Lazy Linda the whole weekend and sixty fags to pick off the name of a very famous multi-national corporation before we could use them.

Lori did us all a favour by not being there. Instead, she and her nursery nurse college mates were handsomely paid to take all the kids off to McDonald's and the mall and the cinema. There was a bit of a sticky moment when Amber came back with her ears pierced, but fortunately I was too harassed to say too much. And anyway, she was so thrilled, I didn't want to spoil her joy. We'd just have to remember to take them out before visiting Granny, that's all.

Gloria was in her element. She was dressed as if she was starring in a Dulux commercial, blonde (just for today) hair in a little sticky-uppy high ponytail, dungarees and far too tiny vest straining at the seams underneath, with purple sparkly bumper boots. I didn't actually see her do any painting, but she had an attractive blob of emulsion right on the tip of her nose all day.

She threw herself into the project whole-heartedly. Anything we needed, she found. She quite literally set up shop in the corner, and every plumber, electrician or man-with-a-van who called in was given a free haircut. Over that weekend, she had people dropping off anything from brass light-switches to a thousand loo rolls; she seemed to have contacts everywhere, we were even given a tank of colourful tropical fish, for nothing.

By Sunday night, the Down Undernet Café had been given a complete facelift. At midnight, we downed tools and crossed the road, to look at it from the other side. Jimmy's handpainted sign said 'Global Village' (Oz had wanted to call it Surfers Paradise – fortunately he was outvoted) in big gold letters, and it was bright and friendly and positively twinkling with invitation.

We stood there, in silence, admiring our work. 'Wow,' said Oz. And 'wow' again. After the third one, we told him to shut up.

Now if this was a movie, it would all turn out beautifully from now on. The café would be a roaring success, Oz would get back with Rosheen, I would become Businesswoman of the Year, forget about Joe completely, and Amber and I would live happily ever after.

But this was Hammersmith, not Hollywood. And in real life there are no happy endings, just on-going situations.

The café was not an overnight success. We did get a few more customers but they weren't exactly queuing outside when we opened up in the mornings. Even though we'd quadrupled our regular clientele, we only just managed to cover our bills for the first couple of months.

307

Oz wasn't interested in getting back with Rosheen, even if she'd have had him – he'd discovered internet dating. I lost count of how many women I saw coming down the stairs from his flat, followed by oz@ripper-root.com grinning like the proverbial Cheshire Cat. He thought it was clever – I thought it was tragic.

As I wasn't exactly rushed off my feet, I had far too much time to sit and stare into space, thinking. Well, OK, obsessing. About Joe, of course.

# CHAPTER 11

'Forgiving is not about forgetting, it's letting go of the hurt.'

Mary McLeod Bethune

I'd finally given in to Gloria's campaign to do a makeover on me and had said she could come round tonight to do the dreaded deed. So Chris(tian) had come along too, as he needed help with a solicitor's letter. So Lazy Linda had accompanied him ('well, it's Friday night, innit') and was in a bit of a huff about it, not saying much.

Lori had an urgent appointment to hang out outside McDonald's harassing posh boys, and Mrs O'Nions' sister was ill (food poisoning, apparently) so Chanel had to come too, which put Amber into a sulk because they were either just about to fall out or just had, I can't remember.

And no babysitter meant that Rev and Max and May had to come as well. The twins obligingly fell asleep under the dining-room table as soon as they arrived, and Rev was happy to sit on the sofa with Chris(tian) watching the football on TV. Lazy Linda started the evening off squashed between them glowering, professionally, for Britain, but soon caved in and joined us girls in the kitchen, where Gloria had set up her portable beauty salon on the table, and – to the delight of the assembled audience – did her best to transform me from Charlotte Small Housewife into Charlotte Small Superstar.

In true makeover tradition, I wasn't allowed to look into a mirror until she'd finished. And in true makeover tradition, I was shocked at what I saw.

Staring back was a more modern version of me. Gloria hadn't done anything outrageous – just cut my hair into a more definite style, shaped my eyebrows, put a bit of colour on to my face and cleverly erased the shadows under my eyes. I looked – well, pretty. Like a nice person. The sort of woman you wouldn't mind having as a friend.

'Well?' Gloria couldn't bear it any longer. 'What d'you think?'

Tears welled up in my eyes. It sounds silly, but I felt like the old me had gone for ever, and I was just a little bit sad to see her go.

'Oh no, don't bloody cry, Char!' shrieked Gloria. 'You'll mess it all up. Linda, get 'er a piece of kitchen roll. OK, Chanel, you get it then, quick!'

She made me bow my head so that the tears didn't run down my face, but dropped straight out of my eyes and on to the taut piece of kitchen towel instead. It must have been a pretty funny sight.

'Mum,' said Amber's concerned voice, as I wept away, 'are you all right?'

''Course she is, love,' Gloria spoke with softness, as she rubbed my back, 'she's just doing a bit more of that defrostin', intcha, Char?'

God, I really love that woman, and I know that she loves me too.

I'd never had a female friendship like that before, not an equal one, anyway. I'd spent a lot of time trying to hang around girls who were way out of my league, and when I wasn't doing that I'd spent the rest of my time shaking off the creepy girls who were trying to hang around me.

Sometimes Gloria was in charge of us, and sometimes I was. My strengths made up for her weaknesses, and vice versa. It was good, it was fair, it was right.

I now believe that the healthiest friendships are the equal ones. Wonder if the same principle applies to men?

Next, Gloria showed me how to do an evening make-up. Now that really was a transformation. For the first time in my life, I had big smoky eyes and dark shiny lips, and if you didn't know me you'd say I was a sophisticate. (Gloria said not to even attempt the chignon myself, one of those big clips from Claire's Accessories would do the same job.)

Then she offered to go through my clothes, which was the part I had been absolutely dreading. I liked my dark wardrobe, it made the choice of what to wear easier, and I didn't want to be transformed into a one-woman fancy dress party. Fortunately, it was nearly midnight and I was exhausted, so I chucked everybody out. Well, tried to.

Chris (tian) and Lazy Linda had already left to go clubbing as they were young people and it was the law; Amber wanted Chanel to sleep in her bottom bunk, it seemed they'd made up now and had to be in each other's pockets once more. I said yes, because the twins were still fast asleep under the dining-room table and so I put a blanket over them and told Gloria I'd bring them all back in the morning.

Rev's Nan was coming round for him first thing in the morning, and so Gloria took him with her – and just as well, I found out after they'd gone that he'd stuck all my postage stamps to the wall in the downstairs loo.

It was past midnight by the time everybody left. I'd read the riot act for the final time to the girls, who'd fallen asleep at last. I'd just started to take all that make-up off when there was a knock at the front door.

'Come on then, what have you forgotten?' I asked, as I opened it.

But it wasn't Gloria.

It was Joe.

He had bleached blond streaky hair, combed into the sort of brushed-forward style you see on the male models in twisted Levi's adverts. It was a more modern version of Joe, he looked the same but different. He was tanned and skinny and his blue eyes were not piercing but pale now. Faded, even. He'd aged, I'd remembered him as a young man. Tonight he looked as clapped-out as I felt.

'Hi.' He said that, not me.

I was too shocked to speak. I'd known this was coming, but I wasn't ready for it. Why couldn't he phone, or write, like a normal person? Why the late-night doorstep dramatics?

'Nice look,' he said. He smiled that really ooh smile. 'Is that the latest thing?'

I realized with horror that I'd only got one smoky eye on, I'd taken the other one off. I must have looked like half a panda.

'Can I come in?'

In an out-of-body experience by now, I silently stood aside and let him over my threshold. (I didn't even remember until much later that I used to keep that knife in the radiator for exactly this moment. Who'd have thought that when it came to it, I'd open the door and let him walk in?)

'Cool,' he said as he looked around the hallway, and in through the open sitting-room door. 'You've done lots to the old place – s'great.'

'Yup,' I replied. He needn't know the details, not yet. 'Tea?' I asked, it was all I could think of.

He did that half-frown half-laugh thing that people do when they want you to think they've misheard, but you know they haven't. 'Got anything stronger?'

'Nope.' I didn't feel the need to explain, and he didn't feel the need to ask. 'I've got coffee, but it's late . . .'

'Cool,' he said again, 'I'll have that. Two spoons, no milk, lots of sugar.' At least his coffee requirements hadn't changed.

'Right.'

He followed me into the kitchen, and whistled as he looked round. 'Nice.' He nodded his approval. 'You working?'

I explained that I was now the co-manager of an internet-based business. (Which was true – he didn't look nearly surprised enough, but it impressed the hell out of me.)

'Cool,' he said, 'that sounds very grown-up.'

I wanted to say that it wasn't at all, it was very hard work and we hadn't made any money yet, but I didn't.

He put his mobile on the table and sat down. He fumbled in his denim jacket pocket. It was the same denim jacket he'd always had. Big hole in the left elbow, button missing from the top right-hand pocket. Where he kept his fags and somebody else's lighter. He got out a little tin, and some papers. 'All right if I –?'

'Er, no, sorry, it's not.' I couldn't believe I'd said

314

that. 'This house is a smoke-free zone.' Why was I sounding like my mother all of a sudden?

'Yeah, but, y'know, I thought it might help . . .' Oh, I got it, he wanted to roll a joint.

'Not for me, thanks, I don't do that any more – but you can.' Why did I say that? There were kids in the house. 'Outside, in the garden, that is.' Very forceful, Charlotte, good. And then I ruined it a bit, by adding 'if you don't mind.'

He rolled it anyway, while I busied myself with the kettle. I wanted to phone Dr Lichtenstein, or Gloria, or a late-night radio phone-in, to ask what I should do. Every nerve in my body was jangling, I was sure he could see my heart thumping. I suddenly remembered Upstairs and had a quick word. By the time he'd skinned up and I'd made the coffee, I felt a little calmer.

'So,' I said. I wasn't able to look him in the face, not yet; I studied my camomile tea intently. Yes, it still looked like wee-wee.

'So,' he said back. He'd put the joint down, but couldn't take his eyes off it, he must be really nervous. He was clasping his coffee mug with both hands, as if he was cold – it was late May, I think, quite a warm night. I noticed his hands weren't their usual soft lilywhite, and his nails were ingrained with dirt – maybe he'd been doing some gardening.

'How's your sister?' I asked, desperate to put off The Moment.

'Dunno,' he replied. 'She's moved again,

changed her number. Fucked off without leaving a forwarding address.'

'Oh?' I asked, waiting for more details.

Which never came. 'And your lot, what's the deal with them?' he asked.

I told him about Matt moving to the States, and that I saw much more of my parents these days, in fact we were quite good friends. I prattled on for as long as I could, avoiding The Breakdown of course, but just as I was about to get into the story of a great-aunt who'd recently remarried her first husband for the second time, he said, 'Can I see Amber?'

'She's not here,' I lied, I don't know why. 'She's at a friend's house.'

I do know why, I wanted him to go through me first before he got to her. I wanted an explanation, an apology, a full police check before he was allowed anywhere near her.

He stood up. 'That's a shame, I was wondering what she looks like now.' He walked towards the door. 'Does she look like me?'

'Where are you going?' I demanded.

'To use the loo,' he replied. 'That all right?'

''Course,' I said, 'of course. Sorry. You remember where it is?'

He grinned. 'Just about.'

As I watched his beautiful bedenimed bum leave the room, I had to acknowledge that I still fancied him. He still looked like bad news, but – well, he'd always had this irresistibility, there was just something about him that I wanted more of and was completely powerless over. Maybe it was his wasted smile, his smoothly fluid sexy movement, the way his hair tried to curl round his ear – maybe it was all three, I couldn't say. Despite the young-person's clothes, I could tell he was much more ragged around the edges now, a slightly more faded version of his former self, but he still did it for me. Horribly, and very much against my will, I could feel a slight flickering in my loins. I knew I should be trying to pull myself together, but I found myself undoing a shirt button instead.

He came back into the room, shocked, white-grey through his weathery tan.

'Joe? What is it?'

'Is he here?' He looked frightened.

'Who?'

'Their dad.'

'Whose dad?'

'Those, er, babies out there.'

'Oh!' I could have had some fun here. I'm still sorry that I didn't. 'Er, no.'

'Cool.' He relaxed – a little. 'You and him – er . . . ?'

'What?' I knew exactly what he meant, but I wasn't going to fill in the blanks for him.

He backed down instantly. 'Nothing.'

'Where've you been, Joe?' I blurted it out, I couldn't hold myself in any longer.

'What, this evening? Yeah, sorry I came round so late, I –'

'No, not this evening! For the last nine years, where were you?!'

'Oh, right.' He leaned back in his chair, put his hands behind his head, and sighed. 'Do we have to go into this now?'

'Yes, we do. I'd say let's meet up sometime and discuss it over coffee, but I have a hunch you wouldn't turn up.'

He smiled. 'Still funny, Carlotta.'

I'd forgotten he used to call me that. It seemed strangely inappropriate now. Too intimate. 'Don't call me that.'

'Why not?' He leaned forward, touched my hand. An ice-cold electric shock ran up my arm.

I pulled back, away from him. Folded my arms, for safety. 'I just need to know, Joe, that's all. Why did you leave us?'

'I dunno really.'

'I beg your pardon?'

'I dunno.'

I hadn't been angry for a while, but I could still remember what to do. 'You don't know?' I laughed nastily, like someone in a bad melodrama. 'Oh come on, Joe, you can do better than that!'

He seemed surprised that I wasn't as chilled out as he was about 'back then', as he called it.

So I let him have it. I told him how it had been, what had happened, how it was now. While I was talking, I marched round the kitchen, I sat down, I emptied the dishwasher, I stared out of the window into the blackness beyond, I sat in another chair, I walked some more. I did my best not to blame him, not to add on any extra bits or lay any traps, I just told the truth. Well, OK, there was a little bit of finger-pointing and quite a lot of 'you bastard!'s, but anyway, I did my best.

To his credit, he didn't interrupt me. When I'd finished, he said, 'I think you're amazing.' He was smiling that smile again, damn him for being so beautiful.

'What d'you mean?' I sat down at the table again, I was exhausted.

'Well, y'know, you're really together. You're a survivor, Carlotta. Brilliant.'

I know it was a nice thing to say, but I couldn't receive his admiration just like that. I had to know who was admiring me. 'And what about you, Joe? What happened to you?'

It was a pitiful story, and he didn't tell it very well. He didn't have much clarity, in fact I noticed he was getting more confused as time went on. Details didn't match up, it was hard to get the full picture. There was more coffee, more attempts to dodge my questions, more not wanting to tell me what I had a right to know. But I got the gist of it, in the end.

He claimed he hadn't thought he was good enough to be Amber's father; once she'd arrived, the whole concept of parenthood had frightened him away, he couldn't handle it.

When he left, the plan was to hit the big time and come back for us, as a millionaire – surprise!

So he'd poured all his energy into his career, apparently. He'd done it for us.

How selfless of him. I wanted to rant and rave at the unfairness of it all, leaving me to pick up the rest, but somehow I managed to keep my mouth shut.

It had taken the band a while to realize that they were never going to make it big. Years, in fact. Not that they hadn't tried, they'd lived in Japan for a bit, and Australia after that. They'd done well in New Zealand, even got to limo-from-the-airport status.

How nice. A limo, you say. Beats the hell out of pushing a buggy in the pouring rain to the bus stop, doesn't it?

Sadly, not one country managed to recognize them as the big stars they deserved to be. It was one of the Great Unexplained Mysteries of Life.

I didn't say anything.

Then the rest of the band discovered they'd grown in different directions, and so, shockingly, it had all fallen apart. Their differences weren't just musical, they were global. The lead singer had disappeared into an ashram in Goa, and the guitarist was now a milkman in Devon. The drummer had been arrested in Canada with a gun in his hand, having shot his stepfather in the groin. It was your typical rock'n'roll suicide story, really.

So Joe had been forced to 'go it alone'. Few bass players enjoy huge commercial solo success, but this hadn't put Joe off. He was determined to make it big, you see, for us.

Yeah, right.

As far as I could gather, he'd been travelling all round Europe for the last few years, chasing deals and gigs and getting into all sorts of scrapes. He found his tales of derring-do and debauchery hilarious; I couldn't help but be resentful that he didn't have to find a babysitter first.

He'd done session work, mainly – I was amazed to discover that it was actually him I'd seen on *Top of the Pops* at Christmas! I'd thought I was delusional, but no, he'd become quite the gun for hire, musically speaking. Been everywhere, done everything. Had plenty of stories with no punch-lines, that's for sure.

Then late one night, in a bar in Paris, he'd had an epiphany of sorts, and realized that it was time to come home and face the music, so to speak.

'So here I am, babe, I'm back.'

He smouldered across the table at me, but I had to know more before I could melt.

'Have you got a girlfriend? Or even,' the thought was almost unbearable, 'any more children?'

'Yeah, well, that's part of the reason I'm here, really. I want a divorce.'

A divorce!

I hadn't been expecting this. It hit me between the eyes, I hadn't been expecting it. It hadn't occurred to me that he wouldn't want to be with me; I had assumed the choice would be mine. For once in my life, I didn't know what to say.

'Well, I did want a divorce anyway.' He shook his head, rubbed his face. 'Miyuki's my manager as well as my lady,' he said, wearily. 'I've been with her a few years now, on and off, she's great – really together, really sorted, you'd love her.' I doubt it. 'She really believes in me, Carlotta. But she's gone and got herself pregnant, says she wants to get married.'

'Not very rock'n'roll, is it, getting married?' was all I could think of to say.

'Well, y'know.' He shifted in his seat, at least he had the grace to look a little uncomfortable about it. 'I stalled her for a bit, of course, but in the end I had to tell her about you and Amber. She went bloody mental.'

I could feel myself about to go the same.

'Trouble is, now that I'm here, it's all gone pear-shaped. I'm all confused. Especially now I've heard your side of things. I didn't think I'd – well, thing is, I can see now that I don't love her like I love you.'

What?

'Never have. She's not a patch on you.' He looked me straight in the eye; God, I just loved looking at that face. 'I'm not sure we shouldn't get back together, Carlotta, but I don't suppose you'd have me back now, would you?'

I was flabbergasted. This was all going far too quickly, it made no sense.

He picked up the joint. 'All right if I smoke this outside?'

'No, no, have it in here.' I hated him, but I didn't want him out of my sight. It was like I'd been winded, punched in the stomach. My mind was racing. Who was this Japanese woman? Did he love her? Did I love him? How would I know? Did I believe him? How would it work? How much of this bullshit was true? Did he really want to come back, or was he just saying that?

He inhaled deeply. 'Want some?' he asked, through held breath.

'No thanks.' I did, though, I wanted anything that would take me away from here and now. I wanted to run, but I had to stay. Dr L had said I'd always got Fight Or Flight round the wrong way; here was the chance to get it right.

He finally exhaled. 'You've always been special to me, Carlotta, you know that. There's not a day gone by without me thinking about you two.' His bright light was on full beam now, I too could remember how it had been between us. But –

'This is killing me, Carlotta,' he said, 'I don't know what to do.'

Neither did I. A thousand thoughts were piercing through my brain, each one completely different from the one before. 'Don't fall for it.' 'Maybe he's turned over a new leaf.' 'He can't just come in here – he can if you want him to.' My head was spinning, my body was turning somersaults.

'It would be good, wouldn't it, you and me and

Amber? Just us three, starting again? I've missed you. And I know you've missed me.'

'Well, yes, but why didn't you –'

'We could be a team, Carlotta. It would be us against the rest of the world, just like the old days.'

'I don't know, Joe, I can't just –'

'I know.' He took another drag and placed the joint in the ashtray. 'Fucked-up, isn't it?' he exhaled. 'Look,' he said as he stood up, 'why don't I go and you can sleep on it? I'll come back tomor –'

'No!' I didn't want him to go, not now that he was here. But I didn't want him to stay either, it would be a mistake. I didn't know what I wanted. I stood in the doorway, and said 'I've missed you, Joe. It's been really hard, I've felt – well, so ugly and bad, and –' I couldn't speak any more, my throat was full of sobs and pain and confusion.

'Sssh.' He stood up, and came over to me. 'I'm here now, aren't I?' He spoke softly. 'Come on, Carlotta, I can tell you still fancy me.' He looked deep into me, like he used to. 'It's still there, isn't it? Our Big Love?' I'd forgotten about that too, but he hadn't. My chin wobbled like a little girl's. 'It's OK, it's all going to be OK now.'

I looked into his eyes, and even though there was something amiss, I could see my old Joe in there somewhere. It was cloudy, smoky, foggy, but he was here. I wanted it to be OK again.

He keeps my gaze as he walks towards me. Before I can look any deeper into his soul, he's holding me and his lips are on mine. Just a slow, tender kiss at first, and an embrace, just like it used to be. His mouth is hard and soft, just right. He's stroking my hair now, and whispering into my ear, 'I'm back, I've come back for you. Just like you always knew I would.' I can feel my armour dissolving, as he undoes another button of mine and I slip his jacket off and he lets it fall to the floor. My hand is cool as it makes its way up his T-shirt on to his smooth back with its silky skin, we're both soft and warm and vulnerable for each other. He feels like he used to feel, I feel like I used to feel. I lean back against the doorpost, he leans into me, we're heading for a world only we know about, on the kitchen table his phone rings.

He put me down and picked it up. 'Yo,' he said.

He walked away so that I couldn't hear what the other person was saying. It was a man, I could tell that much. I looked at the clock – it was nearly three o'clock in the morning, for goodness' sake. Who would be ringing at a time like this?

'I've got to go,' Joe said. He looked shocked, harassed, preoccupied.

'But –'

'Sorry.' He gave me a quick peck on the cheek, and said, 'I'll be back.'

He left immediately.

I sat up for a couple of hours, on the sofa, waiting.

'I'll be back.' That's what he'd said on his note all those years ago, the last time he left.

I came to with a jolt. What a fool I was being! Did I really think he'd changed?

I didn't allow it any more headspace as I went upstairs. I didn't even cry as I got ready for bed. I was tired, I wanted to sleep and work it all out in the morning, when it might all make more sense.

It was my job to look after myself now, I knew that.

Now that made a change.

Needless to say, I didn't sleep a wink that night.

My head was doing Olympic gymnastics, my duvet was too hot. Upstairs didn't seem to be too interested either, there were no bolts of lightning with messages attached coming through my bedroom window that night. The pain was unbearable, I had to take action.

So I got up again, and sat at the kitchen table and wrote it all down in one of Amber's Aladdin exercise books. Everything I could remember Joe saying, everything I was feeling, all the hatred and yearning and bitterness and loneliness and fear and anger and envy and fucked-offness I could spew out on to that page, I did. My reasoning was that if I could get rid of the past, then I could carry on with the future, whatever that may hold. Then, for added drama and a bit of ceremony, I threw the jotter into a metal bin and set fire to it out in the back garden. That shut the neighbourhood cats up for a bit.

I felt much better after that. I went to bed feeling much lighter – I lost a few stone in emotional weight that night.

'Mum, whose is this?' Amber woke me up, prodding me with one hand and holding up a denim jacket with the other. Chanel was behind her, wide-eyed.

'What time is it?'

'Whose is it?'

It was as if she knew.

'I don't know,' I lied. 'Can you go and check on the twins, see if they're still asleep under the dining-room table?'

'It's got this in it,' she said. She opened her hand – inside it was what I recognized from various TV documentaries as the paraphernalia of a heroin user. There was a little white packet folded origami-style, containing some brown powder, assorted folded pieces of tin foil, a disposable lighter, and an old biro casing with the top end snapped off.

'It's not got the ink bit in it,' said Amber, puzzled.

Fortunately, we were interrupted by the twins crying in tandem – they wanted their breakfast and they wanted their mum, thankfully in that order.

Some unsolicited advice:

If you want to go out with a pop star, don't date a musician. Date a pop star.

And if you want to go out with someone who's not a drug addict, don't date someone who's still using. Date someone else.

Don't fall in love with someone's potential.

'Oh.'

Joe was back!

It was later that same Saturday; we'd dropped the kids off at Gloria's and stayed for lunch. Then we'd done a bit of shopping, looking for a cheap but expensive-looking suit for me to wear to Sabrina's forthcoming high-society New York wedding, which didn't exist; and some school shoes for Amber that were acceptable to both of us, which also didn't exist.

Then we'd popped in to see Oz at Global Village; he'd given us the video of *Gone With the Wind* (Rosheen had left it behind, even though it was her favourite movie ever) and the plan was to watch it this evening, curled up on the sofa with pizza and chocolate ice-cream.

And now we'd arrived home, and were face-to-face with Joe, who'd clearly been waiting some time. He stood up when he saw us, he looked agitated and nervous.

You'd think that after the previous night's

shenanigans, I might be able to be nice to him, wouldn't you?

'I threw your stuff away,' I spat, as I groped around for the key in my smugly tidy handbag.

'Oh Jeez,' he said, hands ruffling through his hair, 'that's not why I'm here.' He didn't even bother to deny that the drugs were his. 'I've come to see you,' he said, squatting down to Amber, who was now taller than him. 'I'm your dad,' he said, as he stood up again, and stooped over her, in a bothering-hovering sort of way.

Amber looked at me, I tried to give her a smile back, but it was a bit crumpled. Heart pounding, I opened the front door and let myself in. Amber looked at me again.

'You'd better come in,' I sighed, holding the door open for him.

Now what?

'D'you want to see my room?' Amber asked Joe.

'Yeah,' he grinned, 'that'd be cool.'

So I watched, unable to do anything about it, as she led him upstairs and into her world. I stood there open-mouthed, horrified. My daughter was upstairs with The Enemy. It was one thing to perform a burning ritual of forgiveness on someone in the middle of the night, but quite another to have them back here so soon, tampering with your daughter's heart strings.

I asked Upstairs to take care of the situation whilst I worked out what to do next.

I phoned Gloria, she was out and her mobile was off. I left a message.

I phoned Dr Lichtenstein, forgetting that it was the weekend. I left a message.

I phoned Arthur, he wasn't answering his home number and he wasn't answering his mobile. I left a message on both.

I phoned a couple of Gloria's friends, but their lines were engaged, they were probably on the phone to each other.

So I phoned Oz at the café, who told me everything was going to be just fine.

'Fine?!' I screamed at him, as quietly as I could, 'what d'you mean, fine? The man's a drug addict, he's got my daughter trapped in her bedroom, he's probably showing her how to drop acid!'

Oz laughed. 'Listen, just keep an ear out for them –'

'D'you think I should go in there, just to check she's OK? Walk in with the vacuum cleaner, pretend I'm cleaning the room or something?'

'No,' I could hear him grinning, 'don't do that. Just let it all happen. Let them get to know each other. They'll be fine, just don't let him leave the house with her – say it's early days, maybe next time.'

'You're sounding very sensible,' I said. 'How d'you know all this stuff?'

'My mum left me and my sister with my dad,' he replied, 'and then had two more with my stepdad. It wasn't easy, but we got through it.'

'Really?' I'd never heard him talk about his family before; maybe because I'd never asked.

'Yeah, I'll tell you about it sometime.'

'I'd like that,' I said, and I really meant it. He was a good soul, Oz, I could learn a thing or two from him.

'Listen,' he continued, 'let her see her Dad as much as you can. You may hate him, but she doesn't know him yet. She's a bright girl, let her make up her own mind about him. He's nothing to do with you any more, is he?'

'We-ell,' I said, and told him all about last night's *snoggus interruptus*.

'D'you think he'll try it on again now?' he asked.

'I don't know,' I said.

'What will you do if he does?'

'I don't know,' I said again.

'Look, I've got to go, someone's spilt coffee on a keyboard – I'll call you back, OK?'

'Sure,' I said, 'off you go. And Oz –'

'Yip?'

'Thanks.'

I 'busied' myself upstairs after that – well, the bathroom cabinet was over-spilling with stuff that fell out every time you opened it, so that needed sorting out. I'd been meaning to re-fold the towels and sheets in the airing cupboard for ages, so it was good to get that done. And I tried to recreate Gloria's sophisticated make-up at my dressing table, and even though I ended up looking like a vampire, at least I could hear Amber's voice merrily chatting to Joe, who seemed to be laughing in all the right places.

Don't get me wrong, I wasn't fine about all this, it nearly bloody killed me. And if I'd heard so much as a raised voice coming from her bedroom, I'd have been in there like a shot to bloody kill him. I stood it for as long as I could, and then I told myself that as it was nearly 6 o'clock, we'd better start watching *Gone With the Wind* soon, or else we'd fall asleep before the end. Good, huh?

I went downstairs and called up 'Amber!' trying to sound breezy, sounding more like a banshee, 'it's showtime!'

They tumbled downstairs looking very – well, happy, I suppose – and Amber busied herself with finding the pizza number while I cued up the video. Joe hung around in the hallway. He looked annoyingly good, even more handsome than yesterday. I'd adapted to his new looks now.

'I'll go, shall I?'

'No, Mummy, let him stay!' Amber came out into the hallway, clutching the leaflet. 'Please?'

'You go and make sure there's enough ice cream in the freezer,' I said, 'or we'll have to order some more.'

She went back into the kitchen. Joe took my hand. Again, it was electric.

'I've been thinking about you all day,' he said.

'Really?' I said, pretending that I'd been far too busy to do the same.

'Why don't I watch the film with you two tonight? I can leave when it's finished.' He cheeked at me. 'Or we could let Amber watch it by herself for a bit . . .'

My loins were tickling again, I could still feel his kiss, I wanted to smell his skin again. Damn!

He moved towards me. 'OK, have it your way, Carlotta. But at least let me say goodbye properly, until next time . . .'

Oh dear God. His mouth is coming towards me, I shut my eyes and prepare for a delicious assault. I hope my body shuts my head up, I do want this, I do. I can feel his hot breath on my face, he's really close, the doorbell rings.

I opened the door. A man in a motorcycle helmet was standing there, holding a stack of boxes.

'Anyone for pizza?' said a familiar voice.

'How did you know?' asked Amber, coming out of the kitchen. 'I haven't even –'

'Oz?!'

'Hold these,' he said, and he ran back to the street, took off his helmet and gave it to a waiting Pizza Hut moped rider. 'Thanks for the ride, Raoul!' he called, as he came back up my garden path. 'Hi!' He held out his hand. 'You must be Joe!'

'Er, yeah,' said Joe, as his hand was shaken vigorously.

'Hi, Oz!' said Amber, and rushed to hug him. 'That's my dad!'

'I'm Charlotte's partner,' gurned Oz, over her shoulder, 'I've heard lots about you, Joe!'

Before I could say 'not that kind of partner', Joe said 'OK, I'm going to shoot off, er – have you got my jacket?'

'Oh, yes, of course,' I took it off the banisters and handed it to him.

'I'll be back,' he said, 'to see Amber,' he said to all of us, and rushed away, nearly knocking Gloria off her feet as she came up the path.

'Oi, watch it!' she said to his disappearing back, 'bloody junkies. Everythin' OK?' she beamed.

The phone rang. Dr L, just so happened to have popped in to work today, got my message.

Arthur pulled up in a cab outside.

Ever felt like you were really being looked after? Thank you, God.

Looking back now, I can see that I had a lucky escape. But at the time, I was furious. As far as I was concerned, this was none of their business.

Ah, they said, but you made it our business when you asked us for help.

Yes, I replied, but I know what's best for me, I'm the expert, thank you very much.

Not any more, as it turns out. Look where I got me. They knew better than me, I had to listen to them now.

He's not good for you, they said. He can't make you happy. He's sick.

Like I said, I had a lucky escape.

334

Joe checked into rehab quite soon after that.

Then the week after he came out, he scored more drugs on the train home. He just didn't want to give up.

Fortunately, I didn't find this very attractive.

Somehow, however, he managed to keep his new-found relationship with Amber going, after a fashion. So she finally got to hold her head high in the playground and talk about her dad, just like the other girls. She had to learn that he wasn't reliable, and he wasn't rich, but he certainly wasn't boring. Well, it's not every dad that takes his daughter and her friend to television studios to watch him play guitar with this week's best band, is it?

Thanks to Dr L, I managed to let go of Joe in the end, even if he did have scratch marks down his sides. I never thought I'd be able to say this, but I don't have any unresolved feelings for him now. He's just someone from my past, that's all. He's a nice enough man, but he's not for me.

I deserve better.

# CHAPTER 12

'There is a type of person who can show unfailing love to others, but not always to themselves, or to their immediate family. That's how my mother was. Which is why, at the party we held after she died, more than a hundred people came to mourn and – with the aid of cheap wine, cubes of cheese on cocktail sticks and paper handkerchiefs – weep copiously over their collective loss with an intensity of grief which neither I nor my brothers were able to feel.'

Jonathan Self, *Self Abuse*

We had reached crisis point at the Global Village. It was the beginning of the summer and business was definitely not booming. Oz and I were having an emergency meeting, just as we had the day before and the day before that. We were utterly despondent.

Not even the sight of Hugh Grant beavering away at what had now become His computer could cheer me up. Over the past few weeks, I'd tried every tip known to Gloria to attract his attention, but he was having none of me.

Oz wasn't flirting today either, not even with the couple of teenage schoolgirls who'd bunked off school to share one coke. There was no one else there, there rarely was. It was a pretty bleak outlook – we were not going to cover our costs this month, and Rosheen was going to have the satisfaction of seeing us fail.

'I suppose it was madness,' I said, gloomily, 'us taking this on. I mean neither of us have had any previous experience of this sort –'

'You worked at Starbucks!' protested Oz.

'Yes, I know, but only as a barista. I left the day I was promoted, if you remember.'

'Oh yeah,' said Oz. He stared out of the window. 'I was a driving instructor, y'know.'

'Were you?!'

'No. Well, only for a day.' He sighed. 'But I did used to visit sick people in hospo with Suki the labrador and Puffy the rabbit.'

'Like I said,' I held my head in my hands, 'we had no experience. What were we thinking?'

The café door opened. 'Der-ner!' screeched a familiar voice. For some reason Gloria was dressed like Al Capone in high heels, thoroughly upholstered with a pinstripe trouser suit, black shirt, black tie. More to the point, she was waving a wad of cash at us.

'What's that?' asked Oz and I, at the same time.

'Have you robbed a bank?' I asked, perfectly seriously. (Well, let's face it, this woman was capable of anything. And she was dressed for it.)

'Yes, I have, in actual fact!' she proudly announced. 'The Royal Bank of Gloria.' Oz and I exchanged a glance. 'My savings!' she said, 'I've decided you need them more than me. You can pay me back when you can, but I think you should 'ave 'em.'

We refused, obviously.

But she insisted, obviously.

So we refused again.

In the end, Oz cleverly changed the subject by offering her a free computer lesson, right there and then. 'No time like the present, Glo!'

'Er, no thanks, Oz mate, not now. I've got to pick the twins up soon, and –'

'I thought Keko had taken them to Legoland today,' I said.

'Yeah, well, y'know, Rev'll be –'

'With his gran in Bournemouth for half-term, I believe –' I finished for her. 'Amber rang by the way, she and Chanel are having a great time with my mum and dad.' Gloria gave a crumpled smile, she was completely lost without her children. She looked like a little girl herself. 'Go on, Gloria, you might as well take him up on it. This is as good a time as any, while we're experiencing this temporary lull in what is normally a very busy day . . .'

'No.' She looked terrified, for some reason.

'It's not scary, y'know,' reassured Oz. 'Or difficult.

Let's face it, if a dag like Charlotte can do it, anyone can!'

'I don't want to, thanks.' She was looking a bit shifty now, I was determined to get to the bottom of this.

'But Gloria, why not? It's fun, you'll love it. What's stopping you?'

'Leave it, Char, all right?'

She was about to explode. I recognized the signs, but Oz didn't.

'Just tell us why you don't want to, Gloria, then maybe we can help –'

'Because,' she was very red in the face, and speaking through gritted teeth, 'I can't bloody well read, that's why!'

Gosh.

Blimey.

'But, what about all those benefit forms –'

'They know down the social, of course; as it happens, I'm trying to get them to register me disabled.'

'And what about books, newspapers, that sort of thing?' questioned Oz.

'Don't need 'em, and anyway, Lori does what I can't,' she replied. 'Going to make any more of this, are ya, or can we move on?'

She was staring at both of us, proud and furious.

We couldn't think of anything to say.

Fortunately someone came into the cafe at that moment and said 'Charlotte, hi – Dad said I'd find you here.'

'Matt!' What the hell was my brother doing here? Shouldn't he be in America? He didn't look right here, in fact he didn't look right at all. 'Are you OK?'

'Mum's very ill. Dad won't leave her, and he didn't want to tell you over the phone. We've got to go down there, now. I hired a car at the airport. I'll explain on the way.'

It was all a bit much to take in. I had to leave Oz to deal with Gloria's bombshell, I couldn't deal with it, I had to go.

As I hugged a somewhat subdued Gloria goodbye, I whispered into her ear, 'Now you leave my little brother alone, you naughty girl!'

She whispered back, 'Don't worry, darlin', he's not for me!' She really was unpredictable, I thought, as I got into the car – not only was he filthy rich, but he was also one of the most hand-some men I'd ever seen. But maybe I only thought that because he was my brother.

'Why didn't you ring me, Matt?' I hated last-minute panics, I liked to have enough time to whip myself up into a really good frenzy.

'Dad and I didn't want to – well, you know, upset you. Just in case . . .'

'Just in case what? Just in case I threw all your furniture out of the window, is that it? I should have known – looking after your own skin as usual, Matt.'

He was silent.

So was I. Damn it.

'Sorry.' I just couldn't get away with that kind

of behaviour any more. 'Just – frightened, that's all. Confused. Surprised. I don't mean to take it out on you.'

'S'OK.' He was sickeningly forgiving, as ever. 'You're probably in shock, as I was. I had to drop everything, jump on a plane. I'm supposed to be having my hair cut yesterday morning, I think.'

We left the cafe. It was a lovely warm evening. Matt had taken the precaution of hiring a convertible. He was so bloody stylish it hurt.

'What's the matter with her, anyway?'

'No idea. Dad said he'd tell us when we got there.'

'It's not terminal, is it?' I looked at his face, for a sign of knowing and not telling. 'I mean, it's nothing serious?'

'Don't know.' He kept his eyes on the road, but he was blinking a lot.

'You're really worried, aren't you?' I'd forgotten he had a completely different relationship with her. This was his parent of choice who was seriously ill. 'Would you like me to drive? You must be knackered.'

He managed a sideways glance at me. 'Are you OK?'

'Yes, why?'

'Nothing,' he smiled to himself, 'you're just different, that's all. You've changed.'

'Correction,' I said, 'I've been changed.' I smiled too. 'It's not a totally unselfish offer, though – I've always wanted to drive one of these! Now are you going to pull over, or do I have to physically push you out of the car?'

I went from nought to angry in about five minutes.

As Matt slept beside me in the passenger seat, I found myself resenting the fact that I was doing all the driving, while he got to rest.

Ten minutes later, I was cross that he had longer legs than me, and better-behaved hair, and white teeth.

Fifteen minutes after that, I was seething about his close relationship with my mother – they adored each other, even though he was boring and she was grim.

By the time we pulled into the drive, I was fantasizing about stabbing him with one of the sharp kitchen knives from the wooden block just to the right of my mother's spotless stainless-steel sink.

I hadn't felt like this for ages. Surprisingly, it didn't feel that good.

My poor dad was beside himself. He'd been waiting for us at the window, and as soon as he saw the car, he rushed out to greet us before I had even turned the engine off. Matt was still asleep, lost to the coma of the jet-lagged – mouth open, probably full of flies by now. I decided to leave him there for a few minutes more while I, being the elder, went in to assess the situation.

I followed Dad into the not-quite-as-spanking-clean-as-usual kitchen – she really must be ill – firing off questions as we walked. 'When did it start? Has she got a temperature? Have you called the doctor? Why not? But you must bother him, she's ill! Have you tried arnica? Echinacea? D'you know what that is? Is she eating/sleeping/moving her bowels regularly?'

He couldn't remember which ones he'd answered and which he hadn't, and I was having difficulty linking his replies to anything I'd asked, and so we made a pot of tea and started again.

She'd not been right since they came home from staying with me, apparently. There had been a lot of 'work' to do and the neighbour and the cleaning lady and the gardener had all done their best, but to my mother it must have seemed an unclimbable mountain. Dad had tried to help restore the house back to manageable, of course, but he'd only succeeded in getting under her feet.

'So how bad was it?' I asked. 'Had a pipe burst or something? Was it rat-infested? Did you have squatters?'

'No, no, nothing like that,' replied Dad, who was a bit pale and a bit shaky, he'd obviously been living with this for some time. 'Poor old darling stayed up cleaning and polishing all night, started vacuuming at dawn, that sort of thing. Checking the sell-by date on all the tins in the larder, drawing up charts of what to throw out when, you know.'

I certainly did know, this was the kind of madness I'd had to endure as a child. I'd since found out from Dr L that it's called Obsessive Compulsive Disorder. I don't care what fancy name you give it; she was a control freak, a cleanliness freak, just a general all-round freak in fact. I haven't heard of many other families where you not only have to take off your shoes as soon as you get in the door, but also have to wrap them in clingfilm.

'Don't know what to do with her now, completely flummoxed.' Suddenly my father looked like a little boy who'd lost his way. His kind eyes were filled with tears, I couldn't bear to see it.

'You really love her, Dad, don't you?'

He nodded.

'But why?' I shook my head. 'She's a nightmare!'

'Don't be rude!' he snapped.

It was a slap on the hand for me, and fair enough. I'd never gone this far with him before. He knew Mum and I didn't necessarily adore each other, but I'd never been so honest about it until now. It was one of our family's many Unspoken Subjects.

Dad folded his arms, leaned against the sink, looked down at the floor. 'Look after each other, you see. Spent too long apart, catching up now.'

His career had taken him all over the world, sometimes for months at a time; she'd refused to go with him, preferring to stay in England. 'But why didn't she travel with you, Dad, it's so selfish of her to make you live abroad on your own. You must have been so lonely.'

'Wouldn't leave you lot behind,' he said, into his chest.

'But I was at boarding school most of the time,' I protested, 'and I'm sure Matt would have gone to the top of the class wherever he was in the bloody world.'

'Wanted to give you lot stability,' he sighed, 'couldn't afford to keep flying you lot around the world, never was anywhere for very long, y'see.'

I hadn't known that. I'd always assumed –

'Never seen her like this before,' he looked up at me, so concerned, 'she going to be all right, d'you think?'

I shrugged my shoulders, I didn't know.

He marched into the pantry – the rest of the world would see it as a walk-in store cupboard, but we had to call it The Pantry. 'Couldn't bear it if something happened to the old darling,' he said from the inside, his voice wobbling a little, 'couldn't manage.'

I laughed. 'Yes you could, Dad, big old blunderbuss like you!'

'Couldn't.' He stood in the doorway, holding a catering-size box of sugar lumps. 'Wouldn't want to. Life without your mother – unbearable.'

He put the box on the kitchen table and opened it, warming to his theme as he slowly unwrapped each fiddly pair of cubes and put them in a tiny bowl.

'Lights up my world, you see. Still get a thrill when she walks in the room. Most beautiful creature I ever saw, heart of gold, very clever woman. Family first, herself last. Lets me know I'm important. Looks after me very well, my job to do the same.'

He looked up. 'Love, you see Charlotte, is all about how someone else makes you feel about yourself.'

This was astonishing. Not only had I never heard him talk like this, but it was also the first time I'd heard him say a complete sentence.

'So we've got to love them back, or else it's stealing.'

Gosh.

He carried on unwrapping. There was a muffled thump from upstairs; he looked up.

'Cats,' he told me.

'Cats?'

'Got a couple of kittens for her, make her feel like she's got something to get up for. Called 'em Spick and Span. Didn't work.'

'Right.'

'Mustn't get into the bedroom, new carpet. Smell of cat piss almost impossible to get out, y'know. Make your mother even more worried . . .'

'Look, you stay here. I'll go up and have a word –'

'– No!' His tone changed in an instant. 'Mustn't upset her, don't know if she can take it.'

My own father, afraid of me. Protecting his wife from their daughter. In the old days I'd have flounced out, probably through the wrong door. Now I suppose I could see why he felt like this. I had been a bit of a monster, a bit of a thief in Dad's terms. I'd taken, but I hadn't given back. Yet.

In the kindest voice I could manage, so as not to alarm him, I said, 'Don't worry, Dad. I just want to help, that's all. If she shows any signs of distress, I'll call you.'

He didn't look convinced.

'I know, why don't you make Matt a really strong cup of proper coffee? I'm sure that's what he'll want when he wakes up, it's all they drink in California, isn't it?'

Grateful for the diversion of doing something practical for his son, he pottered about finding the coffee machine's new place, tracking down the filter coffee, and the papers, and the measuring spoon. (That new-fangled contraption The Cafetiére had not reached their corner of darkest Surrey yet.)

I went up the stairs, smiling at the familiarity of the house. Nothing had changed, nothing. The stair carpet was getting a little threadbare on the treads, but it wouldn't be thrown away yet, they'd only had it about ten years. (As far as I could remember, their old bedroom carpet must have been at least thirty years old before it had been replaced.)

The staircase walls were lined with old family photographs; stiff Victorians in uncomfortable hats, children in strange knitted bathing costumes on cold beaches, my father and his father and his father too in various military uniforms, trying to look frightening, but looking frightened instead.

The landing was lined with bookshelves, bursting to overloaded with old hardback novels from the 70s by long-forgotten book-club authors. There were strange china ornaments on top, figurines of shepherdesses and pan pipe players, looking as if they had been randomly dotted around the place in their prettiness – but us insiders knew that each one was exactly where it was supposed to be, and that she'd know straight away if anything had been moved.

(Needless to say, neither Matt nor I ever attempted to have a party when they were away. Nor did our friends even bother to try and persuade us. Mind you, we couldn't; we weren't allowed to be in the house on our own at such times, we always had to stay with friends or relations. I did try to explain that I wouldn't necessarily want to set my own home on fire, but she was having none of it.)

Every door upstairs was tightly shut, to keep the dust out and the spiders in. If I'd entered one of the rooms, I would doubtless have been punched in the nosebuds by the usual overpowering aroma of Mr Sheen and Shake 'n' Vac and mothballs, with more than a hint of citrus, spring meadows, pine forests and floral bouquets exuding from the abundance of plug-in air fresheners in every available socket. It was enough to give you hay fever, even in winter.

'Mum?' I knocked on their bedroom door gently.

Guess what, no reply.

I turned the handle silently, so as not to wake her up. I knew exactly how to do this, as I used to creep in at night when I was little and watch them sleeping. I don't know why I did that, and now it strikes me as slightly weird – I suppose it made me feel safe.

I could see from the chink of light creeping in through the blackout curtains (my father was incapable of shutting them properly, as she'd told us, many times) that she was asleep. Her tiny frame seemed swamped by their big bed. I was always surprised that they'd never moved into single beds, like my friends' parents. I think she'd tried, but he'd refused, cleverly citing the expense of two new duvets and extra sheets, and the waste of a perfectly good double bed. The real reason, I now understood, was that he wanted to sleep beside her, to touch her and care for her and hold her close to him, for comfort and protection, because he loved her.

But she wouldn't understand that. Or would she? As I stood at the end of their bed, I realized that

I didn't really know this woman. She'd always been My Mother, never a real person. What would I think of her if I met her, got to know her as a normal human being?

The photographs on his chest of drawers told her story. I'd seen them a hundred times before, but now I studied them with a different eye. She'd been a debutante, but despite some clever hairdressing and the matt powdered make-up of the time, not a pretty one. The uniform of the 1950s had given her a well-cut elegance she'd never captured since. Her eyes had something, however; a sparkle, a glint, a hint of mischief. I'd never noticed that before. She looked as if she'd been quite good fun; she'd probably been a jolly companion for him, popular at business functions, a big hit with the husbands as well as the wives.

Their wedding looked like it had been a very stuffy affair, full of maiden aunts and chinless uncles. The bride and groom's mothers were standing at opposite ends of the line-up, where they were to remain for the rest of their lives. Both had thought their son/daughter could have done a lot better, and both had let their views be known to anyone who would listen. I assume this only went to strengthen my parents' resolve to make the marriage work, and work it they did. They were coming up to their forty-fifth wedding anniversary later on this year. That's an astonishing length of time to be married, isn't it? Even if I met someone this afternoon, it would be unlikely I'd ever achieve anything like that.

Her whole demeanour seems to have changed by my christening. She's holding me with a grim determination, smiling through gritted teeth. What's the matter with the woman? Wasn't she pleased to have me? Didn't she know what a precious gift a child is?

Then it hit me. Wasn't I exactly the same, when I had Amber? OK, my circumstances were different, but didn't I used to smile at the camera with the same forced grin? Until very recently, I had been a great exponent of the 'having kids is awful' school of thought – maybe my own mother had felt the same way, but in those days she'd never have been allowed to say it. Come to think of it, Dad was away mostly during my early childhood, not Matt's. To all intents and purposes, she'd been a single parent too.

But how would that explain this beaming photograph of her with Matt? In my bedroom. (I was very familiar with this one, of course, having studied it for so long when it arrived at school.) Aha – my father had started his company by then, he was home much more. Of course. They got to be a real family.

It all came together in that moment. Like me, she hadn't had the emotional resources to cope with a baby on her own. Like me, she'd found it very difficult, a thankless task. Unlike me, she'd gone on to have another child with the help of a

351

loving and supportive husband, and she'd managed to be happy this time.

No wonder she didn't like it when I showed up, I just reminded her of her old pain. And maybe Dad had been aware of this, and overcompensated, and loved me too much. She must have been so jealous. No wonder she gave it all to Matt.

And here the three of them are, at his graduation ceremony at Oxford, so proud. (I remembered being invited, but I'd said I was too busy to go. Too busy trying to find a knife to cut off my nose, probably.) How different she looks! Radiant, almost pretty. Why couldn't I make her that happy?

*It's not too late*, said a voice in my head – spookily, Upstairs had recently begun to talk to me.

I was just about to start arguing back when the door was opened so roughly it banged against Mum's bedside table, causing the precarious pile of Georgette Heyer paperbacks and Women's Institute literature to topple to the floor. A tiny black kitten ran out from under the bed and escaped through the open door, nearly causing Matt to fall flat on his face.

'Come on, Mum.' Matt's voice still managed to be loud in the muffling room. 'Wakey wakey!' He began to open the curtains.

I thought she'd sit up, thrilled to see her favourite child, but she didn't. She rolled over and turned away from him.

I silently quizzed across the bed at Matt, puzzled. He looked down at her and shook his head, not like someone who was sad that their mother was ill, but more like someone who was frustrated by a stubborn child.

'I tried to tell her when they came over at Christmas,' he said to me, as he sat down on the bed. 'But she made damn sure I didn't get the chance.'

'Tell her what?' I asked, sitting on the chair by the window, where my father's clothes were laid out for him every morning.

'Every time I tried to broach the subject, she would talk about something else, or turn on the TV, or leave the room. It was as if she knew what I was trying to say, but didn't want to hear me.'

'What were you trying to say?' I asked.

'I think she probably knew anyway, she just didn't want it to be true.'

'Knew what?' My last attempt.

'And Jesus, when I think of how I could have done it. She was lucky. Some guys can be really brutal with their parents, you know?' He sighed. 'In the end, I wrote her a letter. I thought that was the best way to tell her. I think that's why she's taken to her bed. She's furious.'

For fuck's sake. 'TELL HER WHAT?!'

Just as my father walked into the room with the best coffee pot and milk jug from their wedding service and four matching bone china cups and saucers normally reserved for visitors and/or the Queen on a tray, Matt said, 'I'm gay.'

Dad dropped the tray.

Mum's whole body winced.

There was a moment's silence, followed immediately by the bedclothes being flung back and Mum leaping out of bed and into action. There was much activity involving the children being sent downstairs for cloths and stain removers and not-at-all helpfully bringing back salt and white wine instead, whilst the grown-ups kept telling each other as they scrubbed away that it didn't really matter, knowing perfectly well that it really did.

Fortunately the carpet had been scotch-guarded, twice, and we found all the fragments of china that had been flung far and wide in the impact, which were put back on the tray, ready for my mother to spend the next few weeks and months and possibly years carefully sticking back together again. The whole mess was cleaned up within ten minutes. Crisis over.

Matt was still gay, though.

Gay!

Of course!

But what kind?

Maybe he was one of those wannabe ones, the type Arthur's always making jokes about. Q: What's the difference between a straight man and a gay man? A: About eight pints.

He couldn't be a screaming queen, or we'd all have known years ago. Neither had he grown a dormouse on his upper lip, worn a lumberjack shirt, gone all hi-energy on us.

No, he was definitely the same kind as Arthur. The same-sex thing wasn't worn like a badge, it was just a part of his life. Matt was a gentleman gay, a professional man who just so happened to be homosexual. A fruit in a suit.

Cool.

By the time we'd had supper and done the washing-up and were ready to leave, the atmosphere had lightened up a bit. Dad seemed to be dealing with it by pretending he hadn't heard a thing, he'd been rendered temporarily deaf. Poor Mum was still in a mood, but it was hard to know whether it was the end of the previous one or the start of a new one, they all sort of ran into each other. Nobody talked about it, of course – this was the Small family, why would they?

I didn't think my new-found perspective on Mum would make a difference, but it did. When we went to air-kiss goodbye in our usual way, I wanted to let her know that everything was going to be fine. So I did.

'Mum,' I said, looking her in the eye, 'I'm sorry I've been difficult. I understand now. This will change, I promise.' To her horror, I flung my arms round her and gave her the most almighty hug. I was surprised to feel how frail her frame was beneath my grip. I hadn't actually touched her in ages, I hadn't realized she was getting old. Suddenly I wanted to be kind to her. Odd.

Anyway, we both told her we loved her, which must have finished her off completely, as she ran inside the house and shut the front door behind her.

Dad came out to the car to see us off. 'Thanks,' he said, shaking Matt's hand. (He couldn't quite manage a hug, not yet. Lot to think about.)

'What for?'

'Sorting your mother out,' said Dad. 'Hadn't realized. Thought she was sick. Feel a bit of a fool.' He looked apologetic. 'Sorry for the false alarm.'

'Doesn't matter, Dad!' Matt grabbed the car key out of my hand and walked over to the driver's door. 'Don't worry, she'll get over it. At least she knows she'll always have beautiful drapes.'

Giggling, I snatched the key back again. Dad returned to the house as we argued over who was going to drive back to London, shaking his head as he knocked on the door and waited to be let back in.

The drive home was extraordinary.

Not because we aired our grievances, listened to each other and immediately became the best of friends, but because we didn't have to do any of that. Now that the 'gay' thing was out in the open, Matt's need to be the perfect son had been lifted. And

356

he seemed more human to me now. We could both relax.

So we chatted away like people who'd known each other a long time, which, in essence, is what we are.

He told me that he'd kept it quiet from us all these years because he wanted to wait until he'd met The One. Stu and he had decided to buy a house together at Easter, and instead of a baby they had a dog called Louis, which is what they would have called their son. Aah, bless 'em!

(He'd tried to tell me all this when I'd phoned him that day to say thank you and couldn't wait to get off the phone; he thought I knew already, and was in as much denial as Mum and Dad.)

But more importantly to me, Stu is a very successful restaurateur. Matt was good enough to pass on a few business tips; words like 'advertising' and 'promotion' were mentioned. By the time we got to London, I knew exactly what we had to do with the café, and how to do it too. I phoned Stu many times after that, and his advice was always very sound.

So once again, my brother had bailed me out of trouble. Only this time I wasn't annoyed, I was grateful.

It was about midnight by the time we turned into my road. It was a beautiful warm evening, and the moon was full and bright, so I shouldn't have been so surprised to find out that there was just one more Biography Moment to be had before I'd get to bed that night. But it wasn't going to be mine.

Ever since Residents' Parking had been introduced it had become impossible to find a space near the house, so Matt dropped me off while he drove around the block. There was a joke in there somewhere about cruising, but both of us were too tired to find it.

Arthur was slumped in the doorway. (I read somewhere once that a person's life gets played out largely in one location only – mine was obviously my doorstep.) Once I'd got him inside and in the light, I could see that he was distraught – his face was ashen and tearstained and his hair was all over the place. 'What's happened?' I asked as I shut the door behind us, although I could guess.

'You'll never guess,' he said hoarsely, poor love had obviously been crying for a very long time, 'Jimmy's gone.'

'No!' I said, trying really hard to sound surprised.

''Fraid so,' he said, as he threw himself face down on the sofa, just like he always did when they'd had a big fight.

I made him a strong cup of tea with lots of sugar, and I had a camomile tea with honey. (And a whole packet of chocolate biscuits too, I hadn't gone macrobiotic or anything.)

'What happened?' I asked, as I placed his mug on the coffee table and settled myself into the armchair, steeling myself for hearing the same old stuff, secretly hoping it wouldn't take too long.

It didn't. Jimmy had gone off with the Punk Peacock again. (I never did tell Arthur about the show that was put on for me that day in Starbucks – I'd decided to let Jimmy do his own dirty work.) She'd been blissfully unaware of Arthur's existence until the café makeover weekend, which was once again an attempt by Jimmy to get someone else to sort it all out for him. Rather admirably, she'd made Jimmy choose between them. She didn't mind him being bisexual because she was too.

Arthur was distraught, he'd always thought he'd lose Jimmy one more time and now he had. I felt sorry for him – compassionate even. I must be going soft.

(I didn't let him know that, of course – poor man would have been terrified at such a change, it would have thrown the whole friendship.)

Anyway, just as I was saying, 'Poor Arthur, you deserve so much better. I'm sure someone will turn up, you just wait,' there was a soft knock at the front door.

Arthur raised his unhappy head. 'Who'd have thought?' he said, 'that it would be this soon?'

'Glad to see that Jimmy didn't run off with your sense of humour,' I said, as I got up to open it.

For as long as I live, I will never forget the expression on Arthur's face when he saw Matt. It still makes me smile.

Later, Arthur said that Matt was his guardian angel, sent to show him the way forward.

I wanted them to get together, and so did Arthur, it would have been just perfect. But it wasn't to be. Matt didn't fancy him, and anyway, he was in love with Stu. But this didn't stop them going to dinner the next night, and I don't know what Matt said, or if anything happened afterwards – it's a gay thing, the rules are completely different, we wouldn't understand – but they became very good friends after that.

Arthur decided not to pursue the young boy line of questioning any further, and since then has very much enjoyed interviewing men of a similar age and social standing to himself, although he hasn't found The One yet. Jimmy's name has never been mentioned again – Arthur says he wants a co-pilot, not a passenger.

I don't buy it for a minute, but if it makes him happy, who cares?

As it turned out, Arthur wasn't the only person who got dumped that summer.

Business at the café had slowly begun to pick

up, and that day was a little bit busier than the day before. There were several customers dotted around both inside and out, reading newspapers while they waited for the caffeine to kick in. I was on my way out to the tables on the pavement to ask Elaine (our local tramp) to stop heckling the passers-by, and to keep her thoughts about them to herself. It was a lovely sunny morning, and I was bribing her with an iced coffee, her favourite, and a couple of croissants we'd kept back from the day before for her, as usual. So there I was, trying to juggle the plate and the glass in one hand, and open the door with the other, when who should be right in front of me but Hugh Grant.

'Hi!' we both said, at the same time.

God, he was just so handsome! He hadn't been to the café for a while, but I'd been too busy to notice. And I'd forgotten how much he made me blush. Almost immediately, I was back at school-girl.

Then 'you must be Charlotte,' said a breath-lessly high-pitched girlie voice behind him, 'hi!'

He moved aside; the sun was in my eyes and I had to squint, but I could just about pick out a happy little face with pale glossy lips shining out from beneath a baseball cap, one of those dark blue ones with 'NY' on it in white letters. She had very long blonde hair, and was wearing a tight little pale pink T-shirt with jeans, which showed her perfect figure off completely. She was perky and petite and pretty. Everything I should have been but never was, and was never going to be.

'This is Mandy,' he said. 'My wife.'

'Hi!' I said, not at all in shock. 'How absolutely fantastic to meet you,' I carried on, 'a totally and completely brilliant pleasure!!! All right if I just drop these off first?'

I kerfuffled my way out to Elaine, issued a firmer than usual warning to her, and came back in to the café, hoping my heart would have stopped beating so hard by then. It hadn't.

'We just got married!' Mandy announced inside, in an American accent, one of the cute ones. She took off her baseball cap and ruffled her hair so that it looked like she'd just got out of bed; not like when I did that and it looked like I'd been dragged through a hedge backwards. 'In't that great?'

'Yes,' I said, 'I'm so happy for you.' (That may or may not have been true.)

They went on to describe in gushing lovey-dovey sickifying terms how most of their romance had been conducted online, in this very café, over the past year. Mandy was a dancer, who up until a month ago had been appearing in a musical on Broadway. Hugh Grant had spotted her whilst on a business trip (he was in insurance) (yes, I know, *insurance*) and waited for her backstage and she hadn't wanted to give him her phone number and so she'd given her email address instead and – oh well, y'know, the rest was history. They'd been conversing transatlantically via msn hotmail ever since, and then finally Hugh Grant, the old romantic, had proposed to her on bended knee in Central Park, just after a ride in one of those horse-drawn clichés, and they'd decided to tie the knot the next weekend in Las Vegas with an Elvis impersonator, and in't that just the most romantic thing you ever heard?

Now I'm no cynic, but – well, OK, I am – how unoriginal.

'Breathtaking,' I said, busying myself with some dirty cups, 'absolutely breathtaking!'

'And it's all thanks to you!' chirruped Mandy.

'Me?'

'Yes. When Keith –' that name still made me wince, 'said that the café was in danger of closing down, we were devastated. It was our only method of communication, you see.' They fluttered at each other, she continued. 'We couldn't afford long transatlantic phone calls. Keith used to come here every lunchtime for a bit of privacy from the guys at work, and I would just be getting up in the morning back in New York, so it was a good time for both of us –' I think she could tell I was losing the will to live, she put her hand on my arm – 'and so we were really excited when you saved it from closing down.' She looked momentarily grave, as serious as a Baywatch babe could look. 'Charlotte, I wanna thank you. You held our relationship together.'

Who'd have thought?

'Isn't the innernet a wonderful thing?' she gushed.

'I'll second that!' agreed Oz, who had been sorting out another new customer with a coffee and a computer, ching ching.

'Oh my god! You must be Shane! Oh my god! I don't believe I'm actually meeting you, oh my god!!!' Even Elaine peered in through the window, to see what the shrieking was about.

Hugh Grant and I watched Oz listening intently as Mandy described the part he had played in Romance of the Century. 'Isn't she great?' he asked, grinning from ear to ear.

'Isn't he great?' I wanted to ask back. Oz was so kind, he was listening to her boring story as if his life depended on it.

'I must be the luckiest man on earth,' Hugh Grant whispered, amazed at his own good fortune.

Unfortunately, I was too wrapped up in my own rejection to be big enough to be pleased for him. I felt such a fool – why on earth had I even thought I had a chance? I was almost old enough to be his mother! I'd always known it was just a silly crush, of course I did, Gloria and I joked about it all the time, but I still felt ridiculously disappointed.

My cheeks were burning with shame, but somehow I managed to wave the happy couple off into the sunset. I felt so upset, even their request to book a party here for all their friends and relations didn't cheer me up. I waved them off through a gritted smile.

'C'm here,' said Oz, and he gave me a great big hug. He smelled of cinammon and olives and too much fabric conditioner. I'd never discussed my Hugh Grant Thing with him, I didn't have to – he was one of those people who just knew. I sobbed into his chest, I felt like the girl who never got picked for the netball team. 'Silly bugger,' said Oz, he was hugging me too tight now, I could hardly breathe. I loosened his grip but stayed in the embrace, and looked up at him.

'I really love you, Charlotte Small,' he said to me.

'I love you too, Oz,' I said back. And I knew I did, I really did.

That was our moment. Sometimes I wish we could have stayed there for ever.

But I had to open my mouth, didn't I? 'D'you think we should . . .'

'What, you and me? Get it together? Be an item, as you would say?!' He was looking at me, he was looking for clues. He was looking very serious. 'You're joking, aren't you?'

There was a pause, a long pause. I looked at his funny face while I was waiting. No, I didn't fancy him. But yes, he was the loveliest man I'd ever met . . .

*Hold out for what you want*, said Upstairs.

Thank you.

'Yes, Oz,' I replied slowly, but sadly, as I released my hold on him, 'I'm only joking.'

'Well thank God for that!' he said, a little too

loudly as we broke away from each other. 'I thought you'd gone stark staring mad!'

'Yes,' I said, as I started to clear a table for the next customers, 'thank God for that.'

And that was our moment.

Stu's advice had really helped us to get going, but now Oz and I needed to get creative. When we'd been choosing the name for the café, we'd wanted to make Global Village just that – connected to the rest of the world, and yet villagey.

So we started lots of clubs and meetings based around our local community, and Oz cleverly found a way to link them up to the internet at the same time. This proved very popular with West Londoners – our huge city had become so sprawling and impersonal, it was nice to have a 'local' that wasn't the pub.

We did our best to offer something for everyone. For example, we had an after-school computer club for kids who didn't have a pc at home. The mums got to natter over a (proper) cappuccino whilst their kids talked online to school kids on the other side of the world who were just starting their day, and Oz helped them with their homework. Well, OK, did most of their homework for them, if we let him.

We started a Silver Surfers Group on a

Tuesday lunchtime, which became very popular with the wrinklies, who learnt how to send emails and track down old buddies, find cheap rail fares, comfy trousers, that sort of thing.

Friday night was Teenage Night, when we had a special licence to keep the café open until midnight and only teenagers were allowed in. Oz used to spend all week looking up groovy websites, only to discover that they were so 'out' that he earned the nickname of 'Grandad'. Needless to say, they all tried to spin one Fanta out to last four hours, so we were forced to put Lori on the door and charge a small entrance fee. This wasn't a problem though, their parents were happy to pay for them to be kept off the streets for at least one night of the week, in an alcohol-free zone. What they didn't know was that we let the teenagers smoke – I have a horrible feeling that was the main attraction . . .

I rang Wendy and invited her and her chums along to an online quiz evening – she took great pleasure in telling us how to make the café more wheelchair-friendly. Fortunately she didn't win the quiz, that would have been too much to bear.

Team Gloria played their part too, of course. There was a single parent lunchtime group on Mondays, during which Gloria would unofficially dispense invaluable practical tips, and advice on how to play the benefits system.

And after that had finished, Oz would set Gloria up on a computer. Yes! He'd found a really good program for adult illiteracy, which after a lot of complaining, Gloria grew to enjoy. Learning to read really opened up her world, it was wonderful to watch. Only of course we weren't allowed to say anything, we had to pretend we hadn't noticed.

Chris(tian) and Lazy Linda were asked, then begged, then threatened with slow, painful death unless they made pre-packed sandwiches for us; once they could see there was money in it, there was no stopping them. I had to persuade them to be a little more adventurous than just cheese and pickle, but they got there in the end. Lori was my number one barista in the school holidays.

It was hard work, but it was fun. I pushed Oz, and he pushed me. As a result, Global Village turned into a busy, buzzy place to hang out. We were popular with the locals, people seemed to like the fact that we were a small friendly business – and the coffee wasn't bad either.

It was December again, and I'd booked myself in for a session at the clinic with Dr Lichtenstein. I hadn't spoken to him much since the Joe fiasco, and I hadn't seen him for months.

I'd like to say that snow was softly falling on to the shoulders of the carol singers as I picked my way through the central London streets towards the clinic, the twinkling Christmas lights winking their cheery way into my warm and open heart. I'd like to say that, but I can't. It was bloody freezing, a passing taxi had just splashed a dirty slushpuddle all over my new suede boots and I was madly stressed about not having done any of my Christmas shopping yet. I may well have become a nicer person, but I still hated bloody Christmas.

My mobile diddly-deed – *All You Need Is Love,* of course – it was Gloria.

'Listen darlin', is it all right if I bring a new friend of mine round to yours with us on Christmas Day? Only she's going to be all on her own – her son's away with his dad for the first time this year, she's really upset –'

'– of course.'

'You sure you can fit us in?'

'I doubt it very much, Gloria,' I replied, 'but I don't think we'll let as trivial a detail as enough space get in our way, will we?'

'Trouble is, where are you going to put everybody? I could get hold of a couple of wallpapering tables – you could cover 'em with a cloth and stick a few crackers on, it'd go right out into the hall, mind you . . .'

'Whatever, Gloria!' I laughed. 'I'm sure we'll muddle through. Listen, I've got to go, I'll call you on my way home, OK?'

'Dr Lichtenstein said for you to go on through, Miss Small,' said the short fat receptionist who clearly thought five days before The Big Day was a good enough excuse to wear flashing snowmen earrings.

'Ah, Charlotte,' Dr L greeted me with a handshake, peering over his Central Casting glasses with concern, 'come in.'

He waited until I was settled comfortably on the sofa before asking with his customary mix of interest and sincerity, 'now, how are you?' He was obviously worried that I was in trouble again.

'Were you surprised to discover I'd made an appointment to see you?' I asked.

'Not really,' he replied, straightening his pen so that it was exactly parallel to his telephone pad, 'most of my patients get a bit twitchy around Christmas. And, of course, it was about a year ago that you had your breakdown, wasn't it?'

'It was, Dr L, it was.'

And how things had changed. I spent most of the hour filling him in on the latest developments in the soap opera that was now my life. I told him all about me and Gloria doing a Thelma and Louise from the east coast of America to the west, after Sabrina's wedding; she'd secretly made Keko give her driving lessons, so that we could take it in turns to map read.

I told him all about me and Matt throwing a surprise party for my parents' forty-fifth wedding anniversary, during which my mother shut herself in the bedroom and wouldn't come out. Dad had sent Matt up a ladder to peek through the window; she was lying on the bed, flat on her back, fast asleep. She wrote a very touching letter to us both afterwards, however, to say thank you.

I told him all about the success of the café; how we'd managed to buy Rosheen out, and even had a few offers to expand the business, but we'd decided not to, not because we didn't want more money but because we didn't need the stress of it all. How I'd learned independence from Oz, and he'd learned responsibility from me, and how much more confident we both were.

'This is all wonderful news, Charlotte – but why have you come to see me?'

I had come to thank him for introducing me to the concept of Upstairs – I still prayed every morning, and every night I thanked God for a good day. I didn't know how it worked, but I knew I was going to be all right now, no matter what happened. I had learned to trust.

Dr L had a question for me. 'And have you found the love you were so desperately looking for, Charlotte?'

'Yes, Doctor Lichtenstein, I have.'

'New man?'

'No.' I smiled. 'A new woman.'

'Oh?' He raised his eyebrows.

'Me.'

371

# ACKNOWLEDGEMENTS

During the writing of this book, I had an ear operation, a bladder operation and an ovarian cyst removed, my daughter Molly ran away from home, my son Ted was diagnosed with several serious behavioural problems, and I nearly lost two years' work when my study roof leaked on to my computer.

At the same time, I gave up alcohol and went organic, I fell in love and we've all moved home together, Molly's become a pop star and we've found the right help for Ted. But none of this would have been possible without sterling support from the following people:

Dr Tania Abdulezer, Carla Ashford, Suzanne Bryson, JC, Jim Davidson, Gilly Greenwood, Benn Haitsma, Nichola Hill, Rachel Junior, Carmel Murphy, Mrs Pink, Kathleen Tessaro, Jill Robinson and the Wimpole Writers Workshop, and those good people at Starbucks.

And last but not least, Hugo Brooks and Mari Evans, without whom both me and this book would have been a bit of a mess . . .